M
(The Connor Family, Book 3)

LAYLA HAGEN

Dear Reader,

If you want to receive news about my upcoming books and sales, you can sign up for my newsletter HERE: http://laylahagen.com/mailing-list-sign-up/

Cover: Uplifting Designs
Photography: Sara Eirew

Chapter One
Paige

"To the squad finally being reunited," Luna exclaimed, holding her glass of wine for a toast.

I'd moved back from Paris two nights before and had immediately planned a reunion with my two best friends, Luna and Faith. I'd asked them to meet me at my grandmother's old inn because I'd stopped by to visit the property this afternoon. We ended up ordering pizza and drinks and staying in. It was fitting. We had many memories here.

"I can't believe this space still looks the same. It's like a time capsule," Faith said.

"Except for the coat of dust," I chimed in. The place had been empty and boarded up for a few months, and now that I had returned, my parents had asked me to look into selling it.

"We're so glad you're back." Faith hugged me with one arm.

"I'm glad too." My three-year work stint in Paris had been exciting, but I hadn't seen myself settling down there. I was an LA girl at heart. I'd missed my friends, my parents, my siblings, and nieces. I'd also missed the near-constant sun. I couldn't wait to hit the beach. I tanned quickly, and even though my hair was almost black, some strands earned a reddish hue after spending a few days in the sun.

"So you're really going to sell this place, huh?" Faith asked.

"Yep. No other way." My grandmother had run a successful B&B, but my parents wanted to enjoy their retirement doing nothing at all, and my siblings and I all had full-time jobs. I couldn't see myself running a B&B on top of that, so better to sell the place than leave it to decay. The house would need some serious repairs before putting it on the market as it was.

The doorbell rang as we carried the empty pizza cartons to the kitchen.

"Are you expecting someone?" Luna asked.

"No."

I dashed to the front door, swung it open, and came face-to-face with a very tall and *very* handsome man. He looked at me, then behind my shoulder at Faith and Luna.

"Can I help you?" I asked.

"I'm Detective Will Connor."

A detective? Not what I had been expecting. Were detectives supposed to be this hot? I would have pegged him for a guy trying to break into the modeling or acting business. He certainly had the looks for it. Tall and well built, with chocolate brown, messy hair. His eyes were a smidge darker, and the bone structure of his jaw reminded me of the models in those aftershave commercials: defined, strong... sexy.

"Oh, and what's the reason for your visit?"

"A neighbor called. Said he saw lights here and that the place had been boarded up for a few months."

"It used to be my grandma's inn. Now it's mine. I came to take a look at it."

"So you're the owner?"

"I am, Detective. My name is Paige Lamonica. Would you like to see an ID?"

"No need. The neighbors thought someone broke in, what with the place being empty. Are there any signs of forced entries? Boarded-up houses attract burglars," he explained.

"I haven't checked the whole house yet, but all doors and windows on the ground floor are still boarded up. The boards will come down, though. I'll be renovating the place."

He folded his arms over his chest, and I took in those biceps for the first time. Holy hell. He was wearing a short-sleeved shirt, and I had to practically force myself to look away.

"You didn't see anything out of place either, right, girls?" I asked, turning to look at them. They nodded wordlessly, too busy checking out Will to answer. I'd mentioned earlier this evening that I wanted to date more, and now I could practically feel them measuring his *dating potential*. I turned my attention back to Will.

"Looks like you made this trip for nothing. Sorry for keeping you from problems that really need your attention."

"I'm off duty, but I was in the area when the call came through."

"Well, nothing going on here except some old friends catching up and celebrating the Fourth of July three days late."

"Make sure you're not too loud." His tone was teasing.

"Why, Detective, will you arrest us?" I asked playfully.

Something glinted in those dark eyes, making my insides tighten. His lips curled into a breathtaking smile. Well, honestly, he was a breathtaking man all-around.

"Since you're off duty, can we offer you a drink to make up for the inconvenience?" Luna asked.

"I'm headed somewhere, but thank you for the invitation." He pulled a card from his back pocket, handing it to me. "This is my number, Paige. If you do find any signs of forced entry, call me."

"Sure."

"Have a nice evening, ladies."

I closed the door and turned to the girls.

"Who knew detectives were so sexy?" Luna asked.

Faith clapped her hands. "I certainly didn't, but now that I do, I think it's time I reevaluate my dating pool."

I ran my hands over the business card. *Detective William Connor.* Below was a cell phone number and the address of a police station. I pocketed it.

We went through the house looking for any signs of forced entry. All the boards on the ground floor were firmly in place, and even though I couldn't imagine thieves climbing through the windows on the upper floor, we checked those too. The inn had been spared.

"So, I'd say it's high time I give you your gifts," I announced when we returned to the living room. They both squealed, hugging me. I'd brought an extra suitcase just with gifts for my friends and family and my work colleague Ashley. She and I had started working at Three Emeralds, a nonprofit focusing on human development, right after college. When a position at the Paris office came up, Ashley bowed out, saying that with a husband and two kids, she had too many strings here. I had reeled at the opportunity to spend time in another country, especially in France. The team was much larger, and I'd learned a lot from my colleagues there. I'd always liked my no-strings existence, but lately I'd started thinking that some strings wouldn't be bad. Some roots. Maybe it was seeing my two sisters and brother getting married. I had no idea, but the idea was growing on me.

"How about some music?" Faith asked, pouring herself another glass of wine.

"I've got an excellent playlist." I took out my smartphone and tapped the screen, bringing up a list with upbeat, fun songs. They were perfect for a reunion evening. As I turned the volume to the max, I wondered if it was loud enough for the neighbors to hear, and if they'd come knocking at the door to tell me to turn it down or if they'd report the disturbance to the police. Would the hot detective stop by again?

Chapter Two
Will

I was still chuckling when I drove away. Though calls like this were usually answered by patrol officers, not detectives, I was glad I'd stopped by. The brunette had made my evening, standing there in her short dress, showing off her perky little body and asking me if I'd arrest them. I should have suggested that she install an alarm. Statistically, renovation sites were a magnet for burglars.

I headed straight to the restaurant where my sister Lori's wedding would be taking place in a few weeks. She'd invited me to the menu tasting. I arrived at the same time as my younger brother, Jace. Lori and her fiancé, Graham, sat at a table.

"Hey! Long time no see," I joked. We'd seen each other last Friday at dinner, as we did every week. "Just the four of us?"

"Val will be a few minutes late," Lori explained, referring to our oldest sister. I knew our two other siblings, Landon and Hailey, couldn't make it, but I was surprised that Lori's eight-year-old son was missing.

"Where is Milo?" I asked Lori.

"Declared that he'd rather spend the evening

with his friend Jilly."

Val arrived shortly afterward, and during the tasting, she and Lori were deep in wedding talk.

Midway through the main course, Val turned her attention to Jace and me.

"So, you two are going to bring dates after all?"

Jace whistled, handing me a five-dollar bill. "You win."

"Always do." I pocketed the bill, grinning at Val's inquisitive look. I might have been thirty-three, but I still loved a good bet.

"What was the bet about?"

"How long it'd take until you or Lori asked that. Jace thought you'd hold back until dessert. I gave you until the main course."

Val laughed. "Bringing a date is purely a defensive mechanism. We can't save you from Pippa."

She wasn't wrong. Weddings were an occasion for well-meaning members of our extended family to meddle, and my cousin Pippa loved to play matchmaker. She was good at it too… when it came to her own siblings. My Bennett cousins—all nine of them—had married within a couple of years of each other. Pippa liked to brag about having a hand in a few of those couples finding each other. Jace and I had barely escaped her plans during Landon's wedding. I didn't think lightning struck twice, but I was going alone. I dated plenty, but for months I'd been on a string of first dates, none of which led to a second one. I wasn't interested in taking just anyone to my sister's wedding.

Jace had other problems. "I can't take anyone to the wedding, because it'll be in all the papers. People might get the wrong impression."

Val tapped her fingers, smiling sweetly. "You mean they might think that the soccer world's *sexiest player* was off the market?"

Our brother had been awarded that title by *GQ* this year, and he was reaping the benefits.

"Exactly."

"Now that would be a tragedy, wouldn't it?" Lori asked with a grin.

"Girls, stop hazing your brothers," Graham said. I liked him, though it was still strange to think about Lori, Milo, and Graham as one unit. For years, it had just been Lori and Milo, because his jackass biological father had taken off before he was born. I had tried to be not just an uncle to the boy but also a father figure, trying to pass on things I'd learned from my late dad. Now that Graham was in the picture, there was less need for me to play that role. I missed it, but I couldn't deny it: being just the fun uncle had its perks.

"No can do," Val answered. "They flex their overprotective brother muscles, we haze them. It's a two-way street."

Jace shook his head mockingly. "Thanks for trying, Graham."

I enjoyed our family time immensely.

"Will, is your Lake Tahoe rental free the week

after the wedding?" Lori asked. "We still haven't decided where to go for our honeymoon, but I do love the lake and your cabin."

"Let me check." I pulled out my phone, looking over the spreadsheet I kept. While I was in college, I built a network of rentals in California, and the caretakers for each one filled the spreadsheet as the bookings came in.

"It's free. I'll tell my administrator not to take any bookings until you decide."

Lori looked up at Graham, batting her eyelashes. He laughed and kissed her forehead, then informed me, "We'll take it."

We left the restaurant well after midnight. The route home took me by Paige's inn. I figured if the lights were still on, I could talk to her about the alarm. With a property this large, she needed one of the more expensive options, with motion detectors on at least the windows on the ground floor.

When I arrived at the inn, all lights were off. I was surprised at how disappointed I was. Judging by their excitement, I figured they'd planned to party the whole night. My body reacted instantly to the memory of her curves. She was small enough that I could scoop her up with one arm. I bet those legs would feel amazing wrapped around me.

I laughed, shaking off the image. Damn, I hadn't even asked for her phone number. But I planned to rectify that.

***

The next afternoon, I had a pleasant surprise. While I was discussing a case with my superior in his office, a familiar voice filtered in through the open door. Was I imagining it because Paige had been on my mind the whole night? Because I'd planned to stop by the inn today to ask for her number? I turned to look, and there she was. What was she doing here? Had something happened to her? She was half turned, talking to one of the officers. I couldn't see any signs that she'd been in an accident or attacked.

"Will?"

"I apologize, sir. An... acquaintance just walked in. Can we table this conversation so I can check out the situation?"

I was out of my chair before he even nodded. I strode past the desks, straight to Paige. I got a better look at her as I came closer. She didn't seem hurt or scared. She was talking to one of our youngest officers, Stan. He was eager to help. Too eager. He stood too close and smiled like an idiot.

"Paige, what are you doing here?"

She stopped midconversation, turning to face me. Those lips were even prettier than I remembered. Her hair was down, obscuring her neck, but the bit of skin that was showing looked kissable as fuck.

"Hi, Will. I looked through the inn like you suggested. Didn't find any vandalism inside, but someone stole the side mirrors of my car, which was parked in the backyard for a long time. I have pictures and I'd like to file a complaint. I need it for my insurance."

"I'll take it from here," I declared.

"But this is in my job description," Stan protested, clearly wanting to spend more time with Paige. My jaw ticked.

"I said I'll take it from here."

Stan knew better than to challenge a superior, even if he was right. I wasn't about to let over-helpful Stan take this.

"I meant to call first to see if you were here, but I lost your card," she said. "I googled the address of the station."

I ushered Paige to my desk, walking one step behind her. Her hips swayed on every step, and I had the sudden urge to check if the skin on her thighs was as smooth as that on her upper arm. Every inch of this woman was lickable.

When we reached my desk, I brought a chair for her from one of the vacant desks, and we both sat down. I searched for the form we needed in the database. Paige crossed her legs, and I couldn't help looking. They were toned and strong, like a runner's or a swimmer's. They'd look gorgeous wrapped around my waist as I held her against a wall, getting my fill of her. *Well, hell.* I'd thought my reaction to her the other night was because she'd looked so... rumpled in that short dress, with her hair piled on top of her head. But now she was dressed in business attire, and I was still itching to find out how those legs would feel wrapped around me.

I focused on the form as we filled it in together. After I pulled up Paige's license number in the database, I scrolled to some of the archived information.

"Paige… you have a dozen speeding tickets."

I turned to her. She was blushing, but not looking away.

"I got those before I left for Paris. I paid them all."

"How exactly did you manage to rack up twelve speeding tickets in two weeks?"

She shrugged a shoulder, and the strap of her dress shifted an inch, revealing a string of freckles.

"I couldn't take my car to Paris, and that baby runs so smooth that I wanted to say goodbye properly."

I sat back in my chair, barking a laugh. I'd been in a shitty mood this morning. A case I was working on was proving to be difficult, which always ate at me. But Paige had changed my mood as if she'd flipped a switch.

"Most people don't own up to that."

"I tried to talk my way out of them, but my sweet-talking had no effect."

Something about the way she said *sweet-talking* made me sit up straighter.

"You tried to flirt with an officer of the law?"

"Is that an offense?" Her tone turned challenging as she jutted her chin forward. I wanted to kiss that sassy mouth.

"No."

If I'd been the one pulling Paige over and she'd flirted with me, I definitely would have turned a blind eye.

"Clearly it didn't work anyway."

"This day just got so much more interesting. You come in to file a complaint and I discover you're a law breaker."

Her eyes were snapping fire. And in that moment, I didn't just want to kiss her. I wanted to pin her against the desk, holding those wrists captive above her head, and ravish her right here, right now, with half the station watching. Jesus, I didn't even know the woman.

She uncrossed her legs, then crossed them again. I looked straight at her until she broke eye contact, licking her lower lip. I wanted to lick that lip too, even bite it a little.

"Don't get any more tickets," I said eventually.

Paige mimicked an army salute. "Yes, sir."

"And you should upgrade the inn's alarm system."

"Why?"

"Renovation sites are a magnet for burglars."

"I'll look into it. The last thing I need is for someone to break into the inn." There was affection in her voice.

"You're fond of that place."

"Yes. It belonged to my grandmother. My whole family loves it, but selling is the best option. We'll probably throw it a proper goodbye party right before we hand over the keys."

I liked the warmth in her voice when she spoke about her family.

"I'll look on Amazon for an alarm, see if they can ship something quickly."

"It's easier and quicker if you go to a specialty store." I pulled a Post-it from the stack next to my computer, intending to write down the address, and then I had a better idea.

"I'll go to a store with you. There's one a few blocks away from here."

"You don't have to do that, but I'll take you up on the offer, otherwise I'll procrastinate and never get around to doing it."

"Do you have time to go now?" It was six o'clock. The store was open until eight. I could take her to dinner after.

"No, I have dinner plans."

I nodded tightly. Were those plans with a guy? The thought annoyed me more than I wanted to admit.

"Tomorrow?" I pressed.

Paige laughed. "You think I need protection that badly?"

"Judging by your speeding tickets, the city needs protection from you."

"Touché, as the French like to say. Tomorrow works. Six?"

"I'll meet you out front." I wrote down the address of the shop on a Post-it, then handed it to her together with another business card. "Don't lose this one."

Paige opened her bag and retrieved her wallet. "See? I'm putting it here for safekeeping. I had the other one in my pocket, and it must have fallen out."

"You have me at a disadvantage. I don't have your number," I said as we both stood up.

"Oh, of course. You should have it in case something comes up and you can't make it."

Yeah, that isn't going to happen, I thought as she jotted down her number. She hunched over the desk, giving me a direct view of her cleavage. Christ, she was magnificent. My mouth was almost watering at the thought of tasting the skin between her breasts, stroking my tongue against her nipples.

I shook her hand afterward and kept my gaze on her until she was out of the room. Judging by her easygoing nature, I could tell she wasn't taking the need for the alarm seriously. But that was why people like me existed: to protect people like her.

Chapter Three
Paige

As I was getting ready for work the next morning, I fussed way too much about my appearance. I put my hair up in a ponytail, then pulled the elastic out, letting the wild waves free. Yep, definitely down. Oh, what did it matter? I was going to buy an alarm. I had no idea why I was fussing so much. Well, I did... sort of. I wanted to make a good impression when I saw Will in the afternoon. I couldn't shake the feeling that he thought I was some kind of a ditz. I wanted to rectify that. My dad used to be an Army man, and I'd been around plenty of his peers, so the whole badge/uniform thing didn't hold a special appeal to me. Quite the contrary. But I couldn't get Will out of my mind.

I yawned, despite already having had two coffees. I hadn't been able to sleep a wink the last two nights. Damned jet lag.

It was a good thing that my first two days back in the LA office were mostly filled with paperwork and setting up my desk. Not much had changed in the years I'd been in Paris. We still rented the same office space on the ground floor of a high-se. Even the team was the same.

"I can't believe you gave up Paris," Ashley said for the millionth time.

"I didn't give it up. We just weren't a good fit."

"Girl, if I didn't have a husband and two kids, I'd move in the blink of an eye."

"Trust me, Ashley. Paris isn't all they make it out to be. Sure, the touristy stuff is nice. The Eiffel Tower and the macaroons. But it's also crowded, and rents are ridiculous. I was paying half my salary to live in a matchbox outside the city. Commutes took up so long that I didn't have time to do anything more than work and sleep."

Ashley sighed. "Don't ruin my buzz with practicalities."

They were a fact of life, though. I'd never intended to move for good, I had just viewed it as a great learning experience. I was a development director, and there were more projects there. But I felt I could make more of a difference here, and that was what mattered after all. Plus, I had the opportunity to get a new project off the ground. I still had to hammer out a few details with my boss, but I'd bring those up once I'd put the jet lag behind me.

That master plan was nixed when my boss knocked at the open door.

"Paige, is this a good time to talk about the education center program?"

It was an awful time. My brain worked

backward. But you didn't tell your boss no.

"Sure."

"I'll leave you two," Ashley said. After she left, Greg got right down to business.

"I was expecting you to be one of those people we lost forever to Paris."

It was clear from his tone he'd hoped I wouldn't come back. Greg wasn't my biggest fan. He saw me as direct competition, even though I'd never wanted his job. The dislike was mutual. He had a misogynistic streak that reared its ugly head from time to time. When I'd started working with him at twenty-one, he'd intimidated me. Seven years later, I'd learned to ignore him.

"I looked over your proposal. It's bold."

Translation: crazy.

I wanted to set up an education center for people who'd grown up homeless. Theoretically, that shouldn't happen, but enough of them slipped through the cracks of the social system, reaching adulthood without any meaningful education or skills to get a job, which continued to keep them on the streets. It was a vicious circle. We could change that, teach them employable skills. I'd toyed with this idea since the last time I'd been home for a visit, when I'd ran into a group of homeless teenagers. They had hopes and dreams like everyone else, but absolutely no means to make them happen. My parents had always worked hard so my siblings and I would have everything we needed. Where would we be if they hadn't? I knew I shouldn't be so involved, but I couldn't help it. It felt personal.

"I can pull it off, though. No one thought I could set up the cross-European program in France, but I did."

"You drive a hard bargain. I see Paris hasn't mellowed you."

"Not one bit."

"I'd rather you focused your efforts elsewhere."

"This isn't the only project I'll be working on." But it was the one I cared most about.

"No grant funding for this one."

"Why not?"

"Because we have a quota for those, and I'd rather you use it for other projects. Focus on private donors."

That made my job significantly harder.

"Tell you what. Get letters of intent for at least 25 percent of the financing from private donors, and then I'll reconsider. You know the drill."

I did, which was why I instantly knew that Greg wouldn't be swayed by 25 percent. I'd need at least 50 percent to convince him this wouldn't be a waste of time.

"I'll leave you to settle. Keep me updated."

"I will."

Ashley returned after Greg left and hovered around my desk, bringing me up to speed. In the afternoon, I started feeling human again. I drew up a list of companies I could approach for funding. I'd already worked with most of the firms on my list. I'd kept in touch with them, because I'd learned early on how important connections were. I'd have to tailor my pitch for each of them. Some would be interested in the cause itself, others only in how much PR they could milk from their contribution. That didn't bother me. Most companies donated because it would look good in their annual report and on their website, but money was money.

I headed to one of my favorite coffee shops in Venice Beach to work on the pitches. It was far away from the boardwalk and the tourists. Greg didn't much care where the work was done—one of the only things I appreciated about him—and now that I was back in LA, I planned to take as much advantage of the sun as possible, soak it all in. I relished feeling the fine sand under my feet, smearing sunscreen on my arms and ankles. Sitting in the outdoor section of the coffee shop, a large hat on my head, I tinkered with the pitch presentations for hours. I'd finished three of twenty-one by the time I had to leave to meet Will. I had my work cut out for me for the rest of the week.

I stopped by the restroom first, taking in my appearance. Despite the hat, the tip of my nose was pink. That was the first step in getting a tan. In the second step, I'd look like a lobster for about a week before my skin turned golden brown.

I refreshed my makeup, dabbing some mascara. I'd forgotten my comb at home, so I ran my hands through my tresses.

Will was in front of the store when I arrived,

leaning casually against a wall. I took in every detail. That defined jaw covered by a faint stubble, the planes of his cheeks....

He was wearing a black leather jacket that was stretched taut over his shoulders and muscular arms. It was unzipped, so I also had a clear view of his torso. His bone structure wasn't the only stunning thing about him. I couldn't get over how hot he was.

Then I noticed the motorcycle a few feet away. Wowza. Add another few points to the sexiness factor. Good thing he hadn't shown up wearing that jacket on my doorstep.

"Good evening, Detective." I walked up to him. He fixed his gaze on my nose. I suspected I looked like Rudolph the reindeer right now.

"You were out in the sun."

I nodded, taking my hat off, rolling it tightly and placing it in my tote.

"Worked from a coffee shop in Venice Beach for half the day, sitting at a table outside."

"What do you do for work?" he asked as we entered the store. It boasted a large array of electronics.

"I'm a development director at a nonprofit. Three Emeralds; you might have heard of it."

"Of course I've heard of it." His eyes went wide, like he had a hard time reconciling the job with the woman in front of him.

"You expected something else?"

"I thought you worked in fashion. A model, maybe, because you mentioned Paris."

He lowered his gaze, and I felt tendrils of heat licking everywhere he looked. Hell, I felt them even where he *didn't* look. My nipples perked up.

"You didn't think I was a detective either when you met me, though, did you?" he asked.

"Well, no. I thought you were an actor."

He winked, then straightened, rolling his shoulders. The badge flashed at his belt as he pointed to the stack at our right side. "Stick to these. They're more expensive, but they're harder to trick. Thieves have become more proficient at fooling old-school alarms."

He explained the ins and outs of various models. They all sounded the same to me, so I intended to go with my gut feeling and the price. I didn't need any fancy add-ons, but that didn't keep Will from giving me the nitty-gritty on the newest models.

I found myself paying more attention to him than to what he was saying. He really had incredible arms. He'd taken off his jacket and was wearing a black shirt with short sleeves that hugged his biceps.

"Pay attention. Not everyone knocking at your door will be as harmless as me. Or as handsome."

He wiggled his eyebrows, and I couldn't help laughing. "You did *not* say that."

"I did. You disagree?"

"Maybe I do."

"So you thought I was an actor because of my hideous looks?"

I folded my arms over my chest, attempting to come up with a smart-ass answer. But I had an inkling that I'd met my match in that department.

"I can't believe you're punishing me for that."

"I'm not punishing you. Just enjoying this too much to stop."

"Bad form, Detective. Making others uncomfortable for your own amusement."

He came a little closer. "Am I making you uncomfortable, Paige?" He leaned in even closer. "Tell you a secret? Looks to me like you're enjoying this too."

Yep, I'd met my match, no doubt about that. I was tongue-tied, and the answer was a resounding yes. I was enjoying this. Ridiculous, wasn't it? A trip to buy an alarm shouldn't be this fun.

I broke the eye contact, finding my voice. I wouldn't go down without a sassy reply.

"You're so boastful." I took one of the alarm systems from the shelf, and we started walking toward the registers.

"My sisters would agree with you."

"Good to know. How many do you have?"

"Three."

"Big family."

"Also two brothers."

"Cocky like you?"

"They try. Takes a special kind of talent to make it work."

My entire body shook with laughter as I paid for the alarm.

"Thanks for your advice," I said as we left the store. The sky had turned a dark orange. Sunset was approaching. "Can I buy you a taco? As a thank-you for helping me out?" I pointed to the taco truck on the other side of the street.

"Sure."

We ate side by side at one of the two high tables in front of the truck. The light breeze from earlier turned chilly, and I put on the lace cardigan I'd tucked in my tote that morning. Will slipped on his leather jacket. What a shame he covered all those muscles. I was conflicted. On the one hand, he looked mouthwatering with that jacket on, but without it, I could admire those biceps to my heart's desire. His phone kept buzzing from one of his pockets.

"What's with all the messages?"

"My sister is reminding me about some of my tasks for her wedding. Seems to think I'll forget them if she doesn't send reminders."

"Does she have reason to believe that?"

"Not at all. I'm a very responsible older brother."

I couldn't imagine Will as anything but a cocky troublemaker, but maybe there was more to him than packs of muscles and a panty-melting smile.

"So, she's just a regular bridezilla, then?"

"Nah, but she's a wedding planner. Loves her checklists." The warmth in his voice was a dead giveaway that he wasn't really annoyed with her.

While we ate, Will kept looking around us. I

knew that behavior. I called it *the silent vigilante.* It reminded me of how I felt every time I went somewhere with my dad. He'd retired from the Army years ago, but old habits died hard. He was constantly on the lookout. He always said, *"Don't worry, honey. I'll keep you safe."* The ironic thing was, seeing him looking for danger everywhere had made me feel unsafe. I'd always been too consumed with worry that something could happen to him.

"Relax, Detective. You're making me nervous, looking around for trouble."

"Sorry, it's habit."

"Are you on duty now?"

"No."

"Then enjoy your time off. Go back to making me feel uncomfortable with your cockiness, not the broody forehead."

Chapter Four
Paige

A look of pure incredulity passed over his face before morphing into a grin.

"So, tell me about the wedding," I said.

"It's in three weeks, and my entire family is in a frenzy."

"I know the feeling. I've got two sisters and a brother, and they're all married. We all had wedding fever before every event. My mom was freaking out before each one. How is yours faring?"

He set his lips in a firm line. "My parents died in a car crash when I was a teenager."

"Oh. I'm sorry for your loss."

He nodded, focusing on his taco. I wanted to lighten up the mood again.

"I hope there isn't a singles' table at the wedding. They should be banned. I went through that horror once."

He barked out a laugh. "There isn't. My family isn't that cruel."

"Neither is mine. Just clueless. My brother got married first, and they had that terrible table. My sisters were also single at the time. We still torment him about it. He's since paid for his sins, but we're evil little things."

Will scrutinized me in silence for a few seconds, as if he was trying to make up his mind about something.

"What are you doing Saturday in three weeks?"

I grimaced. "Trying to weasel out of a meeting with some high school classmates."

"High school not your favorite scene?"

"Not really."

"My sister's wedding is that Saturday. How would you feel about going with me?"

"Very funny," I said. He wasn't smiling. "Wait, you're serious?"

"Yes."

"Why would you take someone you don't know?"

He moved closer. Our arms were touching, and it had the inexplicable effect of making my entire body heat up.

"I know essential information. You blatantly disregard speed limits and have a sassy streak a mile long. Plus, a wedding is a good excuse to give to your high school crowd." He winked, looking at me expectantly. I was a little stunned, and I scrambled to gather my wits. I was so very tempted to say yes.

"That's very flattering, but… no offense, I barely know you. Why do you need to take anyone anyway? Go alone."

"I risk giving my cousin Pippa a reason to exercise her matchmaking skills."

I cocked a brow, taking a swig of my soda. "You're asking me to be your protector?"

"Not how I would put it." He shifted his weight on the leg closest to me, bending slightly at the waist, towering over me. The effect was overpowering. Fire danced in those deep brown eyes as if daring me to say no. Which I did, of course.

"Answer's no. I still don't know you." I liked him, and I'd had a lot of fun this evening. But I'd still met him just two days ago. "And I should get going."

"I'll walk you to your car."

"I Ubered here."

"Where are you going? I can drop you off."

"I'm headed to Venice. Is that on your way?"

He nodded, but I hesitated.

"I've never been on a bike."

"Come on, first time for everything. Including going to a wedding with a guy you just met."

I laughed as we crossed the street to his bike. "Don't get ahead of yourself, Detective."

"When do you have to be there?" he asked.

"I'm meeting someone at a bar near the beach in forty minutes."

His posture changed. The easy smile from before faded. He shrugged out of his jacket as we reached the bike.

"Just one protective jacket. You're getting it."

"The jacket is about five sizes too large."

"It'll protect you anyway."

I put the jacket on, then a helmet. He had two of those. I felt like RoboCop as I climbed behind him on the bike.

"Hold on tight," he said after I told him the address.

Oh, yeah. Guess what holding on to him meant? I got to keep my palms on the front of his torso. The six-pack complemented his biceps just right. I had to really work at keeping my hands still. I wanted to touch more…. How did he get so ripped? My arms were pressing in on his waist. He didn't have an ounce of fat.

Will Connor was pure muscle.

Riding a bike was an adrenaline rush; there was no other way to put it. The speed, feeling the wind on my legs. My dress was loose enough that I could spread my thighs comfortably but not be afraid the wind would blow it away. I had the craziest impulse to take my helmet off, feel the wind against my face and in my hair, but I knew it wasn't safe.

I held on even tighter when Will took a narrow turn, bending the bike at an angle that made me break out in a sweat.

We came to a stop in front of my meeting point with Luna all too soon. I climbed down, careful not to flash Will my underwear, then took off the helmet and the jacket. I smelled a bit like Will now.

Luna was waiting in front of the bar. Her jaw hung loose when she noticed me getting off the bike. Her gaze moved between Will and me.

"Detective, I wasn't expecting to see you so soon," she told Will.

I held up the bag. "He helped me pick an

alarm for the inn."

"Want to join us for a drink?" she asked.

"Just the two of you out for girls' night?"

"Yes," I confirmed.

Will held his hands up, but his smile was back. "I have it on good authority that crashing a girls' night isn't a good idea. My sisters drilled it deep in my mind."

Luna crossed her arms over her chest. "I like you."

I liked him too. Very much so.

"I insist," Luna continued. "One cocktail on us?"

"We don't want to keep you," I said. "I've taken up enough of your time. I'm sure you have plans."

Will flashed me a devastating smile. I could feel one knee weaken, then the other. He was concocting a plan. I couldn't shake the feeling that it had to do with me.

"I don't. One cocktail." That deep baritone voice was exquisite. "Why not?"

One cocktail turned into two, then three. All nonalcoholic for Will. I was mixing it up. The bar was crowded, but we found a table for two. It was tiny, and the three of us crammed around it rather awkwardly. Will was sitting next to me.

He was fun to be around. He knew how to keep the conversation going, shared a lot about himself without dominating the conversation. I learned that in addition to three sisters and two brothers, he also had a one-year-old niece and an eight-year-old nephew that he was quite fond of. He was the son of the sister who was getting married.

Then he told Luna about the wedding, and his relative's propensity for matchmaking. I was wondering why he brought it up, when he said, "I asked Paige here to go with me and save my ass, but she declined."

Luna blinked. "Why would you say no?"

"My thoughts exactly," Will replied.

Well, well, will you look at that. The good detective was playing dirty.

"I'll let you ponder that, Detective. Some soul searching now and then is healthy, I've heard." I fished a cherry from the bottom of my glass, looking at him over the rim. Sometime during the exchange, he'd moved his hand to the backrest of my seat. One of my shoulder blades was pressing into his bicep. He laid his palm at the end of my other shoulder blade.

"I'll put in a good word for you," Luna informed him.

"I'd appreciate that, Luna," he said, without taking his eyes off me. He was drumming his fingers on my back, and the muscles strummed tightly together.

"I'll get going and leave you to enjoy the rest of your girls' night. Paige, let me know if you need help installing the alarm."

As he pushed his chair back, our thighs

touched. The contact electrified me, sending a bolt of heat from the tips of my breasts right to my center.

"Have fun," he called before he left. I had a feeling it wasn't the last time I'd be seeing Will Connor.

"Holy Moses," Luna exclaimed. "That's one hot man. Wanna tell me why you're not going to the wedding with him?"

"I just met him."

Luna slurped from her cocktail, rolling her eyes. "I think we can rule out him being a serial killer. He's asked you to a wedding, not a dark alley."

"I know. But he's just... I don't know. Kind of cocky, asking a woman you just met to a wedding."

"Honey, a man who looks like him can afford to be cocky. Why don't you tell me the real reason you're not all over him? You were saying the other night that you'd like to give dating a real shot. Here comes a bachelor who looks like a god, and has a sense of humor and a good job. Explain yourself, friend."

I pondered this. "I think I'd prefer dating someone whose job doesn't include the possibility of getting hurt."

"Oh," Luna said softly.

"I don't know... it's silly. I just don't like that kind of worry." Luna would know all about it. We'd been friends since the time my dad was still in the Army.

"Well, it makes more sense than you not

being into the kind of hotness Will Connor has going on. I wonder if he's got a six-pack."

"He does," I confirmed. "Felt them when we were on the motorcycle. Had a great excuse."

Luna raised her glass. "That's my girl. How's the inn coming along? Found a handyman?"

"Sent requests to three, waiting to hear about their prices. I've made a list of repairs needed—that I could tell, at least. It won't come cheap. I also want a new coat of paint. Apparently newly painted spaces haul a 5 percent higher price on average."

"Thank God you don't have to live there. Living in a place that's being renovated is my own personal hell."

Luna had renovated her house last year.

"Was worth it though. I'm still jealous of your place."

We hung out another two hours at the bar, long after happy hour passed. I'd missed this. In Paris, I'd made a few friends, but I'd never grown as close to anyone as I was to Luna and Faith.

Once we both decided we'd had enough cocktails, we each hopped in a cab.

But by the time I arrived at my apartment, I felt wide awake. So instead of slipping into bed, I started sorting through some old clothes I planned to donate. I should have done this in Paris instead of hauling everything with me, but I hadn't had time. I set aside a scarf I knew Mom would like, and a lace cardigan. I ended up with a sizable pile of clothes for charity. I filled my largest suitcase with them, which I set by the entrance door, and looked around at my home. I hadn't wanted to let go of this apartment, so I'd sublet it while I was away. The apartment was in a two-story U-shaped building that boasted an inner courtyard with ferns, small palm trees, and a pergola. The living room was small, but the white kitchen appeared more spacious than it was. As a plus, it boasted a walk-in pantry where I stored clothes.

The occupants hadn't been careful. Some walls were chipped in places, others had grease stains. My mother had suggested I find another place to live when she'd seen it. She'd also made another offhand comment that had stuck with me.

"Oh, honey, Dad and I bought our house when we were your age. And we had you a few months later."

The thought that I wasn't moving forward was nagging at me. I'd peaked in my career two years ago. I'd rejoiced at the time because I'd been the youngest development director in the company. But the next career jump was only possible if my boss quit, and honestly, I didn't want Greg's job. I liked mine. On a personal level, I'd had two "serious" relationships before moving to Paris, but I'd never seen those going anywhere. I hadn't felt either was the one. I was in a funk, that much was clear. But thinking about it in the middle of the night was only going to make it harder to fall asleep. I walked across the cream-colored tile to my bedroom, which was as girly as it got. Most of my sheets were a shade of pink, or flowery.

I had one more thing to do before going to bed: put the alarm in my tote so I wouldn't forget it in the morning. I grabbed the package, and when I turned it around, I laughed. Will had written his number with a black marker under the instructions.

Here is my number again, just in case. Call me if you need help with the alarm. ;) These things are hard to install.

Chapter Five
Paige

Will hadn't been kidding about the alarm being difficult to install. I made it to the inn one week later, and I intended to take care of the alarm business before work. But despite reading the instructions a dozen times, watching explanatory YouTube videos, and even perusing a blog by a fellow homeowner who'd installed a similar model, I had yet to make it work, and I was running out of time. One of the companies I'd e-mailed last week had answered, saying their general manager had an opening this morning. I had to leave now to make it in time. I'd tinker with the alarm again in the evening.

The heat was a killer, even at eight o'clock in the morning. I'd forgotten how hot LA could get in the summer, and it was only the second week of July. I foresaw a lot of sweating in my near future. I'd suited up, wearing pants and jacket, and a silk blouse underneath. It was on the conservative side, but experience had taught me that people took me more seriously when I wore a suit.

I was pleased I'd scored a meeting with the general manager. That was usually an indication that he was interested in the project, not just looking for a

PR boost. In those cases, I only dealt with the PR and Finance departments.

The offices were on the top floor of a building opposite city hall. I paced the meeting room while waiting for the general manager to join me, going through my pitch. I turned on my heels when I heard the door opening.

"Good morning, Ms. Lamonica. Thank you for coming on such short notice. I'm Christian Lackeroy."

"Good morning, Mr. Lackeroy."

"Call me Christian."

I typically didn't like to be on a first-name basis so early, but the fact that Christian appeared only a few years older than me put me somewhat at ease.

We got right down to business. He interrupted my pitch with well-considered questions, even offering to put me in touch with other businessmen who'd be interested in supporting the cause.

"I'll be honest. I don't see this coming to fruition. It's so specific, and doesn't scream PR material like green projects."

"I'm confident I can find other businessmen like yourself who are interested in the cause rather than PR."

"I like your confidence, Paige. You have my support on this. You're already in touch with my assistant; e-mail her the documents you want signed. A letter of intent, you said. I'll have the legal department look over it, and if nothing jumps out, you'll have it back by the end of the week."

"Perfect."

I had a great feeling about this as I exited the office, smack dab into sweltering heat. I took off my jacket, trying to decide where I should work today. I could reach Venice Beach in forty minutes, park myself there for the rest of the day and work on more pitches as well as the redistribution of some incoming funds. But I'd stick out like a sore thumb in my suit. In the end, I decided to head to the office. Air-conditioning beat the ocean breeze when you were wearing a suit.

At lunch, Ashley stopped by with takeout. She was one of the few who preferred to work from the office daily. Midway through our lunch, a bouquet of red roses was delivered. I thanked the delivery boy, bringing them to my office.

"Wowza, those are nice. Who are they from?"

"Christian Lackeroy," I said, reading the card.

"I'm guessing he liked you more than the project."

"It would seem so." I'd felt an overly friendly vibe toward the end of the meeting. The card read *I had a lot of fun today. I'd love to take you to dinner.* He'd actually signed with his name *and* position, which I found very tacky.

"Is he attractive?" she inquired.

"You could say that."

"Take him up on it. You'd have a lot in

common."

Maybe… but as I put the card back, all I could think about was Will Connor in his black leather jacket, smelling like the ocean and the woods, looking like he could fulfill every sinful dream I'd ever had.

Five finished pitches later, I was ready to call it a day. Even though I was in the mood for another girls' outing, I did the right thing and went by the inn again. I was determined to tackle the alarm. I was also cooking in my suit, so I went through some boxes labeled *Paige*, hoping I'd find anything to change into. I'd had some old clothes here, and Mom had packed them all up after my grandma passed away so they wouldn't gather dust.

Bingo! I found a box with clothes from the high school era, back when I'd thought skimpy was the new cool. The only thing that fit me was a very short dress, but it would have to do. I'd been overweight as a teenager, and in the summer before my senior year, I'd gone through a drastic diet and lost thirty pounds. Out went my baggy, tent-sized wardrobe. I'd replaced it with an array of short, tight dresses like this one that were inappropriate for any place except a strip club. I'd wanted to feel beautiful, and I relished the attention I was receiving from boys. Until I realized not all attention was good attention.

I watched the explanatory YouTube videos again, working in tandem to set up the alarm—to no

I couldn't make it work.

I turned to the back of the package, reading the instructions again… and Will's number. I'd saved his number in my phone after he gave me the second card, but I liked a man who covered his bases. And well, if the sexy detective had offered his help, why not take him up on it? I could call my father too, he was handy with security systems, but he and Mom had a date tonight, and I didn't want to interrupt. My brother wasn't much of a techy, and neither were my sisters. And I couldn't deny it; I looked forward to hearing Will's sexy baritone voice.

"Detective Will Connor," he answered. His voice was even sexier than I remembered.

"Hey, Will. This is Paige. The alarm is giving me headaches. Maybe if I walk you through what I'm doing you can tell me where I'm going wrong?"

"I'll do one better. I'll stop by and show you how to install it."

My pulse intensified. "Are you sure? I mean, I'm sure I'm on the right path."

"It'll be quicker if I do it. I'll bring dinner too. Do you like Thai food?"

"Love it. Especially masala curry with shrimp."

"I'll stop by with curry."

After ending the call, I took a good look at myself in the mirror hanging on the bathroom door. Maybe I'd been too harsh on the poor dress. I'd always been extra judgy of my past fashion choices. No way was I changing back into my pants. My silk hirt had perspiration stains at the armpits. This dress would have to do.

I was glad that he was bringing dinner because I was starving. I had some wine left from when the girls had been here. I hoped Will liked it. I was wringing my hands for no reason at all, so to give myself something to do, I looked up real estate prices, trying to estimate how much we could get for the inn.

It had two stories and ten bedrooms, most on the upper floor. My grandma had called it a home for the unpretentious tourist. The bedrooms were spacious, but sparsely decorated, with simple wood double beds and matching small closets. Some rooms even had a small desk. The ground floor had a towering double-story ceiling and walls of glass to give the impression of a larger area. The living room was separated in a dining area and a seating area with an assortment of couches that didn't fit together, ranging from leather to floral prints. The kitchen was completely separate. It had been the family space and grandma's favorite room. We'd spent a lot of time in here, Grandma cooking and me eating everything.

When the doorbell rang, my self-imposed cool demeanor flew out the window. The second I opened the door, I knew I hadn't been extra judgy with the dress.

Chapter Six
Will

Was this woman trying to kill me? She was wearing an extremely short and tight dress that didn't leave much to the imagination.

"Hi," she said cheerfully.

"Hi," I said back, though it sounded more like a groan. I swallowed, looking to the side, pretending to inspect the alarm unit she'd already hung at the window. I had to gather my wits, but the sight of her toned thighs and narrow waist was burned into my brain. Those breasts looked ready to pop out of her dress.

She took the plastic bag with the curry boxes from me, heading to the kitchen. I remained in the foyer, inspecting the base unit of the alarm. Out of the corner of my eye, I saw her tugging her dress, as if she could make it longer just by pulling at it.

"Let's take care of the alarm first," I suggested. "We can eat afterward."

"Sure. I have wine. Do you want a glass?" she called from the kitchen.

"No, thanks."

I was already tinkering with the alarm when she joined me by the door with a glass of wine for herself.

"Hey! Don't do it without me. I want to learn."

I motioned toward the alarm.

"The trick is to get the contacts right."

"But I did it the way they explained it in the instructions."

"Let's do it again together."

I forced myself to slow down, so she could see me setting up the contacts. I liked her curiosity, the way she watched me, clearly intending to memorize what I was doing.

"There, done," I said after all the wires were set. We tested the alarm, and she clapped her hands when it worked. Her pink lips puckered before she gave me a wide smile, and I focused on that—on her lovely, beautiful smile. It was easier to resist taking the rest of her in if I focused on her mouth.

"Thanks! I can finally cross this off the list. Let's have dinner."

She led me to the living room, and I walked a few feet behind her, watching that perfect, round ass swing on every step. The skin of her thighs was lighter the further up it went, as if she hadn't exposed it to the sun.

We ate at the low coffee table, sitting on the floor. Paige was fidgeting, clearly trying to find a sitting position that wouldn't be indecent. She tucked her legs under herself and flashed half her ass. Then she stretched her legs out, which... wasn't exactly indecent, but I had a hard time concentrating on my curry.

"Did you find a handyman?" I asked. She'd mentioned it during cocktails.

"Yes, he's coming next week to do an initial check and tell me what it will all cost." She looked around wistfully. "I'll miss this place. I spent a lot of afternoons here as a kid, came here straight after school. My grandma and I were close."

"When did she pass away?"

"Last spring. I think that's when I first knew I didn't want to be in Paris anymore. I was missing a lot of birthdays and stuff, but not being here for my family when this happened, that hurt. It took me almost a day and a half to come here, and everyone was... well...."

I reached over the table and stroked her hand. Her eyes widened, but she didn't pull her hand away. I wanted to comfort her any way I could. She had a beautiful soul, and clearly she was still beating herself up over the fact that she hadn't been here.

"Tell me about your job. Have you always worked at nonprofits?" I asked, in an effort to distract her. It worked. Her expression lit up.

"Yes. My friend Luna got me into it. She volunteered to run a study group for kids from underprivileged backgrounds in college, and roped me into it. Then we both interned at Three Emeralds. One thing led to another. She works at a bank now, but I stayed there. I like it. I feel like I'm making a difference. Why did you become a detective?"

"Same reason as you, I suppose. Making a

difference." I liked that we had that in common. "I studied criminal justice and law enforcement in college, then enrolled in the police academy."

I had surprised everyone with my decision, especially because as a rebellious teenager, I'd had some encounters with the police. Once they busted me when I'd tried to climb the Hollywood sign. It had been a stupid dare, but I'd been all about stupid dares back in those days. The cop had seen right through me. I wasn't just a kid out on a prank. I was feeling lost after my parents' accident, angry that the culprit hadn't been caught.

He'd brought me to the station with him. At first I'd thought I was going to spend a night behind bars, but then he told me that if I agreed to shadow him for a week, he wouldn't press charges. I didn't have time for that. I had to be home every day after school to watch Lori, Jace, and Hailey. Val and Landon were counting on me. I did a lot of shit, but I hadn't let my family down… yet. But the cop left me no choice. After one week of witnessing him bring in vandals and criminals, I wasn't so hot on the idea of stupid dares anymore. In retrospect, I realized that had probably been his intention. But I had gotten a taste of what it meant to be on the force, and I'd liked it. So much, in fact, that after college, I'd decided to join it. Catching criminals had made me feel useful.

We spoke about each other's jobs while we finished our curry. I'd forgotten all about her short dress until we got up to carry the empty takeout containers and glasses to the kitchen. Apparently, so did she, because she pushed herself off the ground with her back to me, and as the skirt flew up, I had a view of half her ass, since her panties barely covered anything. *Fucking hell.*

My dick twitched. I groaned, turning away. Paige was desperately trying to cover herself.

"Paige," I said slowly, "no matter how you much you tug at it, that dress won't cover much."

She stopped fidgeting. "I wore a suit to work today, and this was the only thing I could change into."

I gave her a cheeky smile. "Works for me."

"Can you at least pretend not to be enjoying it so much?"

"Why? Is it too flattering for you?"

She blushed.

"You sure you didn't choose that dress on purpose? To torment me?" I continued.

"Did you do something for which you'd deserve tormenting?" She tossed me a sassy glance over her shoulder on the way to the kitchen.

"Maybe." I'd had dirty thoughts. I still did.

What I'd do to this woman, right here in this kitchen…. I'd bury my face between her legs until she cried out my name.

"You're flattering yourself now. Maybe detectives aren't my type," she teased as she threw the cartons in the bin. I placed the glasses on the counter, then swept my gaze around the kitchen… and stilled. There was a bouquet of roses on her windowsill. They even had a card. I walked closer until I could read what it said.

I had a lot of fun today. I'd love to take you to dinner.
Christian Lackeroy
General Manager

I swallowed, trying to control the mix of emotions. "Who sent you flowers?"

"A potential donor I met today."

I stepped away from the roses. "I see. You said detectives aren't your type. So I gather suits are."

She ran a hand through her hair. She was agitated. "No, that's not what I meant."

"So you haven't accepted the douchebag's invitation?"

"How do you know he's a douchebag?"

"Wrote his position on the card wanting to impress you." After a brief pause, I added, "Did he succeed, Paige? Are you going out with him?"

She tensed, jutting her chin forward. I could bet that she wanted to challenge me, to flip me off, tell me that it was none of my business. Hell, it *was* none of my business. But then she glanced straight at me, and whatever she saw in my expression made the fight go right out of her.

"No, Will. I didn't accept the invitation," she said softly.

"And you took the flowers with you because…?"

"I'm going to be working remotely for the rest of the week. There was no point leaving the flowers at the office where no one could see them. "

I gave her a tight smile. "You said you met the guy today?"

"Yeah."

"Damn. He moves even faster than I do."

She chuckled. "I don't know, Will. He hasn't asked me to go to a wedding with him yet."

"Have you given that more thought?" I moved closer to her.

"It's a standing invitation?"

"Yes. Why? What did you think?"

"That you'd continue your search for a protector."

I threw my head back, laughing. Then I moved even closer, bracing a hand on the counter right next to her waist.

"You really want me to come to the wedding?"

I nodded, waiting. Just before I'd met Paige to buy the alarm, Lori had called to ask me to give her away. I was sure she'd ask Landon, since he was the oldest and he and Val raised us. But Lori said she'd love it if I considered it, and I said yes, of course. It meant a lot to me. But I foresaw that the day would be more of an emotional roller coaster than I'd originally thought, and I wanted Paige by my side.

"I know we just met," I said when she continued to be silent.

"Well… you did go buy an alarm with me and came by to install it. We can rule out malicious intent." She smiled, but I detected a strange reticence in her expression.

I cocked my head. "Depends on your definition of malicious."

"Nah, you'd make a good friend, Detective."

A *friend*? That was how she was labeling this? Our bodies were almost touching. There was maybe half an inch between our hips. I'd been fighting a hard-on since I arrived. Her nipples were puckered. I could see their shape through the dress. She was leaning *into* me rather than away. But she'd put the *friendship* stamp on this for some reason.

"I'm going to do my best to get out of that thing with my high school classmates."

"Your very best?" I insisted, pushing a strand of hair behind her ear.

"My very best. I promise." Her breath caught a little when she spoke. She was deliciously responsive to my touch. Paige and I weren't going to be *just* friends.

***

"You're outta here already?" my partner, Elliot, asked a couple of days later.

"Friday dinner. Can't be late."

"I still need to finish the paperwork I've put off."

We'd been burning the midnight oil with a case of a string of robberies, gathering evidence, and we'd been putting off a lot of things.

I faked a shudder. "I'll do mine next week."

Elliot hated paperwork as much as I did. He was fifteen years older, and we'd been paired since I joined the force. We made a good team.

My mind was still on our latest cases as I left the station. Some left the work behind when they were off duty, but I'd never managed that. However, I did make a concerted effort right now, because I was heading to Friday dinner. My sisters always picked up on it if I was troubled, and I didn't want to worry them.

Which was why I pushed all thoughts about the case to the deepest recesses of my mind when I climbed the stairs in Valentina's terraced yard. This space would give any botanical garden a run for its money.

My three sisters were on the front porch of the ranch-style home, whispering and giggling. When the words *sexy time* reached my ears, I thought it would be smarter to announce my presence. I absolutely didn't want to eavesdrop on their girl talk.

"Girls, change the subject. I will pretend I haven't heard anything."

Hailey whipped her head in my direction, tilting it slightly. "You look like someone pissed in your cereal, brother."

Hailey was our youngest sister. She looked a lot like Mom—shorter than Val and Lori, and with dark brown eyes, like me. The rest had inherited the green eyes that were part of our Irish heritage from Dad's side.

"Trouble at work?" Val chimed in. Lori

wasn't saying anything, but I knew that didn't mean she was staying out of it. Especially when she was exchanging glances with both Val and Hailey. They were cooking up something. In any case, I still had to work on my poker face and putting my day behind me.

"Girls, no need for an intervention."

Hailey smiled, holding up a finger. "This would be an ambush."

"It's just work stuff. I'm gonna head inside, leave you to finish your girl talk."

"We'll come inside in a minute," Val assured me. "Hailey just needs some advice, and we're trying to keep girl talk away from sensitive manly ears."

"Excellent strategy."

My nephew was inside the house, playing a game of darts with Graham. I joined them.

"Girl talk still going on outside?" Graham asked.

"Yep."

"Accidentally walked in on it earlier. I'm scarred for life."

"Join the club."

Jace arrived just in time for dinner. So did Landon with his wife Maddie and their one-year-old daughter Willow. Landon told us about his latest investment deal while we ate.

The conversation then inevitably turned to Lori and Graham's wedding, as it had done every time we were together over the past few weeks. Val was relentlessly teasing us about Pippa's matchmaking games.

"Actually," I said, "I'm bringing someone."

Jace looked shocked. "What? But we're supposed to stick together. Strength in numbers and all that."

"Who is she?" Lori asked.

"You don't know her. I met her recently and invited her."

"Has she said yes yet?" Jace inquired.

"She'll say yes," I said confidently, even though I hadn't heard from her in a week. I hadn't insisted, deciding to be a gentleman and wait patiently. Except… I wasn't exactly known for my patience.

"Well, let me know as soon as she does, so I can change that in the seating chart," Lori said.

"Looks like you'll be on your own, brother. Don't count on me and Val to save you from Pippa. We'll be busy with wedding stuff."

"Hailey, you're enjoying this far too much," Jace declared.

Hailey patted Jace mockingly on the shoulder. They were the youngest. Growing up, I couldn't tell which one was the worse influence. But by the time they were teenagers, things changed. Jace turned into a fierce guardian to our sisters. Our little Hailey didn't grow up to be a troublemaker. She was sharp and focused, paving her way through life with a sledgehammer. Lori and I were the middle kids, though I'd always considered myself part of the older group. Partly because Val and Landon were twins, which made me the second oldest, but also because I'd been in charge of watching the younger ones, being an authority figure and all that.

After dinner I decided that I was going to get an answer from Paige tonight. I went out on the porch and called her. She didn't answer, but as soon as I disconnected, she called back.

"Sorry for missing the call. My phone was at the bottom of the bag. Took forever to find it. I've been meaning to call you this evening."

"Oh, yeah?"

"Uh-huh."

"I'm warning you, saying no isn't an option."

She laughed softly. "That's quite some swagger you're flaunting."

"Just being upfront."

"I see. Well, now that makes me want to say no just to hear your reaction."

"So you're saying yes?"

She laughed again. "I'm bad at playing this game. I've cleared out my schedule for next Saturday. Took some time, because one of my close friends is flying in for the occasion, but I'm meeting her on Friday instead. But you *were* right. As soon as I mentioned the wedding, I was forgiven. When are you picking me up?"

"Three o'clock."

"I'll be ready."

I couldn't suppress a grin when I returned inside the house and told my sister, "Lori, add a plus one to your list."

Chapter Seven
Paige

On Saturday, I was certain I was going to be late. I hadn't heard the alarm, so I'd slept in. I'd been back from Paris for a while now, so I couldn't blame the jet lag anymore, just my lazy bones. I'd barely made it to the hairdresser appointment, but no way was I attending a wedding without a professional hairstyle. I'd never been handy with that stuff, and following YouTube tutorials usually ended in disaster. I was doing my own makeup, though, because I preferred a natural look, and most professionals applied so much foundation that I felt like I was wearing a mask.

I practically flew back home after my hair appointment, blowing two red lights and driving way over the speed limit. I wondered if Will could retroactively fine me for this. I'd ask him tonight. The thought made me smile. I had no idea why I liked pushing his buttons.

I put on one of my favorite dresses. The light green chiffon was tight above my waist, with a crisscrossing pattern of black lace up to the shoulders. It flowed in a wide A-line to the floor, with a generous split up the right leg. Still, I knew it was a bit too much fabric for this weather. The heat in the second part of July was no less forgiving than it had been in the first part.

I'd bought it from a French designer in a tiny shop two streets away from the Eiffel Tower. He'd been up-and-coming and a total gem of a person. On the plus side, his prices were a bargain because he wanted to get his name out there. If there was one thing I missed from Paris, aside from the croissants, it was the fashion. There were plenty of choices in LA, but I missed what Paris had to offer.

Luna called while I was applying makeup, so I put my phone on loudspeaker, placing it on the shelf under the bathroom mirror while I leaned in as close as possible. I was trying not to poke myself in the eye with the eyeliner. I had no idea what had possessed me to try a smoky eye, but I bore a striking resemblance to a panda, so I wiped it all off and started from scratch. Just mascara, and a smidge of color on my eyelids, cheeks, and lips.

Meanwhile, Luna was grilling me. "A friend? You did not just say that. So let me get this straight. You turned down the Lackeroy guy, and you're going with the hot detective to the wedding as friends?"

"Yes."

"So you're basically dateless and sexless?"

"Jeez, way to make a girl feel better." But my friend had a point. I'd said I wanted to date more. So why had I told Will he could be a good friend?

"Do you want me to set you up with someone?" Luna asked.

"Umm... no thanks."

I still had scars from the last time Luna had tried that. My friend meant well, but... "good intentioned" was the best I could come up with to describe that fiasco.

"Well, have fun at the wedding."

"I will."

After disconnecting the call, I assessed my work. Makeup was decent. My hair was up in an elegant bun. The dress was perfect. I paired it with black flats and a small black clutch bag. I wanted to knock Will's socks off. Because I was too nervous to wait inside, I headed outside, waiting for Will in the shade of a large tree in the inner courtyard. A black car pulled in a few minutes later, and Will climbed out from the passenger seat.

My mouth watered as I took him in. Today he was dressed to the nines. Charcoal suit and tie, white shirt.

"How long have you been waiting? I would have picked you up from your door."

"Not long. I just wanted some fresh air. How come you're not driving?"

"Lori insisted on arranging transportation for everyone so we wouldn't have to worry about drinking and driving."

He opened the car door for me. I was surprised at the pang of disappointment when Will *didn't* check me out. He kept his gaze firmly on my face.

"Great day for a wedding," I said once we

were in the back of the car. It was sunny, even if a little too hot for my liking.

"It's gonna be great. We're going directly to the church. We're meeting everyone there."

"Sounds good. Do you like the guy? Does he have the family's stamp of approval? Come on, give me some dirt."

"We like the guy. He's great to my sister and her son."

"But?"

"I didn't say but."

"It's in your tone."

"You're very curious."

I leaned in closer, whispering, "And you're hiding something."

"Not hiding anything. Just adjusting to the new dynamics. I used to do a lot of activities with my nephew before, even attended school events."

Whatever I had expected him to say, it wasn't this.

"How come?"

"His biological dad was a scumbag. Took off before he was born, so he didn't have a father figure. I tried to fill in that role, so to speak. I spent a lot of time with him."

Will Connor had many layers, and I wanted to discover every single one of them. We made small talk until we entered Pasadena, and the car dropped us off right in front of the church.

There was a crowd gathered already, and

someone was handing corsages. Will and I each took one, and he pulled me a little away from the entrance.

He took care of me first, pinning it on my left side, just under my shoulder. Was it just me, or was his hand lingering longer than needed? His thumb feathered just above my clavicle, where it had no business being. Despite the burning sun, a shiver slithered down my spine. I was dying to know... was I here just as a friend? Or perhaps a date? Sure, I'd been the one to bring up the word friend first, but Will hadn't corrected me. I wasn't even sure what I wanted this to be. Well, I knew what I *wanted*, I just wasn't sure if it was wise.

When my turn came to pin the corsage to his lapel, I took an inordinate amount of time. I was using the opportunity to study him up close. He must have shaved this morning because I smelled the clean scent of aftershave on him. His cheek looked so smooth that I barely refrained from touching it. As I finished securing the corsage, I had no reason to linger... but I didn't want to step away either.

"Just in time," a gorgeous brunette interrupted, approaching us. She was wearing a floor-length dark blue silk dress, but I still spotted her shoes. If I wasn't mistaken, those were Louboutins.

"My sister, Hailey. Hailey, this is Paige," Will said.

Hailey kissed my cheek. "Pleasure to meet you. Will's announcement caused quite a stir. We'll have to wait until he's not around before I start dishing dirt about him, or he'll fight me on every word."

I didn't think I'd ever liked anyone instantly the way I liked Hailey. I loved everything from her impeccable shoe choice to her humor.

"I'll make sure to take notes," I replied. Will glared at his sister.

"Can you at least wait until after the ceremony to give me shit?"

Hailey chuckled. "Absolutely not. Wait until the rest—oh, look, here's Jace."

I jerked my head back when Jace climbed the stairs.

"Jace Connor, *the soccer god*, is your brother?" I whispered.

Will nodded, watching me intently.

"And this must be the lovely Paige," Jace said when he reached us. He flashed a smile that bore a little resemblance to Will's, then shook my hand.

"Dad used to take us kids to the Lords' games. Obviously you weren't on the team then, but I'm a Lords fan through and through."

Jace grinned, looking between me and Will. "Brother, if she's a Lords fan, you've hit the jackpot."

"Oh, he selected me based on that criteria." I was fighting to keep a straight face.

Another woman joined us. She was a little taller than Hailey. Her dark brown hair was tied up in an elegant bun, and her deep green dress matched her eyes. "Okay, Lori is in the car. Will, you should wait at the foot of the staircase. Graham is already inside. And you must be Paige. I'm Valentina, but everyone calls me Val. We should all go inside, except Will."

Will was giving his sister away? He hadn't mentioned that. I said goodbye to Will, then walked inside with Val and Hailey, sitting with them. I saved the seat next to me for Will. When he stepped inside the church with the bride, I saw yet another side of him. Pure emotion was reflected on his features, and he kissed his sister's forehead before stepping away from her and the groom. He sat next to me, and on pure impulse, I wrapped an arm around his. He stiffened at first, as if he hadn't been expecting it, but then he squeezed it lightly.

After the ceremony, a photographer took group pictures in front of the church.

While we waited for the cars that would take us to the restaurant, I was introduced to Landon, the oldest brother, and his wife, Maddie. Landon was carrying a toddler who seemed intent on performing gymnastics in her father's arms. Jace rode with Landon and Maddie. Will and I slid into the next available car with Val and Hailey. Because Will was a mountain of a man, we asked him to sit in the front while we girls crammed in the back, careful not to sit on each other's dresses.

"I think Landon's a bit jealous that Lori wanted you to give her away," Val said as the car lurched forward.

"Well, Landon can walk Val and me," Hailey said.

Val waved her hand. "Speak for yourself, sis. My chances at spinsterhood are looking better and better."

"Ah, this is the second wedding in the family, right?" I asked.

Val nodded. "If you don't count our extended family, yes."

I patted her shoulder, then held up three fingers. "Three in mine already. One brother, two sisters. Just putting it out there, but by the third one, you'll be wondering if it's time for life-altering choices."

The girls laughed, then Val took out a mirror, and each of us checked our makeup. When the car came to a stop, Will opened the door, and all three of us filtered out.

"What's that smile about?" he asked me.

"I'm glad I'm here. This is a fun day."

The restaurant was in a renovated Victorian house, on the ground level. The space outside had also been decorated for the wedding, with tall white bar tables where one could relax with a drink. I was happy the reception was taking place inside though, where there was air-conditioning. Two hostesses were directing the guests around. I became acutely aware that Will's hand was on my lower back. I looked up. Will's gaze was on my lips. Heat coiled low in my belly, at the tips of my breasts. Holy shit.

"Paige, you look incredible." He was *so* close. And he sounded… delicious.

Somehow, I found my voice. "Thank you."

One of the hostesses came to lead us inside. Will offered me his arm, and I took it. I felt more aware of him than before. The point where our arms interlaced pulsed. The occasional brush of our thighs as we moved sent tingles up my leg. I was relieved when he went to bring us both drinks. I needed a break from all that squirming.

Chapter Eight
Paige

I sat down at our table and took in the room. It was a dreamy setup. The strings of lights and white linens had been arranged discreetly so that they complemented the building's character rather than obscured it.

Eat. Dance. Repeat. I lived by those words the whole evening. Boy was I happy I'd chosen to wear flats. Otherwise I would already have had blisters. I'd learned that the hard way. At my first sister's wedding, I'd taken my shoes off to cool my soles on the bathroom floor after a few hours. My feet had been so swollen that I'd barely managed to wedge them back inside the shoes. At the second wedding, I changed from high heels to flats after a while, but the damage had been done. I couldn't wear anything other than flip-flops for the next two days.

I danced with Will and Jace, as well as some other guests, and did a girls-only dance with Val and Hailey.

"You all have dancing in your blood, I swear," I said in a brief moment of reprieve. Val was excellent. I felt like a chipmunk on the dance floor next to her.

Val nodded happily as we stood in a corner, catching our breath. "We do."

We chatted about each other's jobs. Val owned a perfume and cosmetics company; Hailey worked at a PR agency.

"And Landon had a software company, but he sold it and now runs an investment fund," Val finished.

"So Will's the only one on the police force."

"Yep. Keeps us all on our toes," Val said, then fell silent as Will approached. By his narrowed eyes, he'd clearly heard the last part.

He was expertly carrying four glasses of champagne, and we relieved him of three.

"That's why you sent me for drinks? So you could bad-mouth me?"

Hailey batted her eyelashes. "No one was bad-mouthing you. We're just concerned, but that's because we love you so much."

Will shook his head. "You always say that because you know I can't get mad at you."

"Precisely. The tactic works, so I'm going to keep using it."

Val shifted her weight from one leg to the other. "I have to sit down. I need a longer break this time."

"I'll come with you," Hailey said. As the sisters walked away, Will came closer. Too close. I was on my third glass of champagne, and the alcohol was doing a number on me.

"So, from one member of a large family to

another, how do you deal?" he asked.

"Don't be so harsh with your sisters. I know where they're coming from."

"You do?"

"Dad was in the Army. We worried about him until he retired. So, yes."

I sipped my champagne, feeling Will's gaze on me. Damn, here I was starting to squirm again.

"Want to go out for some fresh air?" he asked.

"Yes. It's getting stuffy in here, even with the AC."

We walked side by side, and when we stepped in the yard, the wind, though warm, made me shudder. Will put an arm around my shoulders. The heat of that strong, muscled body was making my knees weak. I felt like we'd been engaging in daylong foreplay.

There were quite a few guests outside, gathered along the round bar tables. We headed toward the nearest one that was unoccupied. It was all the way to the right, near the corner of the building. We stopped along the way at a table where a knockout blonde was scolding two identical-looking girls.

"Ah, Paige, meet Pippa Bennett-Callahan. My dearest cousin, and my nieces," Will said.

The little girls stretched out their hands, introducing themselves as Mia and Elena. I shook Pippa's hand last. Her name tugged at a memory, and then I remembered.

"You're the matchmaking cousin, right?" I asked. Will groaned. I ignored him.

"That's right. Though Will doesn't need my skills, clearly."

Awww. Will was almost puffing out his chest next to me. Didn't the man know that pride was a sin? I could have kept my mouth shut, but oh, how I liked to push his buttons. And this one was begging to be pushed.

"Oh, he just brought me as his protector. My job is to save him from you."

Will expelled a harsh breath. We turned to look at each other at the same time. The side of my left breast was pressed against his chest. Will's next breath landed above my upper lip. The hand resting on my shoulder gripped me tighter. Holy hell, my knees buckled from the intensity of his attention. I focused on Pippa again, who was laughing, looking between us.

"Will, I think you have your hands full even without my meddling."

"That's the first time you've showed me mercy, cousin. I'll take it."

"Girls, let's go inside and find your dad and uncle Jace. *He* does need our help."

Pippa moved past us, and Will nudged me forward until we reached the table we'd been eyeing from the start.

"You are something," Will declared. Those dark eyes held fire. And I wanted more fire still. The champagne had made me bold, and Will's proximity was fueling my blood with adrenaline.

"I have a tendency to misbehave, Detective. What are you gonna do about it, arrest me?" I held my palms in front of me playfully. I realized what was going to happen a second before it did. Will did cuff both my wrists... with his bare hands. Then he moved us around the corner, where it was dark and there were no guests. He lowered my wrists behind my back, still keeping them prisoner in his hands, and then he kissed me. His mouth moved over mine urgently, his lips wreaking havoc. He tasted like champagne too, and when I opened up for him, he stroked my tongue with his. My body reacted to every stroke as if he wasn't kissing just my mouth. My nipples hardened. The muscles low in my belly clenched. We had full frontal contact now. I wanted my hands free to roam those shoulders and chest, but Will wasn't relenting. He had complete control over the kiss, and it made everything about a million times hotter. He was going to explore me until he had his fill of me, and I wasn't sure my body wasn't going to spontaneously combust in the meantime. He stopped only to tug with his teeth at my lower lip, then the upper one. Then he ran the tip of his tongue along both before kissing me again. I became slick between my legs.

His thumbs were pressing on my pulse points. His grip was gentle, and yet strong enough that I couldn't move my hands. He slid a thigh between my legs, lowering our entwined hands to the middle of my ass. The fingers that weren't cuffing my wrists were pressing into my ass cheeks. He was pushing me up on him, and I was practically straddling his thigh. He had me at his mercy, and it felt as if with every stroke of his tongue he was showing me that I was his to ravish and explore, that he was laying claim on me.

He groaned against my mouth before pulling back a notch. I was dissolving in his arms.

"Don't dance with anyone else tonight, Paige. No one but me."

I was still lost in the magic of the kiss, but that seemed like a great idea. Why would I even dance with anyone else? Will was so.... I had no words, but he was what I needed.

***

Will had been holding out on me. We'd danced before the kiss, but not like this. I especially loved it when other guys approached to ask me for a dance. Will threw them one look, and they scurried away. When the wedding reception was approaching the end, Lori announced that she was going to throw the bouquet and asked all the single girls to gather in the center of the dance floor.

I made to head to our table, but Will caught my arm. "You're not participating?"

Before I had a chance to answer, the groom announced that he'd throw the garter after the bride threw the bouquet. Will scrunched up his nose. I saw my opportunity for some more button pushing.

"I'll go with the girls for the bouquet if you line up for the garter later."

"No. That's my sister. Catching that garter... no."

"Who cares? Every single man is supposed to line up."

Will pierced me with those sharp eyes, leaning in until I felt his breath on my cheek. "No."

I wanted to come up with a smart reply, but damn... the way he watched me made me lose my train of thought. I was still feeling those hot lips on mine as if we'd kissed a few minutes ago, not a few hours.

Before I had a chance to give it more thought, the Connor girls appeared at my side. Val got my right hand, Hailey my left one, and they practically dragged me to the center of the dance floor.

Will was laughing, the bastard. I'd plot my revenge on him later on, preferably without looking in those gorgeous eyes. They robbed me of thought and willpower.

The crowd of single ladies was so large that I didn't worry I'd catch the bouquet. I didn't have anything against it in particular, but I wasn't one to put much stock in such traditions.

I was standing between the Connor girls, smack dab in the middle of the crowd. I had to admit, it was fun. I clapped and whistled along with the others, and watched as Lori threw the bouquet with a beautiful arch. Unfortunately, she threw it so high that it hit the ceiling… and then fell smack dab on my head. I didn't have time to duck or even brace myself. The bouquet fell straight on the middle of my head, hitting me so hard that I nearly lost my balance. On pure instinct, I held my hands in front of me, catching it. The poor thing was missing a quarter of its petals. I suspected I was wearing them in my hair. The hit also seemed to have messed with my senses, because I wasn't hearing anything. But then my ears made a little *pop*, and I became aware of laughter.

Val and Hailey were wiping tears from their eyes.

"That's a first," I said sheepishly.

"You never caught it before?" Hailey asked.

"Nope. Though I can't say I caught this. More like it hit me straight on."

I wondered if it was a sign. Ah, but the flowers were beautiful. I admired them as we rushed off to the side, leaving the dance floor for the men. I was surprised at how many showed up to catch the garter.

"Men usually aren't so excited about this part," I murmured to Val.

"In my opinion, the excitement is directly proportional to how beautiful the woman who caught the bouquet is."

"Oh, oh!" *Now* I remembered. The guy who caught the garter was supposed to slide it up my leg. I looked at the crowd of men, trying to detect potential candidates to cheer for. Then I saw Will joining the crowd. He stood out among the dozen or so men. He was taller, and by far the best-looking one. And those arms... *yummm*. I wondered if he could lift me up with just one. He wasn't wearing the suit jacket, and the white fabric of his shirt was stretched a little too tight over his biceps.

Oh, so now he was interested in catching the garter, was he?

I tried to catch his attention, but he was focusing on Graham. It looked like he was serious about winning.

Graham threw the garter up in the air in a swift move. The crowd of men lurched forward, but Will, being taller, had the advantage. Plus his reflexes seemed sharper. He caught the garter with little effort. One of the competing men literally bounced off him. I tried to contain my joy, but it wasn't easy, especially when Will winked at me.

Oh, God. He was going to put his hands on me. In front of everyone. How high exactly did he have to push that garter? I'd never bothered to find out, and asking the Connor girls would be too embarrassing. In any case, I congratulated myself on choosing to shave all the way up today. I'd thought about cheating and only shaving to the top of the split, then decided not to be a lazy ass.

Graham took the microphone, asking me to step forward and explaining the tradition of the garter for the guests. I heard only half of it. Will was looking straight at me, and by the way his gaze traveled up and down my body, I knew he was going to make me squirm. Damn, I already *was* squirming.

After Graham lowered the microphone, Will brought a chair on the dance floor, motioning for me to sit on it.

I did that and crossed my legs before realizing it was counterproductive. Will followed my every move, taking stock of the leg where the split was. He chose the other leg to slide the garter up.

"Thought you didn't want to catch the garter," I teased. Will was close enough to hear me, but no one else could. A catchy song was playing.

"You thought I'd let some other guy put his hands all over you?"

My God, had he somehow become sexier in the past half hour since we'd danced? Something was different....

"Ah, I see. Well, I was rooting for the guy next to you."

Will cuffed my ankle. I was reminded of our kiss and the way he'd held my hands behind my back.

"You're a bad girl, Paige. And I am going to make you pay for every button you've pushed today." His voice was low and seductive, and I knew I was toast. I was at his mercy *again*, only now we had a crowd watching and clapping.

He moved his hand up to my ankle then higher, drawing small circles with his middle finger on the back of my calf. A sizzle went up my spine. Yep, the sizzles were starting already, and he wasn't even at my knee. He trailed the finger up to my knee, then let the garter drop.

He turned to the crowd, shrugging as if to say,

"What can you do?"

Then he started the whole ordeal from the beginning, starting with my ankle. I was clasping the edges of the seat with both hands, willing myself not to squirm.

But when he moved past my knee, I lost the battle. He smiled, as if he knew exactly the effect he was having on me, watching me intently. He'd trapped me with those sinful brown eyes. I couldn't look away even if I wanted to.

"How do you like this, Paige?" Will whispered.

"You're driving me crazy," I whispered back. My entire body was tingling, even though he was only touching my leg. And the pressure between my thighs was intensifying. I couldn't see what he was doing, but I felt every callus on his fingers.

"Good, that's exactly what I'm going for."

I inhaled deeply through my mouth, exhaling through my nose. If Will Connor thought I couldn't push his buttons even when I was at his mercy, he was in for a surprise.

"If you continue to go so slow, you'll never reach high enough to check if I'm wearing any panties."

Victory! Oh, yeah. Will clenched his jaw, his hand tightening on my thigh.

"Paige," he warned. His voice was breathier, which gave me immense satisfaction.

"You were saying, Detective?"

He wiped the sass right off my tongue when

his hand moved higher.

"Tell me if you're wearing any."

"What if I won't?"

His hand inched higher. He was going to call my bluff. The others wouldn't know exactly what was happening under my skirt, but I would. When he moved his hand higher still, I relented. He was only halfway up my inner thigh, but I couldn't risk it.

"Fine, yes. Yes, I'm wearing panties."

He gave me a smile that left me feeling as if my lacy, barely there thong had caught fire. "What kind?"

"Will Connor, I am not going to describe my underwear to you."

"Then I'll check for myself."

"I'd like to see you try."

I knew it was the wrong thing to say a second after I spoke. Will's smile turned wolfish. Holy shit, I'd never met a man willing to go toe-to-toe with me. So, I was surprised when he let go of the garter, which made a tiny snapping sound as it touched my skin. When Will pulled back his hand, I felt a little foolish, realizing he couldn't have called my bluff. He couldn't very well look up my skirt in a room full of people.

The guests clapped and cheered, and I stood up, rolling my dress up so everyone could see the garter. I knew that would get a rise out of Will. Looking sideways at him, I wiggled my eyebrows. That hot and possessive look he gave me in return? It could have melted Antarctica.

Chapter Nine
Will

"Uncle Will, can I talk to you?" Milo asked me as the wedding reception was winding down.

"Sure. What's up?"

I motioned to the chair in front of me, and he climbed on it. I was facing him, but I was also keeping an eye on Paige, who was three seats away. She'd been deep in conversation with my sisters up until a minute ago when they'd gone to bring a fresh round of drinks. They were all tipsy already.

"So, Mom and Dad are going on their honeymoon in two weeks," Milo said.

I nodded.

"And Mom wanted to talk to Aunt Val so I could stay with her, but… can I stay with you? I like Aunt Val, but…."

And now I understood why he'd waited until my sisters left. He hadn't wanted to hurt Val's feelings.

"Of course you can. I'll talk to Lori."

Milo clapped his hands in excitement. "Can we build a birdhouse?"

I ruffled his hair, filled with a strange happiness. "Sure."

Before Graham, Jace and I had been the ones to show Milo the ropes when it came to *manly activities*, as Lori called them. Now Milo was basking in the fact that he had a dad who could show him all those things.

I wasn't ashamed to admit that I'd missed our time together. I was thrilled to spend a week with him.

As Milo hopped off the chair, running straight to Lori, I realized Paige had been watching us and was smiling warmly. Val and Hailey returned, carrying tequila shots. They'd been chugging champagne for the past few hours, and now were topping it off with shots?

I was one to talk. I was buzzed from champagne… and still high on Paige. On the taste of her mouth and the smooth skin of her thighs. She was getting tipsier by the second, but it was endearing to watch her be a goof and have fun with my sisters.

They were talking about her dad. She was telling them about one of his deployments, and I was shamelessly eavesdropping. When she'd said her dad had been in the Army, I realized what she'd meant that day about detectives not being her type. She'd said it jokingly, but paired with her comment today about understanding my sister's worry, and her insistence on the day we'd bought the alarm that my looking around was making her uncomfortable, there might be some truth behind it.

That didn't sit well with me, because I liked

Paige. The sweet way she'd reached out to me in the church completely took me by surprise. The way she'd goofed around the entire day, pushing my buttons even more than usual... somehow she'd known I needed that today. And that kiss... how she'd surrendered to me. My dick twitched at the memory.

When all of the guests had left and only family was around, Paige rose to her feet. She was beyond tipsy. Her gait was steady, but other things gave her away. She grabbed her phone too tightly; her movements were too brusque.

Over her shoulder, I saw her pull up the app for ordering a cab.

"You don't need to order anything. Those cars we all came in are waiting outside."

"Oh."

"I'm taking you home, Paige."

She blinked up at me, giving me a dazzling smile. "That's nice of you. Thanks."

On the way to the car, I tucked her into my side, half supporting her weight. I'd been right about her level of tipsiness.

In the car, I became aware that I wasn't faring much better. The champagne had gone straight to my head. Not touching Paige took a huge effort. Her dress slid off one leg, revealing all that creamy skin. I sat next to her, careful not to make any contact. If I kissed her, the driver would be in for quite a show.

"How did you like the wedding?" I asked.

"It was great. I'm so glad you talked me into

going."

I leaned in, whispering right in her ear. "I'm quite good at talking you into what I want." I could feel her wanting to argue with me, maybe dish some more of that sass. Almost without thinking, I touched her bare thigh on the spot where I'd slid the garter on her other leg. She let out a sound between a sigh and a moan, and when I cocked my head in her direction, I nearly lost all my control. Her eyes were hooded, full of lust. It took all I had not to kiss her.

It became clear quickly that she was also tired. She slid lower in her seat, and her head kept lolling to one side or the other as she dozed off.

"You're tired. Relax, I'll hold you."

I slid my fingers under her chin, tilting her head on my shoulder. Before long, she was asleep. I would have liked to talk to her, but this worked just fine for me too. She made an adorable sound, like a purring cat. Her hair smelled like strawberries.

When we arrived at her building, I rocked her gently.

"We're here, Paige. Wake up."

She blinked her eyes open, straightening up. I climbed out of the car, then opened her door, helping her out.

"This is me," she said unnecessarily.

"I'm walking you to the front door."

I scanned the area and decided it was semisafe. It was a sleepy residential area, with an inner courtyard and free access to the staircase. The corridor didn't have a full wall, so I could watch

Paige walk to her apartment, but there could be plenty of creeps waiting somewhere along the way.

Paige was fidgeting. "Will, I had a great time tonight, but...."

She glanced to the building, then at the car. I realized she thought I was inviting myself into her apartment or her bed. I stepped closer, taking her head between my hands, looking her straight in the eyes.

"Let me walk you to the door. I just want to make sure you're okay."

She bit her lip, then nodded. It was a testament to how tipsy she was that I got no sassy reply. Paige lived on the second floor, and I was satisfied there was no creep inside.

I walked her to the door and stood right behind her while she searched for her keys. I felt the heat of her body against my chest.

"Here is where I leave you, Paige."

She turned around. "You really just wanted to walk me to my door?"

"Yes. You should get an alarm, by the way."

She chuckled, bringing her hand to her temple in an army salutation. "Yes, sir. But only if you help me install it."

"Of course." I brought my lips to her cheek, then trailed them to her mouth, kissing one corner, then moving to the other. Then I kissed her. I hadn't thought a kiss could be hotter than the one at the wedding. I'd been wrong. She leaned back against the door for support as I deepened my exploration. She was free to touch me this time, and she took full advantage. She started with my arms, then moved to my shoulders before descending to my chest. I groaned against her mouth, and then one of my hands was on her thigh, touching her bare skin. She rolled her hips forward. I moved my hand higher just a fraction of an inch and then stopped. My other hand tightened on her shoulder. I was fighting the urge to move my hand even higher. She seemed to realize that... and moved it for me.

She was going to be the death of me. I needed to touch this woman intimately. I'd barely refrained when I kissed her at the wedding, but now, in this dark hallway.... One inch, then another, I trailed my fingers, until I reached between her legs. Her pussy was drenched. I was trembling with the desire to push her panties to one side and sink my fingers inside her. Hell, I wanted to drop to my knees and worship her with my mouth, right now. Instead, I retrieved my hand completely, placing it on the door with a loud thump. I had to tear myself away from her.

Outside the building, she'd been wary of me coming up. Now she was aroused in addition to being tipsy, and I knew that combination meant she wasn't thinking clearly. She'd regret this tomorrow. I was a nanosecond from breaking down the door and taking her inside, spreading her wide and feasting on her, sinking inside her. I pulled on every ounce of self-restraint and almost moved away... but then she lowered her hands to my hips, slamming them against hers.

Fuck, fuck, fuck. I was only human, and I was so turned on, I could barely think. My dick was painfully hard, and the suit pants weren't much help covering it. The length of my cock was pressing against her belly, and the friction was driving me insane. Paige had wound her hands in my hair, and she lifted one leg up my thigh, opening herself up. I nearly came in my pants. I breathed in and out, and finally tore my mouth away from hers. I brought both hands to her hips, pushing them firmly against the door.

"Fucking hell, Paige. You're killing me."

She was looking up at me with pent-up desire. I wanted nothing more than to go inside with her. If I thought I could keep my hands off her, I would. Just to talk to her, maybe find out a little more about her reticence about my job and how deep it went—if it was a deal-breaker. I was content even to just take some more button pushing from her. I wanted to be with her partly because tonight of all nights, I didn't feel like being on my own, but also because I was consumed by her.

I'd always followed my instincts, and I felt it deep in my bones that I wanted Paige in my life, perhaps even needed her. I wasn't sure how I felt about *needing* someone since I'd pushed away that concept at seventeen, but the entire day, that instinct had grown stronger. I wouldn't ignore it.

"Go inside. We're both buzzed from the champagne, and I'm very close to losing control. I'll call you tomorrow."

She blinked, then said awkwardly, "You're right. Thanks for keeping a clear head."

She turned around, but not before I noticed a strange expression on her face. It looked like shame, possibly even disappointment. I wanted to clear something up. I brought a hand to her waist, figuring it was safe to touch her because she had her back to me, so I couldn't get lost in her eyes or be tempted by her mouth and lose all reason.

I brought my mouth to her ear. "Paige, this doesn't mean I don't want you. I do, and when we take that step, I promise I'll fuck you *so* good." My voice was almost a growl. Her knees buckled, and she missed the lock twice. I covered her hand with mine and guided the key inside the lock.

"Will...."

"But I want us both—you especially—to be completely sober and in full possession of our mental faculties." I kissed the top of her back, then lower between her shoulder blades. "And in full possession of our senses, so you won't miss any single thing I'll be doing to you." I spoke every word against her skin. I felt a small quiver snake through her just as I took my hand away from her waist. She turned the key in her lock, then went inside. I fought against all my instincts to keep from knocking at her door.

Chapter Ten
Paige

Next day, I headed to my parents' house for brunch. My sisters and my brother were going to be there too, which made me giddy with excitement. I was going to get some much-needed quality time with my nieces. It had been far too long since I'd played with them. I put on a sundress and a large hat, bagging sunscreen too. My parents had a small pool, and I intended to use it.

I'd woken up with a suspiciously clear head. I'd feared a hangover, but so far, so good. Maybe I'd imagined all those champagne glasses... or the hotter-than-hell way Will had kissed me against the door. Had I imagined the dirty talk too? A sizzle went through me as I remembered his exact words. Nope, my imagination wasn't that good. I appreciated that he'd remembered we were both buzzed, when I'd gotten so lost in him. I knew most men wouldn't have cared about me being drunk when I practically jumped him in front of my door, even though I hadn't intended to let him into my bed so soon.

But his kiss had set me on fire, and well... I *had* been more than buzzed.

I arrived first, and my mother's first comment, as usual, was "Honey, you're too thin."

After which she loaded extra sausage and bread onto my plate.

"We're not waiting for everyone else to arrive?" I asked.

"We can eat with them too," Mom said. I hid my smile. So did my father. Ever since I'd lost weight in high school, Mom had been convinced I was too thin. I'd given up convincing her otherwise, and settled on doing extra laps in the pool after every meal.

I was the only one eating, though. Mom was too busy fussing around me, and Dad was watering some roses that the automatic sprinklers didn't reach. He walked with a slight limp he'd acquired nearly fifteen years ago. It had been one of the worst nights for the entire family. We'd thought the worst. I remembered sitting huddled on the couch with my sisters, none of us daring to talk. We'd put my brother to bed earlier, so he hadn't been aware. They were crying silently, but I wanted to be like Mom, who hadn't cried once.

But by morning, the hair at her temples had gone completely white. I'd researched it, and apparently shock can turn your hair white in a couple of hours. Mom had dyed her hair platinum blonde ever since.

I'd always been in awe of my parents' bond. It had survived for decades, despite the fact that Dad had spent most of their marriage deployed.

Mom had tried to keep most of her anguish to herself, but I noticed every time. She wouldn't cry in front of us, but many mornings she couldn't get out of bed, explaining she had migraines, and would ask me to prepare breakfast for the little ones. She wouldn't even look my way, which I'd learned meant she was trying to hide her face because her eyes were puffy from crying. I'd felt her fear deep in my bones even as she tried to keep the bad news to herself. The intensity of their love had frightened me sometimes.

My sisters, Miranda and Elsa, arrived at the same time, and my brother fifteen minutes later. They each had a little girl, and I hugged the living daylights out of them. When had they gotten so big? God, I'd missed so much. We ate as fast as we could and then jumped right in the pool.

"Hey, brat, how is it going with the inn?" my brother asked.

"I'll tell you when you stop calling me brat. I'm older than you."

"And still a brat." He was smiling.

"A handyman is coming next week to do some repairs, and then… on to selling it. It's going to take some time, though. I can only supervise the handyman after work. I don't trust anyone to give them keys."

"We can take turns watching him," he assured me. My sisters asked me to put them in the rotation too, which helped. My parents offered to watch the handyman during the day, but I refused. There was no rush to sell, and they didn't have to put their very active social life on hold for it. My parents' social calendar was better than mine. They did everything from dancing classes to trips around the country.

When I moved from the pool to one of the lounge chairs, I got out the sunscreen and my phone. I had a message from Will. My heart went pitter-patter. I hadn't ever felt such a strong attraction to a man. It almost scared me.

Will: How are you this morning, fine lady? Head weighing a ton? Hungover?

I smiled, typing back quickly.

Paige: Why such a low opinion of me? My head is perfectly fine. In fact, I'm having brunch with my family :-)

I didn't have enough alcohol in my system, but I definitely had a Will Connor hangover.

Will: What are you doing after brunch?

I hid my phone when Elsa passed me on the way to the house. If I thought my heart had gone pitter-patter before, it was nothing compared to now. Was he... was he trying to make plans with me?

Paige: Don't know yet.

I felt like dancing when his reply came.

Will: Let's do something together.

Paige: Define something.

Will: Not sure yet. Are you game for something spontaneous?

When it came to Will, I seemed to be game for anything. Including letting him kiss me against the door.

Paige: Game on, Will Connor.

Will: How about a trip to the mountains? A short trail?

I stared a little at the phone, wondering if this qualified as a date. Or were we just… hanging out, whatever that meant? After last night, it was clear that Will was interested in doing the horizontal mambo with me, but did he want something more too?

I fiddled with my phone, considering everything. He'd taken me to his sister's wedding, which had been sweet and personal. Way too much effort just to get in my pants—though I couldn't be sure, of course.

Paige: Sure. I love hiking.

Will: I know. You told me that yesterday :-)

I didn't even remember that. I smiled, feeling all sorts of winged creatures in my belly, and chose to view this as a date, hoping Will didn't consider it to be less.

Will: Let me know when brunch is over.

I tucked my phone carefully in my bag before lathering on sunscreen. Hiding my excitement wasn't as easy as hiding my phone, though. I looked at Miranda, laughing with her husband, and at my oaf of a brother chasing his daughter through the water, then joined in on the fun, even though the sunscreen hadn't sunk in my skin yet. I'd be sorry for my impulsive ways when I was eighty and wrinkly, but for now, I didn't care one bit.

I did laps, then played with my nieces and was

generally a brat to my brother. I had to live up to my nickname, after all. I even pulled Dad in the pool when he was passing by, even though he was fully clothed.

"Paige," Mom admonished with a smile, but Dad wasn't mad. I'd never seen the man mad one day in my life. He took it in stride.

When my siblings announced they had to get going, I started thinking about what to wear to meet Will. Which was why, instead of texting him when the brunch was over, I waited until I was home to text him, because not only did I need to change, but by the pool I'd discovered that another pass with the razor was needed. I went even higher this time, and afterward slathered on one of those creams that smelled good enough to eat.

Then I dressed in hiking gear. The fabric stretched over my skin a little too tight, and I grinned, imagining Will's expression when he saw me. He could barely keep his hands off me last night. There was no telling what he'd do today.

Chapter Eleven
Paige

Will arrived on his bike, sporting his usual swagger and grin. He raked his gaze once over my body, and I suddenly felt aware of every inch of my body.

"You have two jackets," I remarked.

"Borrowed it," he explained as he held them for me. *A female friend*, I thought as I shrugged into the jacket. It was a little too large for me, and I wrinkled my nose at the smell of begonia. I'd much rather have worn Will's. It was on the tip of my tongue to ask more about the friend, but I couldn't think of a way to pass it off as sass and not as me poking my nose where it didn't belong.

Was she an ex? A friend with benefits? Someone who looked like Will probably had a lot of both. I imagined that all that kissing ability came from a lot of experience. As we climbed on the bike, I was feeling oddly deflated, which was ridiculous.

Being so close to Will after last night's kiss was going to be torture. I was thankful that he was wearing a jacket, because I couldn't feel him up again. That didn't keep me from trying, though. I drummed my fingers over his abs, thinking I could pass it off as simply searching for the best place to rest my hands… for support, of course. When Will cleared his throat, I froze, then wrapped my arms around his waist. I kept my crotch and thighs a few inches from him, trying to minimize the body contact, but I slid forward in my seat when he used the brakes, or at a turn, and every time my groin collided with his ass, I… simmered, for a lack of a better word.

We took the freeway to Pasadena, exiting at Lake Avenue. By the time we reached the mountains, I was all hot and bothered, and kind of wished we'd gone to the ocean. I needed to jump in the water and cool off.

"There are some lockers here. We can leave the helmets, but let's take the jackets with us. Might get chilly."

"Good thinking."

I took in my surroundings, breathing in the cool mountain air. I'd often wondered why everyone associated LA with beaches when the mountains were equally impressive. Today, the area was full. Clearly Will hadn't been the only one who wanted to escape the heat. After placing the helmets in a locker, Will pulled up a map of trails on his phone.

"How far are you comfortable hiking ?" he asked.

"I can't do more than four or five miles."

He pointed to a track. "This one's got great views."

"Then we've got our trail."

Before starting our hike, Will bought two

bottles of water, which fit into the pockets of the jackets. He surveyed the various groups as we walked the trail, and the hair at my nape stood on end. He was doing that silent vigilante thing again, and I really didn't like it. It made me want to look over my shoulder at every turn. I didn't say anything at first, but after about twenty minutes, I brought it up.

"Will, I have one rule for today," I announced in a cheerful tone, hoping to ease him into it.

He tilted his head, a smile playing on his lips. "And I strike you as a man who plays by rules?"

I had no idea why that sounded hot, but there I was, searching for my wits again.

"You're the police. Rules are your job."

"Exactly. I enforce them. But I, myself, like to color outside the lines."

He'd moved closer, and it wasn't helping me keep my wits.

"Well, well, what do your superiors say about that?"

"I break the rules in my free time. So what rule did you have in mind?"

I took a deep breath. "I don't like it when you do that thing where you look around for danger."

Will's smile faded. "Right. I forgot about that. Sorry, it's force of habit."

I nodded, regretting that I'd brought this up because the playfulness between us was gone.

"Dad does the same thing. It always puts me on edge."

Will rubbed his jaw, then threw the jacket

over one shoulder. "I promise I'll try."

As we climbed further up the trail, Will asked, "How was brunch with your family?"

I clapped my hands. "Fun, as usual. I tried my best to be a brat."

Will laughed. "Why?"

"Well, I was a brat as a kid, which my brother reminds me of at every turn. He insists on calling me that even now, so... if I can't shed that image, I'll embrace it."

Will laughed even harder. "Why doesn't it surprise me that you were a brat?"

I feigned offense. "Meaning?"

He came closer, until he was right in my face. "You drive me a little crazy, Paige, you know that?"

"I do?"

He nodded, tracing my jaw with his thumb. I wished he was touching my lip. Stepping back, he motioned for me to keep walking. As we went up, I began to question him.

"So, I take it you weren't the brat?"

"No. I'd say Jace and Hailey can safely claim that title."

"And you were...?"

"Ask my siblings. I'm sure they'll have no problem assigning me a tag. I went through a wild phase after our parents died though."

"I'm sorry about your loss. How young were you?"

"Sixteen. I was a rebellious teenager, and after that I was a little out of control."

"That's understandable," I said quietly. We were walking side by side, and I slipped my hand in his. It was pure instinct, as it had been at the wedding. And just like then, he squeezed my hand gently.

"Sometimes I think the only reasons I didn't go off the deep end are my siblings. I had to be here for them. Landon and Val did the heavy lifting. They ran Dad's pub, but didn't have time for much else."

"So you watched the little ones?" I guessed.

He nodded. "Supervised them, yeah. Helped with homework. Cooked. They were a few years younger than me. Hailey was crying in corners when she thought no one was watching. I used to make a fool of myself to make her laugh. It worked. But when Jace started copying the stupid shit I did, I realized I had to stop. If not for my own good, then at least for his."

I moved closer to him until our arms were touching.

"You're a great brother."

"She turned into a pain in my butt when she was thirteen," he said with a grin. "Sabotaged my dates."

"I think Hailey might be my soul mate."

"She's a great person. All my siblings are great." I loved the affection in his tone. I hadn't met many families that were as tight-knit as mine.

"Tell me about your family," he prompted.

"Well, when we were little, we moved a lot with Dad. But then Mom said it got to be too much, and we settled in LA, where my grandparents were. Mom started working too. She said she *needed* a career, and she became a real estate agent. So my siblings and I spent most afternoons at the inn. God, it was so much fun."

We chitchatted about Jace and his soccer career for a good portion of the trail, but then it became steeper, and I started saving my breath.

Will laid a hand on my back, giving me a much-needed push. His hand moved lower as we continued, finally settling just above my ass. I swallowed as I felt one of his fingers on my tailbone. Our kiss from last night replayed in my mind. Each time I imagined it, I found it hotter... and felt hotter.

We reached a plateau before long, and I thanked heaven for that because the muscles in my legs were protesting.

"Want to rest for a bit?" Will asked.

"Oh, yeah."

He led me to a small clearing, and holy smokes. The view was impossibly beautiful. A canyon and a waterfall stretched before us, and beyond, the city of angels.

"How far above the city are we?" I asked in wonder.

"No clue. But it's a great view, isn't it?"

"The best."

We sat side by side, watching LA, and Will took a swig from a water bottle. Then he offered it to me, and despite having my own bottle, I drank from his. And there I was, remembering the kiss again.

As if sensing my turmoil, Will moved even closer. Our hips were touching. I looked up at him and found him looking at my lips. I licked them.

"I have another rule," I declared. "You can't kiss me out here like you did last night."

Will chuckled. "Did you not hear my speech about rules before?"

"Oh, I did, all right. But it doesn't mean I have to do what you say."

"Woman, you can't push my buttons like this in public."

That glint in his eyes? Delicious.

"Why not?"

"It's hot, and I don't want to be cited for public indecency."

"Oh."

"Yeah, oh. I'm an officer of the law, after all. It would be embarrassing."

Oh, but now I was getting all these ideas. How far could I take things before he forgot all about citations? Would it take one jab? Two? Three?

"Paige." His tone held a note of warning. He looked at me like he knew exactly what I was thinking. "Don't worry. I won't kiss you."

"Wait... at all?"

One corner of his mouth lifted. Then the other. I'd just given him ammunition, but I didn't care. I wanted my kiss.

"You're very greedy," he murmured, bringing his hand to my chin again, caressing it with his thumb. Then he moved his thumb to my lips, from one corner of my mouth to the other. I held my breath as I waited for him to come closer... and then he finally did. The contact electrified me, even though this kiss was different. It was slow and sweet, a gentle exploration. He kissed the bow of my upper lip. Then my lower lip. I needed his tongue, right now. I fisted his shirt in a silent plea, and he gave me what I needed. He slipped his tongue inside my mouth, stroking mine in a lazy rhythm. It was delicious. God, the way this man kissed had to be outlawed. When we stopped to breathe, neither pulled back, so we were breathing the same air.

Then Will pushed a hand through my hair, tilting my head up slightly, and kissed me again. It wasn't as gentle this time, and I was starting to feel hot for him again. Could this man show me some mercy? I'd admonish him for blatantly disregarding my rule, but I was enjoying it too much to pull back.

"Told you that you drive me crazy," he murmured when we resurfaced for air again. "I want to take it slow, then you're in my arms and...." He didn't need to finish the explanation, because I knew exactly what he meant. It was the same for me.

"Let's enjoy the view, hmm?" he suggested. I envied his willpower because the only view I wanted to enjoy was of him. But I attempted to do the right thing and turned to watch the city. It was getting a bit chilly, so I put on the jacket and hugged my knees as close to my chest as possible. Will moved behind me, practically covering me with his body. His front was flattened against my back, and the insides of his thighs cradled my legs.

"Warmer? Or do you want us to go?"

"I don't want us to go," I said quickly. "We're having too much fun."

"I'll keep you warm."

And oh boy, did he ever. He rested his nose in the crook of my neck. The contact, along with his hot breath on my skin, would have been enough to light me up. But Will went one step further, placing open-mouthed kisses from time to time. Every time he did, I jolted straighter, feeling the contact between my legs.

"How is the funding for your education project coming along?"

"It's still early days, but once I have a few backers things will progress faster. My boss won't be swayed easily, but I also don't give up easily."

"I like that you're so determined."

I took pride in my projects, and for me, there was no greater compliment than when someone praised my work.

Will wrapped his arms around my shoulders, kissing my temple. He chuckled, and I thought I could stay in his arms forever. I played with his right hand and felt the calluses on his fingers. I knew his work could get rough sometimes. I could ask, but I didn't think he liked to talk about it, so I just followed my instinct and kissed each pad.

Will stilled. "What are you doing?"

"Kissing," I explained, without stopping. I lavished each finger with attention, and when I reached his thumb, Will… growled. There was no other way to explain that sound.

"Woman, if you don't stop, we'll get that citation."

Well, damn if that didn't sound like a good idea. But I stopped and laughed when I felt Will's breath of relief against my cheek. We stayed for another hour, chatting about everything and nothing, and then we made our way back down. The closer we got to the bottom, the more crowded it became. Because everyone seemed to come down after sunset, the group waiting in line to retrieve their possessions from the lockers was rather large. I glanced at Will from time to time, and I could tell that he was making a concerted effort not to switch on the vigilante mode. I felt bad for asking it of him, but it *had* made me uncomfortable.

The ride back to my apartment was pure adrenaline. I enjoyed it even more than the lunch ride because the sun wasn't burning anymore. Will walked me to my front door again.

"I loved the trail," I commented.

"Me too. I wasn't expecting so many people. I like it more when it's not crowded, but I'd choose it over the ocean any day."

"Yep, can definitely confirm you're a mountain man and all."

"What exactly are you implying? That I have no manners?"

Hmmm… the man had asked me not to push his buttons in public, but could I really pass up this opportunity?

"You had your hand up my dress during the wedding. If that ain't lack of manners, I don't know what is."

"It was required. And better me than anyone else." Will smiled smugly, and before I knew it, his mouth came down on mine. Holy shit, the man was kissing me *good*. He went all in, tongue and all until I was breathy and turned on.

I was in a daze when he pulled away, resting his cheek against mine.

"I have to go. I have an early start tomorrow," he said.

I nodded, still dazed from the kiss as he left. Then, as I turned to unlock my door, I remembered how Will had kissed me against it last night... and realized he hadn't even hinted at coming inside, and it wasn't *that* late. Was the fact that a man didn't want to come inside still general code for him not being that into you? Had today been disappointing for him? Except for that weird moment when I'd laid out my first rule, we'd had fun. I'd thought so at least. But now pushy, cocky Will Connor hadn't made any sort of move to convince me to invite him inside. Even though he had kissed me as if he'd wanted to make my clothes disappear into a puff of smoke.

Chapter Twelve
Paige

Monday started off with a bang. I went to the same coffee shop in Venice Beach. I could see it becoming my go-to place for working. I intended to finish a few more pitches. I had a great feeling about the day, even wondered why people hated Mondays so much. Then I checked my inbox, and immediately wished I could move forward in time to five o'clock so I could have a cocktail without feeling guilty.

Ms. Lamonica,
We regretfully inform you that we won't be able to support your project. It is not a good fit for our company, but we wish you the best in your endeavor.

Best,
Kennedy Fellows, on behalf of Christian Lackeroy

What the hell? I stared at my laptop, going through every phase of rage at the same time, it seemed. I was used to people changing their minds, of course. Some were too ashamed to turn me down during a meeting, so they sent an e-mail afterward. Others thought it might be good PR, but then crunched numbers and realized they couldn't afford the donation. But Lackeroy had seemed genuinely interested.

I sank lower in my chair, pressing my palms against my temples, breathing in and out. Had he just been interested in getting in my pants? Was that it? I refused to believe it. I wasn't some naive twenty-year-old; I'd done this job for close to eight years. I knew interest when I saw it, and Lackeroy had been ready to attach his name to the project. I'd banked on it, and was even going to use his company as an example in other pitches. Usually when there was one big donor on board, it was easier to nab the next ones. So, instead of letting it go, I called his number.

"Hello, Paige." I'd expected him to get his secretary, so I was thrown upon hearing his voice.

"Christian. Hi! Thank you for taking my call. I'll get straight to it. I received an e-mail from your secretary, saying you can't support the project. Forgive me if I'm too frank, but you seemed completely on board during our meeting."

"Your project is definitely interesting, but I expressed my concerns about the feasibility."

"You wouldn't actually be committing now, just expressing interest," I explained, holding on to the hope that maybe it was a misunderstanding.

"I understand that. Tell you what. Why don't we meet again and talk it through? Dinner?"

My shoulders slumped. I had a feeling I knew where this was going and tried to salvage the situation. "I'll happily come by your office again."

"Not my office. Somewhere more private."

I gripped the phone tighter, breathing in and out. My blood was boiling, but I had to remain professional. "I don't discuss business in my private time, Christian."

"Oh, it wouldn't all be business. We'd get to know each other better."

"I believe I already turned down your dinner invitation once."

"This is your chance to reconsider."

I breathed in and out. Calm. Above all, I had to remain professional.

"My offer to come by your office still stands, but nothing else."

"Well, Paige, I wish you all the best, then. I'm afraid we can't cooperate. Have a nice day."

"You too," I said through gritted teeth, before disconnecting the call. I discovered that I was shaking with all the contained anger. I detested men like Lackeroy, who used their position to prey on others. I loved my job and believed in the project, but I refused to prostitute myself for it. I had a lot of other irons in the fire, and I was going to work on more pitches today. But half an hour later, I hadn't made much progress. I was still too mad. I had to calm down if I wanted to get anything done today. A swim in the ocean would do me good, but I hadn't brought a bikini with me, and in any case, I couldn't leave my bag and laptop unsupervised for so long. So instead I went to the bathroom and splashed cold water on my face. Afterward, my mind was much clearer, and I finished two more pitches within an hour. The issue with Christian still bothered me, mostly because I'd been so gullible at our meeting. Why had I misread the situation? My thoughts flew to Will. Had I misread the situation with him too? I took a swig of my orange juice, refusing to waste any more time dissecting my date with Will. I wasn't that girl anymore, who rehashed every detail, searching for a hidden meaning and doubting herself. I had no time for this. I had pitches to finish and was meeting my brother at the inn this evening. I hoped he was bringing my niece too, because I wanted to cuddle that girl.

***

Will

I knew I was in for an interrogation the second I arrived at Hailey's house. Val was there too, and instead of berating me for being late, the girls were smiling coyly. Hailey was repainting her living room, and Val, Jace, and I had agreed to help. The two of them had already started.

"Girls, why didn't you wait for me?"

"Thought we'd start on our own."

They'd already made a mess. Hailey had a speck of paint on her cheek, and Val had smeared it in her hair.

Just as I took the third roller, Jace arrived. We divided the room equally in four, even though I would much rather have done the job only with Jace.

The girls tended to lose themselves in conversation and make little progress and a lot of mess.

As each of us concentrated on our respective walls, Hailey said, "How was your hike yesterday, Will?"

I'd known the question would come up from the moment I'd asked to borrow her leather jacket.

"Great. Was crowded, though."

"Paige come to her senses, or does she still like you?" Val teased.

"Paige is a smart girl. Knows a catch when she sees one," I volleyed back.

Val whistled. "Woot, brother, she's got you wrapped around her little finger, doesn't she?"

I straightened. "I'm a grown man—"

"Who almost elbowed everyone out of the way to make sure he caught the garter, after swearing up and down he wouldn't do it," Hailey supplied helpfully. She had a point. Paige made me a little nutty. But after she'd caught the bouquet, things clicked in my brain. I saw the herd of men hurrying on the dance floor, and my only thought had been, *Hell no.*

I wasn't sure if it was our respective connections to our families or the fact that her sassy antics were addictive, but being around her was like breathing in deeply for the first time. Yesterday had been a lot of fun, even though reining in my *inner vigilante,* as she liked to say, hadn't been easy. It went against my instincts—against who I was—but the last thing I wanted was to make her uncomfortable. I was excited to explore things with Paige and see where they could lead, even though I didn't have a stellar record when it came to relationships.

I couldn't say I'd had deep ties to anyone I'd dated. It wasn't a conscious decision or something I could explain, but I'd never felt that strong bond that I thought was necessary for a long-term relationship. The few I did have were monogamous and based on mutual respect, but they didn't lead anywhere. Maybe I wasn't even capable of developing such a bond—some women I'd dated certainly expressed that thought.

"You thought bringing a date was so smart. Now you're all...." Jace grinned, waving a hand as if he couldn't find the right word.

"Jace, don't haze him," Val chided.

"But you're doing it."

"Yeah, we're sisters. It's our job. You're supposed to have his back."

"Even Val says it, man," I said with a grin. But truthfully, I liked it when Jace gave me shit. I returned the favor as often as I could. Still, it never hurt to have an ally against my sisters.

"Besides, Jace, you're one to talk," Hailey said. "You were all over that blondie Pippa introduced you to."

"What can I say? Pippa struck right this time. But Blondie was only in town for the wedding, so there goes our great love story."

I listened carefully for the sound of the rollers moving. Jace and I seemed to be the only ones working. I half turned to my sisters to confirm my suspicion. Yeah, the girls were slacking.

"Girls, when are you going to learn to multitask? Either paint and gossip, or own up to the fact that your painting skills aren't worth jack shit."

Hailey and Val looked at each other, then attacked me at the same time. Paint flew in every direction. Jace watched and laughed.

When I left the house two hours later, I had smears of paint on my jeans and shirt. I'd had some on my face and arms too, but I washed them off. We'd finished the job, though. Hailey was content. I was glad to see my little sister finally living like a normal person. For a few years, she'd seemed to be in a race against time, working as a business consultant. To complete projects, to catch flights. I wouldn't have minded if she'd been happy, but she hadn't been. Not that Hailey would own up to it, but she'd smiled far less than usual, and her expression had been haunted when she talked about work at Friday dinners. But now she was here, with a new job, happy, and ready to plan interventions with Lori and Val. Or was it an ambush? I never knew. Sometimes I thought the girls had their own secret language. I'd come with my car instead of my bike, and as I climbed into it, I decided to drive to Paige's inn. She'd mentioned during our hike that she'd be there this evening.

I recognized the car she'd filed that police report for in front of the gate, and parked right behind her. Then I headed straight into the yard, but came to a halt when I saw Paige wasn't alone. She was with a guy. They were pointing at the facade, talking with their heads together.

Their ease with each other made my insides churn. They were obviously familiar. Paige noticed me and strode over, and the dude followed.

"Well, I have to leave now, but call me if you need anything. We're on for dinner tomorrow, right?" he told her.

"Sure," Paige answered him.

Dinner? Call me if you need me? Had I completely misread the situation with her? Damn, I liked her. A lot. Was he a friend?

"Hi, Paige," I said when they were close enough. I was proud that I sounded relaxed, though if the guy was an ex, I'd lose my cool fast.

"Hey, Will. What are you doing here?" she asked.

"Remembered you said you'd be here. Thought I'd drop by."

The guy put a hand on the small of her back. Paige smiled up at him. Dude was getting all her smiles, it seemed.

"Will, this is Declan, my brother."

I'd have felt like an idiot if I weren't so busy being relieved. Declan and I shook hands, and then he left.

Paige ran her hands through her hair, looking me straight in the eyes as if trying to gauge something. "I'm going to get myself a drink," she said. "I still have some wine. Do you want a glass?"

I nodded, following her into the house. So the brother issue was cleared up, but something was still off. By the way she walked—more like stomped— and the slight sag in her shoulders, I surmised that she was upset about something. We went to the kitchen, and I took the wineglass she handed me. She was avoiding my eyes.

"Paige, what's wrong? You're acting strange."

She wasn't her usual self: laid-back, fun, sassy. She hadn't even pushed one button. She drummed her fingers on her own glass, then took a swig. I'd questioned enough people to know what the hesitation meant: whatever was wrong had to do with me.

"Did I do something to make you mad?"

She took another swig, then finally said, "I don't know what you being here means."

My mind went blank. "You don't know... what? You were there with me on that mountain yesterday, right? We had fun, we connected. Why does it surprise you that I'd stop by?"

Paige looked at her glass, then back up at me. She jutted her chin forward, and I saw that some of that fire I loved was back.

"Because when you dropped me off yesterday, you didn't seem too... into me. You didn't even ask to come inside."

I tried very hard to rein in my smile, but I failed.

"You're upset that I didn't come inside?"

"Don't make fun of me," she muttered. She seemed vulnerable, and every instinct in me wanted to right whatever was wrong. I put the glass on the counter behind her, then placed my palms on the sides of her face, tilting her head slightly up. I needed to communicate more clearly with her. It wasn't one of my strengths, but I was going to give it my best shot.

"I didn't trust myself to be alone with you. I want you so badly that I lose control when I'm around you, and I don't want to rush things with you."

"Oooh."

"Yeah, oh."

I took the glass out of her hands, putting it on the counter too. I wanted nothing between us for the way I planned to kiss her. She looked up at me as if she was begging to be kissed, and I moved in on her, hooking an arm around her waist to bring her closer, taking her mouth like she belonged to me. Paige moaned against me, which made me explore even deeper.

"You're tense," I muttered when I moved on to pepper kisses on her cheek.

"Not the best day."

"Want to tell me what happened?"

She sighed, kissing my jaw. "The general manager jerk pulled out of the deal."

I smiled. "That means you won't see him again?"

Paige poked my ribs. "Can you at least

pretend not to be so happy?"

"Sorry, I can't."

"It's bad form to rejoice at my misery," she informed me.

"Can't help it. Why did he back off?"

"Because I didn't go out with him."

I straightened up, looking her straight in the eyes. "What?"

"Yep. His secretary brushed me off via e-mail, then I called, and he was oh-so-willing to discuss this again, over dinner. Get this, when I told him that I don't discuss business in my private time, he actually told me that it wouldn't be just business. Turned him down again, and he said the deal was dead." She spoke quickly, as if wanting to get it off her chest.

"That bastard," I said through gritted teeth. I tried to rein in my anger, because that wasn't what she needed. "I'm sorry. Does that kind of thing happen often?"

"Used to happen more often. Now I'm better at sniffing them out, but from time to time I'm blindsided."

"Thank you for trusting me enough to share this with me." I was proud of how she'd handled the situation. I wished she didn't have to handle *anything*, but nothing I could do about that. What I could do, though, was to take her mind off it.

I kissed her again, and Paige responded with so much passion that my dick started to twitch. I wasn't content with kissing just her mouth. I explored her neck too, kissing just below her ear, licking that spot. She rewarded me with a delicious moan.

"So… now that you know I'm very much into you, you're going back to push-the-buttons Paige?"

"Hey, I don't push just anyone's buttons."

"Does that make me special?"

"Very much so."

Chapter Thirteen
Will

I smiled against her neck, tilting her head to the opposite side so I could feast on her. I traced her clavicle with my tongue and pushed the strap of her dress off her shoulder so I could touch her bare skin. Then I went back to her mouth, savoring her lips before claiming her tongue. When I drew my thumbs over the peaks of her breasts, I felt her nipples respond. Christ, she wasn't wearing a bra. I wanted to yank that dress down and suck on her nipples until she begged me to be inside her. I sucked on her tongue instead, until she pushed her hips against me. She was so on edge.

"God, Will. I need…."

I knew what she needed, and I was going to give it to her in spades.

"You need to come, Paige," I whispered in her ear, and she gasped, rubbing herself against the bulge in my jeans. I needed to lay her down, so I looked around. There was a couch in the living room. Perfect. I kissed her while I walked her backward to her couch. My pulse was pounding at the tip of my cock. If I touched her pussy, if I made her come, would I be able to control myself? I had to.

I sat her on the couch, backing her into the armrest.

"You're trapping me here," she said huskily when I leaned over her, setting a knee on the couch between her thighs. She bent her knees, and the skirt of her dress fell in her lap. Then she spread her knees further apart, opening up for me.

Fuck, she was beautiful. Those toned legs, that smooth skin. I ran my fingers up the inside of a thigh, then moved to the other. All the while, I kissed her, because I couldn't get enough of her mouth. I inched further up between her legs and touched her panties. I moved my middle finger up and down the fabric and felt Paige shudder. My control was hanging from a very, very thin thread. Then she slipped her hands under my shirt, and I stilled.

"You're not allowed to touch me, Paige."

She pouted. "Why not?"

"Because I'm very close to sinking into you as it is."

"What's holding you back?"

I kissed her temple, breathing in that sweet strawberry scent. "As I said, I don't want to rush this."

"Will—"

"So no touching me."

She pouted again.

"If you don't do as I say, I'll stop touching you."

She immediately took her hands away. I brought a hand to the back of her head, pulling her into a deep kiss while I stroked her one last time over her panties. Then I slipped my hand inside, rubbing a finger over her folds. Paige moaned. I felt the reverberations in my mouth. I worked up to her clit, flicking it between my fingers before drawing small circles around it. She wasn't going to last long. I'd hoped to draw it out, but I'd give her seconds. In a brief break from kissing, she moved her mouth on my neck, suckling on my Adam's apple, and I nearly burst in my jeans. Fuck, I hadn't told her she couldn't kiss me. I would have told her now, but I was so turned on that I wasn't sure I'd be coherent. So I kissed her mouth instead.

As I moved my hand faster, Paige dug her heels in the couch, pressing herself against the armrest as if she couldn't take what I was giving her. I didn't relieve the pressure on her mouth or between her legs. I kissed and touched her until she exploded. Her hips arched beautifully, lifting off the couch, and she pressed her knees together, trapping my arm as I kissed the tip of her nose, listening to her ragged, heavy breaths. Her face and neck were flushed, but the tension still hadn't left her body, so I moved on with my plan: seconds. Only now I didn't want just my fingers on her. I wanted to taste her, to have my mouth on her when she surrendered her pleasure to me.

"Sit at the edge of the couch, Paige."

She did what I said, watching me with wide eyes.

I knelt in front of her.

"Now take off your panties."

She didn't ask why. She just lifted her ass off the couch enough to move the panties to her thighs. I yanked them past her knees and ankles. She was ready for me. I spread her thighs wider, moving the tip of my nose up one thigh, then bringing it back to the apex.

"Will," she muttered pleadingly.

"I'll draw this out. Slowly."

"Why?"

"Because you'll come harder."

She swallowed, and I teased her other thigh before lowering my mouth to her clit. I stroked it with my tongue until she gripped the backrest above her head for support with both hands and lifted her hips off the couch again, pressing herself against my mouth, crying out my name.

***
Paige

I felt as if I was floating. My body felt as light as a feather. I went to the bathroom to clean up, and when I returned to the living room, Will asked, "Let's order food. What do you want to eat?"

"Hmmm… hot detective with a side of fries?"

Will laughed, shaking a finger. "Paige."

Damn, I liked how he said my name. It sounded sexy and naughty and affectionate all at the same time.

"I want a chicken salad."

Will tapped the screen of his phone a few times, and then shoved it in his back pocket. His shirt rode up a few inches, and I caught a glimpse of those hot-as-sin abs.

I sashayed to him, and I swear, the extra sway in my hips was not intentional... just my body's reaction to Will's scorching-hot gaze. I stopped right in front of him, rising on my tiptoes to plant a kiss straight on his lips. I smiled against his mouth when he gripped my hips and pulled me flush against him. I took that as a green light to touch him, but I was a good girl and kept my grabby hands just on his arms and shoulders.

"You're a good guy," I murmured.

"Why is that a surprise?"

"Because you're hot as sin."

"And those are mutually exclusive things?"

"Usually. And when I met you, I don't know... you were so full of swagger that I sort of assumed you were..."

"A jerk?"

I shook my head. "You came to buy an alarm with me. Jerks don't do that. I just didn't know what to make of you."

"Now you do?"

I lifted one shoulder, working as much sass into the gesture as possible. "You're still on probation, but I like what I see."

Will grinned. "On probation, huh? I'll take the bait."

The bait? What? I was just teasing him.

About half an hour later, our food delivery arrived. I made to go to the door, but Will got there first, so instead I went to the kitchen. My heart was thumping wildly, and I wasn't sure why. Was it because I had this sexy guy here with me?

I took the food out of the carton and laid it on plates, and then we ate at the small table, like that evening when he installed the alarm. We started talking about my job again.

"So how many letters of intent do you need?" he asked after I'd explained the process.

"Until I've reached 50 percent of the budget."

"But you said your boss only needs 25 percent."

I was mildly surprised that Will was showing real interest, not just making small talk.

"I know how my boss and his bosses think. The project is risky enough that they won't green light it with just 25 percent. With 50 percent, though, they won't discard it as quickly. And if I burn the midnight oil on this, I might be able to kick-start it by the end of the year."

"This project means a lot to you."

"Each project does."

"Do you always take on the most challenging ones?"

I considered this. "Lately, yes."

After we finished dinner, we took our plates into the kitchen. We were side by side at the counter as I washed my hands, but then Will slipped behind me. For a brief moment, he wasn't touching me at all, and then his hands were on my thighs, drawing small circles. At least he was only teasing my outer thighs. Whew.

Wait... I spoke too soon. Daredevil that he was, he slipped one hand to my inner thigh. "You're distracting me," I muttered.

"You didn't mind before." He pushed my hair aside, kissing between my shoulder blades.

"Mmm... I didn't. In fact, it was so worth it that I can't wait to get upset again so you can distract me."

He turned me around.

"I'd like for us to set some rules, Paige," he whispered against my lips. "This thing we're doing here... I don't know what it is, but I'd like for us to be exclusive."

My heart felt like it was about to burst. I rose on my tiptoes and bit his earlobe gently. When I faced him again, I realized he wanted me to say it out loud. He swallowed, his gaze hard, and... a little vulnerable. I'd only seen him this open and raw when he walked his sister to the altar.

"Of course I want us to be exclusive."

His expression didn't soften. "Are you sure? Don't say it if you don't mean it. I know some like to have open relationships and whatever they come up with to excuse cheating, but I'm old-fashioned that way."

"I meant what I said," I assured him. I placed my hands on his chest, rubbing soothingly with my thumbs. "I don't want to see anyone else. I wouldn't

have let you.... I don't do.... I'm old-fashioned too,
I guess."

Will relaxed, finally. I felt the tension leave his
muscles, saw his eyes soften. He took both my hands
in his, kissing my palms, then the backs of my hands.
The chaste kisses touched me deeply. I wrestled with
my thoughts, then decided to voice them. Will
wouldn't laugh or tell me I was overthinking things. I
thought he'd appreciate it. Hoped, at least.

"Thank you for having this conversation out
in the open and not leaving me guessing or doubting.
I appreciate it."

I had the strangest realization that I wouldn't
have to pretend with Will.

Will brought my hands back to his chest, then
leaned in to capture my mouth. God, the man could
kiss. He was an expert. Each kiss felt different,
better... hotter. How could he turn me on just by
kissing me? I had no clue, but I planned to enjoy it
thoroughly. I wished he wasn't keeping my wrists
hostage though. I wanted to touch and explore. Oh,
wait. I wasn't supposed to, right? Hmm... that didn't
sit well with me.

He deepened the kiss, and my hips arched on
pure instinct. I slammed right into Will's hips, and
discovered that he was hard. Will groaned, a delicious
sound I ate up. I wanted to lure more sounds like
that out of him. I was so greedy that it scared me. I'd
always been the ten-dates-before-sex kind of girl, but
with Will... I didn't feel the need to be on the
defensive.

He let go of my hands, instead putting his hands on the counter. Well... slamming them actually.

"Jesus, woman. You drive me crazy."

"I love that I do."

"How often will you be here?"

"A few times a week. My family and I are taking it in shifts to oversee the handyman."

"When are you free this week?"

"Thursday. Why?"

"I want to take you out."

My stomach cartwheeled. "Okay. What are we doing?"

"Dinner."

"Dinner it is. So... we've talked about my day, but not yours. How was it?"

He stiffened a little, straightening.

"I don't like to talk about my work."

"Umm... then how will I know when you need to be distracted?"

He placed his hands on the counter at my sides, leaning in until he spoke against my lips. "I'll tell you."

He feathered his lips on my cheek, and I suspected he was using his exquisite seduction skills to avoid talking about work, keeping me at bay. My hunky detective was putting up a protective shell. He would be a tough nut to crack... but I was nothing if not persistent.

When we came up for air, I debated pushing the issue, but I let it slide instead, because... well, this was new, and my pushy tendencies tended to alienate people, and I really, really didn't want to alienate Will.

"You're amazing, you know that?"

I relished the compliment but felt compelled to point out something.

"I think my skimpy outfit may cloud your judgment." I was wearing one of my high school dresses again. I had to bring some clothes here.

"Trust me, your outfit affects many body parts, but not my mind."

I felt my cheeks heat up. Will grinned.

"I made you blush."

"You do that a lot."

"You look sexy in this dress. So sexy, in fact, that I just want to keep you here so no one else sees you."

"Like I would walk out like this. Don't worry. My brother was the only one who saw me." On a whisper, I added, "I like that you're possessive."

"Why are you whispering?"

"Because I don't know if I should admit it. It might enable you."

Chapter Fourteen
Will

On Thursday, I was ready for the day to be over so I could pick up Paige for our date. Unfortunately, it simply refused to end. Elliot and I had made an arrest, and it had taken hours to fill in all the paperwork and bring everyone up to speed. I didn't have time to go home and change, so I just hopped in the shower at the station. Luckily, I kept a spare change of clothes in my locker just for such occasions.

As I walked out of the locker room after changing, I rearranged the collar of my shirt and swore loudly. The arrest had involved a physical altercation and had earned me an ugly scratch on my neck, right at the base.

"What did that shirt do to you, Connor?"

I hadn't heard my colleague Hensley come up to me.

"It's not the shirt. I got a cut today on my neck, and it shows."

"Wear your collar up."

I grimaced. "I'd look like a nineteen-year-old schmuck trying hard to impress."

Hensley folded her arms over her chest, sizing

me up. "You are trying to impress, aren't you?"

"I'm going on a date, yes."

"Well, the scratch makes you look more of a badass, so where's the harm?"

Usually I wouldn't care, but I suspected it might make Paige uncomfortable.

"Or I can give you some foundation to put on it," Hensley continued.

I drew the line at makeup. "No, thanks."

I left the station, feeling energized despite the tiring shift. The prospect of seeing Paige excited me like nothing else. I revisited my plan on the drive to her office building, where I was picking her up: dinner and a stroll through the park.

I made mental notes of a few contingency plans in case she wasn't too hot for a walk, because I wanted her to enjoy the evening. I wanted to please her. When I pulled the car in front of her office building, I realized I hadn't given the case a single thought. Usually after making an arrest, I was consumed by it, playing out possible outcomes. Now, I only had Paige on my mind. I texted to let her know I was already here—twenty minutes early— assuring her she could take her time and I'd wait. After a few minutes, I got too restless to just sit, so I decided to wait inside.

The offices were on the ground floor, and when I walked in, I was surprised by the flurry of activity. One person worked the small reception, where several people were waiting in line. I leaned against the wall near the elevator until a petite blonde came up to me.

"You're here to sign up for volunteering?"

"No, I'm here for Paige."

The woman blinked at me, then smiled. "Detective Will Connor?"

I had no idea why the fact that she'd talked to a coworker about me made me so happy.

"Yes."

"Come on, I'll take you to Paige." The blonde led me to the left of the reception, through a narrow corridor until we reached a half-open door. Paige was on the phone, but when she saw me, she motioned for me to come in, mouthing, "Sorry."

I just shrugged and smiled, watching her. As far as I could tell, she was discussing a financing deal. She was magnificent, standing tall and proud, wearing a little suit. It was the first time I'd seen her wearing one, and as she turned with her back to me, the sight of her perfect little ass made my mouth water.

The person on the other end wasn't easy to deal with, but Paige wasn't going to back off. She was a fighter, and that turned me on even more than her perky little ass.

When the call ended, she gave me her undivided attention. She was standing in front of her desk, and I walked to her until we were inches apart. She looked up at me with so much warmth that I lost my train of thought. Had she looked forward to this moment as much as I had?

"Hello, beautiful."

"Mr. Handsome. Welcome to my office. How

did you find me?"

"A helpful coworker showed me the way. She knew who I was."

"Of course she did."

"Have you been bragging about me?"

"Duuuh. Have you looked in the mirror? You're super bragworthy."

I kissed that lovely mouth, intending it to be nothing more than a quick peck, but I lost that battle as soon as our lips touched. She tasted too good, and the way she responded to me was too addictive. She parted her lips, allowing me access, and I took everything she gave me. Then I became hungry for more and fisted the edge of the desk to keep from lifting her skirt up to her waist and touching her bare skin.

"Will," she admonished when I pulled back. "This... you can't kiss me like this at the office." She was blushing, which gave me immense satisfaction. "I'm just going to refresh my makeup, and then we can go."

I still had her trapped between me and the desk, but I lifted one hand. As she made to move, I set my palm on her belly.

"Don't wear lipstick."

"Why not?" she whispered.

"It'll be in the way."

She squirmed a little, and I let her go. She returned a few minutes later.

"No lipstick," I said with satisfaction as I offered my arm and she laced hers through it.

"Maybe it just didn't go with the outfit."

I'd expected the sass.

"Or maybe you just want to be kissed, Paige."

She swallowed and looked away. I pushed on. "Don't worry, you don't have to admit it. I plan to do it until you beg me for more."

***

Paige

Will picked an excellent restaurant. Unfortunately, while delicious, the portions had also been tiny. We were both still hungry after we finished, but for some reason, instead of taking him up on the offer of ordering seconds, I said, "We can go back to my place, and I'll whip us up something."

I had no idea what had possessed me to say it. I was a shitty cook. I had ingredients for dinner, but truthfully, I never shared my cooking. With a cocky grin, Will had taken me up on my offer.

I wasn't sure I was going to pull it off. Especially with him in my kitchen. I felt his presence, even though he wasn't in my line of vision, and I had trouble concentrating on following the recipe, which meant the risk of this ending up tasting like dog food was higher than usual. *Focus, Paige. Focus.* I reread the last two steps. Goddamn. I'd done step two, but had forgotten about step one. I was nervous.

"Paige, you're sure you don't want me to take over?" Will asked for the millionth time. He'd been a great help chopping the vegetables, but I'd assured him I could do the *actual* cooking.

"Nope. I'm fine."

"Just saying, that doesn't smell like cinnamon."

Oh, crap. I looked from the pan to the ingredients... and realized I'd forgotten the cinnamon. I turned to inspect the drawer to the left. It had to be there....

While I was searching through piles of useless stuff, several things happened at the same time. First, a foul smell assaulted my senses. Then Will crashed into the kitchen, just as I turned around to see the sauce spill over. Will removed it from the stove, but it was too late. It had already spilled.

"Crap, crap, crap," I exclaimed. Then I realized Will was... shaking with laughter. I'd seen him laugh before, but never like this. He was laughing with his entire body, and I couldn't help but join in. We cleaned the stove together, and as I washed the sponge, Will came up behind me. He set his hands on the edge of the sink, trapping me. Then I felt his lips tugging at my earlobe.

"Not much of a cook?"

"Nope."

"Why didn't you say so from the start? We could just order in."

"I wanted to do something nice for you." The admission felt intimate. I hadn't had the urge to impress a man in years. Will's hands were still grasping the counter, but his chest was pressing against my back and his lips were torturing that spot just below my ear.

"Aren't you hungry?" I whispered.

"I'm starving. I'm starved for you, Paige."

My body moved on instinct. I pushed my hips back, seeking as much contact as possible. When I felt his hard-on against my ass, I moaned. Heat shot straight between my thighs. Will moved one hand to my right hip. He kept the other hand firmly on the counter as if he didn't trust himself to touch me with both hands.

"I've been thinking about you the entire day. About how much I want you," he murmured, and his mouth was now moving down the side of my neck, then back up to my earlobe. I was shuddering. He was barely touching me, and yet my entire body was responding to him. How could he do that?

And when those light kisses turned more passionate and I felt the tip of his tongue just below my earlobe, I gasped out his name, moving my hand to tug at his hair, desperate to touch him—any part of him.

"Paige...."

Will flipped me around, and I caught just a glimpse of the fire in his eyes before his mouth descended on mine. He'd never kissed me like this. He wasn't just exploring me. He owned me with that one kiss. He moved to my neck again, and then he stilled. I felt as if I was in a haze. Everything around us blurred. I was only aware of Will's hard body backing me into the counter, of my nipples tightening.

"Paige, if you want us to stop, say something, and say it fast."

His hot breaths against the sensitive skin on my neck wiped away every thought. His lips were so close to my neck, almost feathering on my skin.

"Ten seconds, Paige," he murmured. I became aware of a light tremor in Will's chest and realized that he was barely reining himself in. This desire was all for me. Instead of saying anything, I kissed his jaw and moved my hands to his torso, slipping them under his shirt. A deep groan tore from within him. My knees buckled from feeling the sheer force of his desire. I'd never, ever felt so wanted.

Chapter Fifteen
Paige

One of Will's hands move up to cup the back of my head, tilting it up so he had better access. With his tongue, he parted my lips. With his thigh, he parted my legs. Then he lifted me off my feet. Instinctively I held on to him, lacing my hands behind his neck, my legs around his middle.

"Bedroom," he murmured in between kisses.

"Second door to the left."

He moved with me wrapped around him. When we barreled into my bedroom, he laid me on the bed. I pushed myself up in a sitting position, turning on the light from the switch near my bed, watching him. He undid the first button of his shirt, starting at the top. I worked on the button at the bottom, then moved to the one above. Will was quicker, but when he reached the last unopened button, he tugged too hard, ripping the button and the shirt. I soaked my panties through at that small popping sound, at the realization of how much he wanted me. Then Will's chest was bare and my hands were all over it. I worked his belt next, drawing circles with my tongue just under his navel.

"Paige." He was almost growling the word.

He threw his jeans and boxers across the bed, keeping his eyes on me all the while. Then he yanked down my skirt. My blouse went next.

My skin burned everywhere Will's fingers touched me. When I wore nothing but underwear, Will moved over me. His knees were propped at the sides of my thighs, his elbows at the sides of my shoulders. He had me trapped underneath him, watching me with that molten gaze of his. He brought his face a breath away from mine, feathering his lips against mine before claiming my mouth. He kissed me until I thought I might come just from the way he was stroking my tongue. I pushed my hips up, desperately searching for friction. When my soaked panties collided with Will's erection, a small, ice-cold tremor spread through me. My thighs began to shake. And Will released a sound…. God, that sound.

He pushed my panties down, then climbed from the bed, grabbing his jeans. He was frantically searching his pockets, and I felt myself get even more aroused when I realized he was searching for a condom.

I turned flat on my belly, reaching to the nightstand, intending to switch off the lights when I heard him roll on the condom. I was still on my belly and still wearing my bra when the mattress shifted and Will came up behind me.

"Don't turn off the light," Will murmured. "I want to see you. Don't hide from me."

The kiss on the back of my thigh was unexpected and it made me jolt. He moved up to one of my ass cheeks, kissing it, then biting slightly. He was kneading the other cheek in one of his big hands. He moved over me, pressing my belly into the mattress. When I felt his cock between my inner thighs, I spread my legs wider. I wanted to turn around to see him, but I wanted him inside me more. Will pushed inside in one soft move, filling me so thoroughly that I let out a gasp.

"Will, oh fuck."

He stilled, and my inner muscles pulsed as my body accommodated him.

"Baby, this feels good," he whispered, and then started to move in and out. He was moving slowly, but he still knocked the breath out of me every time he slid back in. I wasn't used to being so full. Just when I thought I couldn't take so much *sensation*, Will slid a hand between my pelvis and the mattress and touched my clit. Pleasure washed over me in quick, powerful waves. Will was working me up to an orgasm, and I wasn't sure I could take it. I felt like my bones might liquefy from the pleasure. My center was burning; the muscles in my entire body were strung tight in anticipation. I was so, *so* close, but not there yet. I'd never needed my release so badly. Will was moving his fingers expertly, but instead of giving me what I craved, he said, "I need to see your beautiful face, Paige."

He pulled out, and I felt him open the clasp of my bra. I tossed it to the side as I turned around. Will settled between my legs again, and then he pushed all the way inside me. I clenched around him.

Fuck, had he grown bigger in the last few seconds? It certainly felt that way. Or maybe it was the new position.

He was moving just as slowly as before, in and out, in and out. I needed the pressure on my clit, so I attempted to touch myself, but Will shook his head.

"That's mine to touch."

"So touch." I knew I sounded desperate, but by God, I was.

"Not yet."

"Don't torture me like that," I pleaded.

He tugged my lower lip between his teeth. "You'll come hard, babe. I promise."

When he finally did press his thumb on the bundle of nerves, I broke out in a sweat. Then he stilled, taking his hand away, and starting the sweet torture all over again. I felt that if I didn't come soon I might start crying, simply because my body couldn't take the *almost-there-but-not-quite* tension. But Will was close too now. His thrusts were faster, deeper, and I knew that he was going to let me come.

I climaxed first, and almost blacked out from the intensity of it. My vision faded; my breath got caught in my throat as I cried out. Will followed me a few seconds later, rocking against me until we were both spent.

I couldn't even feel my body afterward as we lay side by side. I wanted to snuggle, but I couldn't even muster up the energy for that.

Will kissed the side of my head. "Shower?"

"I don't think I can move," I whispered.

"You don't have to. I'll carry you."

"Why can you still move?"

He chuckled. "I guess you didn't wear me out yet. But the night's still young."

My nipples perked up at that. My inner muscles clenched. Yep... I was so exhausted I couldn't even move, but my body was still hot for Will.

My shower was much too small for two people, so we ended up showering separately. I went in first, then felt semihuman again as I waited for Will in the living room, wearing a robe. I was perusing a takeout menu on my phone when he joined me, with a towel wrapped around his lower body.

He sat next to me on the couch, looking over the menu.

"This avocado and quinoa salad sounds good," I muttered.

Will smirked. "I need a steak. Salad won't cut it after that workout."

"I thought I didn't wear you out." I elbowed him playfully, then placed the food order.

"Who knows what other fiendish plans you have for the night."

"If there's a fiend here, that's you. You almost killed me."

"So you didn't love every minute of it?"

"I loved every second." I swallowed as he took the phone out of my hands and pulled me into a kiss.

We made out like teenagers until our food arrived, and then we enjoyed the food on the couch, eating directly from the takeout boxes.

"This is dry as paper," Will commented. He'd been chewing on the same bite of steak for a whole minute.

"Your own fault. Delivered steak is never good."

"Bet it's better than a steak you'd cook."

I opened my mouth to argue, but swallowed the words because the man had a point.

"I will let that mean comment slide only because it's true. And because I'm feeling unnaturally generous, I'm going to share my salad with you."

I used the opportunity to snuggle up to him.

"Unnaturally generous, huh? Why might that be?"

"Just a side effect from that amazing orgasm."

Will laughed and then went on to eat almost half my salad. I took a few bites from his steak, and didn't find it all that bad, but that might just be because I'd gotten used to my own atrocious cooking. We were up late long after we finished eating, talking about everything and nothing, just enjoying each other.

Ping. Ping. Ping.

I opened one eye. The bedroom was dark. I didn't remember walking to bed. Had Will carried me? Speaking of Will... he was putting on clothes.

That was the sound that had woken me.

"Will?" I murmured.

"Shhh… go back to sleep. It's five thirty. I need to get going so I can change before my shift starts. Sorry I woke you up."

"No, that's fine. I need to be up at six."

"Damn, I've been dying to kiss you since I woke up. If I'd known, I wouldn't have held back."

I chuckled, and even though I usually valued even five minutes of extra sleep, I dragged myself out of bed. Snuggling up to Will was an excellent incentive to forgo sleep.

"Coffee?" I asked.

"Would be great."

I moved to the kitchen and started the coffee machine. While I waited for it to warm up, Will came out fully dressed. He buckled his belt, then arranged the collar of his shirt. He grimaced, wincing.

"What's wrong?"

"A scratch. Forgot about it."

"Let me see."

He lowered one shoulder and turned the collar down, revealing an ugly, deep scratch.

"Did I… I didn't do that, right?"

Will chuckled, straightening up. "No. Got it at work yesterday. Made an arrest. Guy wasn't too happy."

I blinked, suddenly feeling wide awake. How didn't I notice it last night? I know we were… busy, but still… "Did a doctor check that out? Looks deep."

"Nah, it's just a scratch."

That blasé attitude didn't exactly reassure me. "You've had worse?"

Will must have heard the tension in my voice, because his smile faded.

"There are rough times. Not often since I'm not out on the field daily, but… yeah…."

I nodded, then turned to the coffee machine. It had warmed up. The light indicating it was ready to brew coffee was green, so I pushed the button.

Will brought a hand to my waist, gently turning me around.

"Paige, what is it? You've gone all… inside yourself, like a turtle."

I tried to muster a smile, but couldn't. "Nothing, I… I just don't like that thought. You getting hurt."

Will was silent for a full minute before saying, "You're not a big fan of my job, are you?"

"I'd love it if your job description didn't include the possibility of getting hurt."

"Someone's got to do the job." I said nothing, so Will continued in a soft voice. "Is this a big problem for you?"

My insides strummed tight. I didn't have an answer for him, but I was afraid that if I owned up to that, this thing between us would be over before it started. So I shook my head. I couldn't tell if Will bought it, so I made the second coffee. While we sipped, Will said, "We're going to talk about this, okay? Not now when I have one foot out the door, but at some point. We're going to figure it out."

"Okay." We'd talk about it some other time. That simple fact reassured me, and I felt tension lift from my shoulders.

I set my empty cup on the counter, and Will sct his next to mine, then pulled me flush against him, lowering his mouth to minc. His kisses were the essence of life. Seriously. Just feeling the tip of his tongue on mine electrified me to the tips of my fingers and toes. He didn't stop at kissing, though. He walked me backward until I felt the wall against my back. His hands were all over me, undoing the robe. He slid both hands to cup my ass. My breasts were pressing against his chest.

"That's how you do good morning kisses?" I teased. Will replied by pressing me against his crotch. "Easy there, or I'm not going to let you walk out the door and kick ass."

Will smiled lazily against my lips. "You're gonna tempt me?"

My seductive maneuvers usually sucked in the morning, but Will was an excellent inspiration.

Chapter Sixteen
Will

I spent the better part of the next few days buried in paperwork for the string of car robberies case we'd been tracking for almost a year, building a case against the top dog of the group. We'd finally managed to make some arrests, getting closer to dismantling the operation. There was nothing like the satisfaction of knowing you'd stopped a criminal from committing any more wrongdoings. Sure the world wasn't a safe place, but at least it was safer than yesterday.

On Monday I picked up Milo from school. Lori and Graham had left for their honeymoon that morning, and Milo was staying with me for a week. It was why I hadn't made any plans with Paige. I didn't know how she felt about hanging around with me and an eight-year-old, but now I was wondering if she'd mind. Man, I was whipped. There was no other word for it. This woman was constantly on my mind. It was a foreign feeling for me, despite having dated for more than fifteen years. Usually I was good at separating my dating life from everything else. It wasn't something I'd done consciously; it had just felt natural. Since I'd met Paige, those lines were blurring.

I'd been texting her several times a day, wanting her to know that I was thinking about her, that I couldn't wait to see her again.

"Uncle Will, can we eat fried chicken tonight?" Milo asked after I picked him up. I fought to hide a smile.

"On one condition: you don't tell your mom."

Milo grinned from ear to ear. "I won't."

"I need you to promise."

"I promise."

"Don't forget. A man never breaks his word."

Milo stood straighter, suddenly serious. "I am a man of my word."

"That you are."

For a kid, Milo was remarkably great at keeping secrets, which was perfect, because Lori would probably have a heart attack if she knew the stunts Milo and I had pulled together. But what Lori didn't know didn't hurt her.

We ate at one of the best fried chicken joints in town, then headed to my apartment. On the way, I thought about Paige again. *Screw this.* I was going to text her and invite her over. Chances were high that she already had plans.

Will: What are you doing tonight? Any chance you'd like to hang out with me and Milo?

She answered a few seconds later.

Paige: I'm on my way home from an out-of-town conference. It's a two-hour drive so I won't be in until later. But I could drop by with dessert.

I lowered myself on my haunches until I was level with Milo.

"Do you remember Paige? My friend from the wedding?"

"Yes."

"Would you be cool with her stopping by later with dessert?"

"Sure. Can she bring nachos? I can eat them for dessert."

I ruffled Milo's hair, texting back Paige. Energy filled me at the thought of seeing her tonight. I knew why Milo liked spending time at my apartment. It was in a complex with seven buildings, each no higher than three stories. There were also two pools and a playground for kids, though he hadn't wanted to use the latter in years.

When Milo and I entered my apartment, it immediately hit me that this place looked like a damn tornado had blown through it. I was usually messy, and the messiness increased by a factor of ten whenever Milo slept over.

"Buddy, we need to clean this place up a bit before Paige arrives."

"Clean?" Milo looked crestfallen. I couldn't blame him. I'd never asked this of him, much to the chagrin of my sister. This was karma biting me back. I mentally went through the arsenal of methods I usually employed to convince Milo. They might include bribing. I decided to go with honesty.

"Ladies don't like messes," I explained.

"Ooooh… you want to impress her?"

"Yes. Yes. That's it."

"You could try jumping from the top of a tree. Marshall and Xander from my school tried to impress Anna, so Marshall jumped from a low branch, then Xander climbed to an even higher branch."

I stared at him. Were boys really that ridiculous? If my young years were any indication, the answer was a resounding yes. "Buddy, that's a very, very bad idea."

"Anna was impressed, though. She even went to the school doctor with Xander when he broke his wrist."

"Yeah, but breaking your wrist to get a girl's attention is stupid. Don't do it."

"And you think that cleaning up will work?" Milo asked skeptically.

"Well, let me put it this way: not cleaning up will definitely not help."

Grudgingly, Milo agreed to help. We spent the next fifteen minutes picking up stuff from the floor, only to place it on the couch or the table, where it also didn't belong. This wasn't productive at all. Finally, we fashioned out a plan. We'd stack the stuff lying around in the empty dresser in the guest room, where Milo was sleeping. We'd almost managed to make the space look presentable when the doorbell rang. I swept my gaze across the room once. Much better than before.

Milo jetted to the door before me, opening up. The corners of Paige's mouth lifted in a smile when she saw Milo.

"Hello, Ms. Paige." He stepped to the side, letting her in. "I'm Milo."

"I know. I remember you from the wedding. You were the most handsome young man there, in your tuxedo."

Milo's smile took up his entire face. He loved being called a young man. Paige stepped inside. I'd been on edge the entire day, but just being in the same space with her made that tension go away.

She came up to me, sashaying her hips, and I was filled with a different type of tension that radiated from below my belt. "Hello to you too, handsome." She was close enough to kiss, and those lips were calling out to me, but I couldn't kiss her in front of Milo—not the way I wanted, anyway, which included pinning her against the wall.

I relieved her of the two enormous bags she was carrying.

"What's this?"

"Dessert."

"Two bags of it?"

"I might have brought some other goodies too."

I carried the bags to the low coffee table in the living room. Paige and Milo followed. "This looks cozy," Paige commented, glancing around.

"We cleaned up because Uncle Will wanted to impress you," Milo piped up. I groaned. Milo wasn't done. Raising a skeptical eyebrow, he asked, "Are you impressed?"

Paige cleared her throat and did a full turn, moving slowly, making a big show of looking around. I suspected she was fighting laughter. When she faced us again, she looked on the verge of tears. But she did not laugh.

"Yes. I'm very impressed."

"Milo," I grumbled in a low voice.

"What?" The little rug rat correctly interpreted my expression. "I wasn't supposed to say? But you didn't tell me."

Right. I stood corrected. Milo was good at keeping secrets… as long as he knew it was a secret.

"You wanted to keep it a secret that you wanted to impress me? Why is that, Will?" Paige asked, parking her hands on her hips.

That sassy mouth!

"Uncle Will doesn't know how to impress ladies. I've never met a lady before."

I was stunned into silence. Paige didn't manage to hold back laughter anymore, but her eyes were full of warmth, and I thought that maybe it wasn't so bad that Milo had let the cat out of the bag. No, I'd never introduced Milo to anyone I was dating.

"Well, I'm very, very impressed," Paige said.

"Milo, you forgot to bring your backpack to your room. Do it now, before we eat."

He nodded, slinging his backpack over his shoulder and dashing to his bedroom, which was at the other end of the apartment. Pocket doors separated the living room and kitchen area from the rest of the apartment.

The second Milo was out of the room, I made my move and kissed her. She parted her lips as my mouth touched hers, welcoming me as if she needed this as much as I did. Had she missed me just as much?

Somehow, kissing felt more intimate tonight. Maybe because the only other time she'd opened up like this for me was when I'd been deep inside her. She pressed her hot, curvy body against me, lacing her arms around my neck. I'd meant to just get a taste, but as usual with Paige, my control was nixed. When had I backed her against the wall? I'd bunched her dress in my hands too. Jesus. I took a deep breath, forcing myself to hit pause, stepping back.

"That was quite a kiss," she muttered, looking absolutely beautiful, all hot and bothered for me.

"I needed a taste of you." My voice was hoarse.

"Mmm… well, if you keep impressing me, I might let you have another taste later on."

"Let me?"

"Oh, yeah. If I'm feeling generous, I might even let you have two."

I stepped back closer, caging her in against the wall, and spread her legs with my knee, pressing my thigh between hers.

"I'll have my fill of you, Paige. Taste your mouth, all of you." I pressed my thumb straight over her clit. Even through all the layers of clothes, I knew it affected her, because she rolled her hips forward.

"I'll lick right there until you're trembling and aching for me."

Paige's breath came out in a rush. I stepped back with a satisfied smile just as I heard Milo skitter back. The boy headed straight to the table. Paige and I followed suit.

"What did you bring, Paige?" Milo asked.

"Well, I brought a little bit of everything," she said eventually and started unloading the bags on the coffee table, averting her gaze. She was so damn cute that I could eat her up. I planned to do just that, later on.

"Wow," Milo exclaimed, taking in the opened food containers incredulously. I was fairly sure Paige was Milo's favorite person in the world right now. "You brought popcorn and nachos and M&Ms. And chocolate chips."

"When I spend time with my nieces, I buy even more."

"You have nieces?" Milo asked excitedly.

"Yeah. Three of them. So I know all the tricks."

Milo drummed his fingers on the table, as if deciding how to test her.

"Can you throw an M&M up in the air and catch it in your mouth?" Milo asked, as we sat on the couch right in front of the glass wall that opened up onto the balcony.

"Absolutely."

To my complete astonishment, Paige popped open the bag and proceeded to perform a perfect throw and catch. Milo clapped his hands. Of course, Milo being Milo, he went on to throw another challenge at Paige, which she took.

I just sat back and watched them. This side of Paige was utterly charming. I didn't remember ever feeling so peaceful and whole in my life.

"Hey, so I think Uncle Will isn't paying any attention to us," Paige whispered loud enough for me to hear. Paige motioned with her head to the takeout boxes, winked, and Milo winked back at her, and I knew I had zero chance of stopping the upcoming food fight.

Three hours later, the living room looked far worse than before Milo and I had cleaned up. Milo had fallen asleep on the couch, and I carried him to the spare bedroom. We'd laughed so much that my abdominal muscles were hurting. When I returned to the living room, I found Paige picking up some wrappers.

"What are you doing?" I asked.

"Cleaning up."

"No, you're not. Come on, let's sit out on the balcony. I want to enjoy you now that you're all mine."

I walked over to her and pulled her to me.

"Watch where you put your hands, hot stuff."

"Why is that?"

"Umm… Milo?"

"The guestroom is on the other side of the apartment, and he never wakes up during the night."

"So sexy activities are on the table?"

He cocked a brow. "Was I not clear about that earlier?"

"Oh, I thought you were just talking big. You know... trying to impress me."

Chapter Seventeen
Will

I led her out on the balcony. As we stepped out, Paige squeezed my hand, and I followed her gaze to the red wine bottle I'd set in a bucket, and the glasses and candles.

"You.... When did you do this?" she asked.

"After you said you'd join us. Figured you'd want to relax after so much driving. If you don't want wine, I have other drinks."

"Wine is great."

She sat at the edge of the comfortable double lounge chair. It was my favorite place in the apartment. Since I lived on the top floor, there was no balcony above mine, so I had a full view of the sky. A tall palm tree right in front of us obscured us from anyone's view. I lit the candles before pouring us wine. Paige was unnaturally quiet during the process. I wasn't an expert on women's minds, but my sisters had drilled one thing into me: when a woman was quiet, it was not because she didn't have anything on her mind, but rather because she had too much.

We clinked glasses, and after the first sip, I asked, "Want to tell me what's on your mind, pretty girl?"

She played with her glass, looking up at the stars, murmuring, "You're very good at... romancing."

I smiled, kissing her forehead. "Come on, let's lie down. It's a beautiful evening."

We both sipped some more of the wine, then set the glasses on the small table and moved to the center of the lounge. I lay back first, holding my arm out for her to use as pillow, and she did just that, coming so close to me that our bodies touched completely. I brought my hand under her chin and tilted her head up, then kissed her slowly. I coaxed her tongue, deepening the kiss. My free hand moved to her dress, bunching up the fabric until I found her skin. Smooth and warm, inviting.

I kissed her until we were both out of breath and then kept my forehead pressed to hers, because I needed the contact.

"I'm glad you could swing by tonight," I admitted.

"Thanks for inviting me."

"I didn't know if hanging out with me and Milo was up your alley."

She laughed softly. "I'm always up for some fun time with kids."

"I know that now. You're quite a woman, Paige. The more I find out about you, the more I like you."

She'd buried her face in my neck, and I felt her smile against my skin.

"Oh yeah? I like the sound of that."

I couldn't be sure, but I thought she might have wiggled her toes. We spoke about everything and nothing for a while, and she even pointed out some constellations. I made note of her interest in astronomy. Who knew when it might come in handy.

Something vibrated between us.

"That's my phone," I said, taking it out of my pocket. It was a notification from the calendar I kept for the rentals.

"You're going away next week?" Paige asked, her eyes on the screen.

"No, I own a few rentals, and this is the booking calendar."

"Holy shit, those are a lot of bookings. How many rentals do you own exactly?"

"Ten, for now."

"Nice."

It afforded me a great lifestyle that wasn't obvious at first glance, which I liked.

"Want to tell me about your day?" I asked, and not just to make conversation. I wanted to know.

"Made some progress with the funding. I'm confident that I'll have at least 25 percent of it in the bag in about a month."

I loved her confidence. It wasn't just blind cockiness. Her confidence was born out of knowing her strengths.

"Man, I just love August," she said, apropos of nothing. We were in the second week of the month.

"Why?"

"I don't know. It's like the heat is more bearable. Or maybe I just get used to it. By the way, I had dinner with my parents. They, err… might know about you."

I squeezed her to me, patting her ass. "What do you mean *might*? I thought I was bragworthy. I'm wounded."

Paige laughed softly, poking my arm.

"What did you tell them about me?" I insisted.

"That you're smoking hot and make me laugh."

"That's it?" I worked as much offense into my voice as possible. Paige was now nibbling on my neck, and I felt every lick of her tongue straight along my cock. I wasn't sure how much longer I could keep the conversation going.

"Trust me, with my mom, less is more. Dad was actually a little shocked you're on the force."

That gave me pause. "Why?"

Paige stopped nibbling my neck and instead wiggled back a bit so she could look at me. "Because at all those annual events he has with colleagues, he's always tried to set me up with sons of his comrades, and I wasn't interested."

I looked at her intently. "This reticence you have about my job is because of your dad, isn't it?"

Paige nodded slowly. "I think so. It was just… hard, you know. Growing up, he was always away. That wouldn't have been half bad if he'd been away on a random job, but what he did was dangerous. We all worried, so much. My biggest fear was that one day another man in uniform would show up at our house to tell us Dad wasn't coming back."

Paige's voice wobbled, and my chest constricted. I pulled her into a hug, and she melted against me instantly.

"It happened to many of his comrades, so I know we were lucky," she muttered in a small voice, but then she continued in a strong tone. "I know what he did was important, though. And so is what you do."

"Paige... my job isn't nearly as dangerous."

"I know." She shrugged, and I held her even tighter because I understood. I knew that bone-deep fear of losing someone you loved, though mine had a different root. Could we work through her misgivings?

"I'm so happy I didn't have to be at the inn tonight," she continued, clearly wanting to change the subject.

"On which evenings are you on rotation?"

"Tuesdays and Wednesdays."

"Mind if I join you?"

"Why would you do that?"

I rolled her on her back and slid over her, propping myself up on an elbow so I could look at her. I touched her face with the other hand.

"To spend time with you."

She blinked a few times, and I felt her relax under me. The candlelight only lit half her face, but I saw her lips curl in a beautiful smile.

"That would be great." On a wiggle of eyebrows, she added, "I promise to make it worth your time. Tempt you with nonskimpy outfits and all that."

I laughed. "I'll make sure you keep that promise. Besides, I know a thing or two about construction. I can be of use."

"Is this a manly thing? My brother and father also think they know *a thing or two*, yet every time they attempt to repair something, mayhem ensues."

"In high school, I worked in construction during summers for some extra money. It's how I got into the rental business. I flipped houses. One thing led to another...."

"Okay, I take all that about manly bragging back."

She lifted her head and kissed me, and I was caught unaware but opened up for her nonetheless. It felt out-of-this-world good. I was enjoying letting her take the lead... at least until the little vixen started sucking on my tongue, and my cock became painfully hard. Then I took back the control.

I unhitched her hands from my shoulders and pushed them over her head. I turned rock-hard when Paige opened her legs wider. The woman was made for me. Her body's response to me was incredible. I enjoyed her mouth until I felt her quivering under me, rolling her hips, looking for friction. But I held my pelvis just out of reach, not giving her what she was looking for. No, I was going to take my time with her. I planned to make her feel insanely good.

"Will," she muttered, fidgeting, trying to break free. "I want to touch you."

"Not yet."

She tried to roll up her hips again, but I pulled my pelvis back.

"How long will you keep him away?" She pouted, nodding toward my belt. This woman was far too cute for her own good… or mine.

"Until I make you come."

She swallowed, snapping her gaze up.

"What?"

"I'll make you come with my fingers, and then I will give you my cock."

She swallowed again. I captured her mouth, sliding a hand under her dress. She smelled so impossibly good. Sweet and spicy, and I found myself wishing the pillows would pick up her smell so I'd have something to remember her by after she left. I went straight for her panties, moving the fabric to one side. She was so ready for me that I slid two fingers inside her at once. I curled them slowly, searching for the sweet spot inside her. She climaxed hard and fast, and I covered her mouth with mine, feeling the reverberations against my chest. The throbbing below my belt was maddening, and I was dying to be inside her, but I held her while she rode out the wave of pleasure.

When her breaths became even and her hands roamed over my back, I reached for the small box under the table, snatching a condom.

"You're… well prepared," Paige said in a low, thick voice.

"It's the only way I can cover my bases with you. Advance preparation. Because when I'm with you, I forget myself."

I got my pants and boxers down below my ass, then rolled on the condom under Paige's watchful gaze. She made to reach for me, but I stopped her. I gripped myself at the base, then squeezed closer to the tip, placing the crown on her lower belly. Her dress was bunched around her waist, and she couldn't see what I was doing to her. She could only feel.

"This is what you want, isn't it, Paige?"

I dragged the tip to her clit as she nodded feverishly, then slid inside her. Her eyes widened, and she bit her lip as her inner muscles clamped tight around me. She braced her arms around my neck, bringing me closer. I pressed my cheek to hers while I moved, because I wanted to be close and hear her. She was quiet, but those soft, barely audible sounds were fueling me. I made slow, lazy love to her, feeling her come apart one thrust at a time. The base of my erection tightened, energy gathering at the tip. She felt so good that I knew I wouldn't last long. She seemed close too, but I wanted to make sure she came again. So I stilled, working one hand between us, touching her clit in small circles until she tightened around me like a fist. Then I slid in and out again, kissing her while she made my world tilt on its axis.

After cleaning up, Paige shuddered a little, and I brought a quilt. I slipped under it right next to her.

"So thoughtful," she murmured.

"I'll warm you up. Brought the quilt just in case."

"You'll warm me up, huh?"

"Yes. I'm a man of many talents."

"That you are. Those fingers are downright magic."

"Just my fingers?"

"Hmm... other body parts might also fit in the magic category." Her voice was low and sweet, almost a purr. "Your chest is the world's best pillow."

"I see." I chuckled while she shifted her head on my chest, looking for the most comfortable spot to rest it.

She yawned. "I should go soon, or I'll fall asleep."

"What would be so bad about that?"

"Explaining it tomorrow to Milo."

She had a point, but was it the only reason she wasn't staying? I moved over her, kissing her bare shoulder.

"Will, what are you doing?"

"You'll see. I'm not nearly done with you."

Kissing her mouth, I tasted wine and chocolate on her lips. I could get drunk on her taste. I didn't want to be without her taste again... without *her*. It was a powerful feeling, and I was sure it was here to stay. And I knew one other thing: tonight, I was going to own her pleasure.

Chapter Eighteen
Paige

"Get a grip, Ashley. You don't see anyone else in this office moping around because one of their kids has a sore throat." Greg was being more of an asshole than usual. He'd come into our office just as Ashley was telling me she feared she'd sent her boy back to kindergarten too early.

I opened my mouth to argue with him, but Ashley silenced me with a pleading look.

"Paige, I want a word with you. I need you on top of the water project."

"The water project?" I blinked, trying to keep calm. That was one of our key projects this year, and as such, Greg was directly responsible for the funding. Why was he adding it to my tasks?

"Yes. Problem?"

I knew better than to argue. He was my boss after all, but I wasn't looking forward to having yet another project on top of the ones I was currently leading. I asked him to send me all the info on it, and while I read through the reports, I kept eyeing the clock, because I was meeting Mom in the evening for a round of late-night shopping.

I wasn't a fan of in-person shopping. I'd been

addicted to ordering online ever since I got my first credit card, and the addiction had only gotten worse when speedy delivery became trendy.

However, on this lovely Thursday evening, I put on my big girl panties and went to meet Mom at the mall. She preferred to shop old school, and she needed an outfit for her and Dad's upcoming fortieth wedding anniversary. Elsa and Miranda were joining us too, so we were making a girls' evening out of it.

Mom arrived first.

"Let's grab a smoothie while we wait for the girls. We promised we wouldn't start without them," I suggested.

Mom nodded, and we each grabbed a strawberry-pineapple combo. I was busy studying Mom, trying to visualize an outfit for her, when I realized my mother was studying me right back. She had a knowing smile that made me cower in fear. That smile usually came with life advice, whether I asked for it or, more often, not.

"How is that detective of yours?" Mom finally asked.

"He's good. We're good." I was choosing my words very carefully. Any excessive display of enthusiasm on my part, and my mother would be choosing baby names and bustling into my apartment unannounced, hoping to run into Will. True, it had happened only once, five years ago, but I wasn't about to risk it happening again. I was saving the gushing for when my sisters arrived and Mom was out of earshot, because I had a lot to gush about.

Will had *not* been bragging about knowing his stuff when it came to construction. He had stopped by the inn over the past two weeks, and a couple of times he even lent a hand to the handyman. And I? Well… I poured myself a glass of wine and enjoyed the view. I liked our casual get-togethers at the inn after work. We could get to know one another without the pressure of preparing for a date.

"When are you going to introduce him to us?"

"It's early days, Mom."

Mom waved her hand as if the tiny detail didn't matter. "I knew your dad was the one on our second date."

I stared at her. "You did?"

"Oh yes. He immediately charmed me." Mom slurped from her smoothie until the cup was empty. "Every couple is different, but when the spark is there, it's there, and you know it. Some don't want to admit it, but they know it." Mom got out a mirror from her bag, inspecting her hair. "My roots are showing a bit. I should make myself an appointment."

"I remember the night you got that white strand of hair," I found myself saying.

Mom smiled sadly. "That was a tough night. There were many tough ones. I'm sorry I wasn't stronger. I tried to keep it together—"

"What are you talking about? You did keep it together. You're a strong woman, Momma."

"I wasn't strong enough, though. I still let grief overpower me from time to time." Her smile turned even sadder, and I wished I hadn't brought it up. "I'm sorry."

"Momma, you have nothing to be sorry about. You're a strong woman, and I look up to you. I always have. We all have. I'm sorry I brought this up."

Mom was quiet for a moment, but I knew her wheels were spinning.

"I know why you did. I think you're a bit afraid of love."

I almost choked. "What? Why would you say that?"

"Just a mother's observation. Maybe seeing me during that rough time scared you. Made you think that truly loving someone gave them power over your happiness, which is true in some respects. But I will say one thing: if given the chance, I would make the same exact choices. Marry your dad, support his decision to enlist. That it was tough doesn't mean we weren't happy, and as a mother, I can only hope you will find that sort of love one day. Actually, not only find it but hold on to it. Fight for it."

I was speechless for a few seconds, before finally saying, "I missed our talks when I was away."

"So did I."

"You have three other kids."

Mom winked. "Only one Paige."

We chatted about our plans for the evening until my sisters arrived. Then we unleashed ourselves on the mall.

We started to bicker almost immediately because, as usual, we couldn't agree on a single thing. This, too, I had missed.

"Wow, it's weird being out shopping without my kid," Miranda said. "It's like I can do everything ten times faster."

While we stormed the stores, I replayed the conversation with Mom in my mind. Was I afraid to love? I'd never thought about it like that. I'd always had an active dating life and even two longer relationships. I hadn't been head over heels in love with either of those boyfriends, but I'd supposed that was because they were simply not meant to be for the long term. But Mom gave me food for thought.

"So, give us the dirty details on Will," Miranda said when Mom disappeared into the first changing room. We were at a respectable distance, but I whispered it all anyway. I couldn't stop bragging about my hunky detective and his delectable ways. He managed to cheer me up even though my project's funding wasn't progressing as well as I'd hoped, which caused me to start every working day with a heavy heart.

I wasn't sure how he felt, though. He wasn't a man of many words, and part of me wondered if Will was even doing it consciously, or he simply didn't know how to open up, let me closer.

Fifteen clothing shops and five shoe shops later, Mom had an outfit. We'd totally knocked it out of the park: a dark green dress that was tailored on her slim torso and flowed in an A-line to her ankles.

Golden sandals with thin straps and a tiny matching purse complemented the outfit.

"Anyone up for buying lingerie?" Elsa asked as we left the shoe store.

To my astonishment, Mom blushed and said, "Umm... I'd... I'd like to see what they have. Maybe try something different... for the occasion."

We all grabbed another smoothie, relaxing our feet for a few minutes before heading into the lingerie shop. It boasted a large selection, even stocking a few items that were on the raunchy end of the spectrum.

"What is that for?" Mom sputtered. "It doesn't even have a crotch."

Miranda threw me a panicked glance. Oh, boy. If this conversation continued, I'd need to slip some wine into my smoothie. Or vodka.

We led Mom into the section of the store where every piece of lingerie had a crotch.

Being surrounded by all that lace got me thinking. I'd already spotted a few items that were screaming "Open your wallet. Right now." I imagined Will's expression when he saw me in some of them. I wanted something classy, but sexy. I was going to buy something to knock off Will's socks. Or boxers.

Chapter Nineteen
Paige

I looked at myself in the mirror critically for the millionth time. The lingerie set looked even sexier than it had in the store, and that was saying something. I was definitely going to knock off Will's socks. It was the first time I'd gotten to wear it since buying it ten days ago. I wanted to impress Will—again.

He'd surprised me by buying tickets to a blockbuster movie I was excited about, and when I asked him how he knew I wanted to see it, he said, "Paige... you talk. *A lot*. And I have a habit of memorizing every detail."

Which was why I was working hard to impress him tonight.

To that end, I'd bought a home-spa kit that had cost almost as much as the lingerie, but the model on the package looked so yummy that it practically begged for my credit card.

While I read the instructions, Will rang.

"Hey," I answered, a little panicked that he might want to meet earlier. I was nowhere near ready.

"Hey. Listen, can I have a rain check tonight?"

"Oh… are you okay? Did something happen?"

"Was a tough shift. I'm tired."

"I can take care of you."

"I'm not going to be much company tonight, Paige."

Now I was panicking for other reasons. He sounded dejected, but I couldn't tell if it was truly just work or…. I ran a hand through my hair, unsure how to proceed. I really wanted to see Will. But should I push? Maybe he just needed time on his own… maybe he wasn't in the mood for me.

Except… I thought I had a good chance at improving his mood. I was afraid of putting myself out there, pushing this and getting rejected. But I was also afraid of creating a precedent, having the kind of relationship where we only met to have fun together and avoided each other on rougher days. That wasn't a healthy basis on which to build… anything.

"Why don't you let me decide that? Besides, I have all these plans to impress you after the movie."

"You going to try and set your kitchen on fire again?"

I laughed. "No. Sexy plans, Will."

I could swear I heard him growl.

"Define sexy plans."

"No can do, Mr. Hunky Detective. You'll have to come and see for yourself."

Will didn't answer, and I felt my heart shrink to the size of a pea. Shit, was I a fool for pushing?

"Okay. I'll be there at seven."

"Can't wait." I hoped the relief wasn't too obvious in my voice. After the call ended, I applied the face mask. Twenty minutes later, I was in a panic, rereading the instructions. Nowhere did the damn package say I would smell like a swamp. I rubbed the mask off. Will was supposed to arrive in half an hour. That was enough time to get rid of the smell, right? I was lucky my fridge was stocked with fruits. I made a mango mask, applying it on my already sensitive skin. Served me right, trying out new stuff instead of sticking to my old tricks. I could feel the mango hydrating my skin.

It did the trick, getting rid of the stink. I blow-dried my hair, then put on the lingerie and a light beach dress. Ah, one of the perks of living in LA. I could wear light dresses even though September was already upon us. I was ready just in time, because my doorbell rang.

After one last glance in the mirror, I headed to the front door.

When I opened it, I tried a casually seductive pose, jutting out one hip, parking my hand just above. Will opened his mouth, then... seemed stunned. His gaze raked over me from head to toe, then back up, and I knew I could have forgone the kit altogether. He stepped inside, closing the door behind him.

"Paige, you look...." He didn't finish that sentence. Instead, he came closer and closer, until he was right in front of me. He touched my shoulder, then my hip. Then my shoulder again. He seemed conflicted as to where to kiss or touch first.

Eventually, he crushed his mouth to mine, sliding one of his hands right under the dress. I was wearing a tiny thong, so my ass was practically bare. Will growled appreciatively. His free hand slid to the back of my head, and he fisted my hair, pulling me in for another kiss. This one was harder, deeper. His passion was igniting me on the inside. His tongue was doing decadent things to mine, moving in a rhythm that made me ache for him.

He ran his fingers down one ass cheek, moved to the other. Then he feathered them over my crack, and I thought my knees might give.

"We should go if we want to make it to the movie on time," he said.

"Sure. Let's go."

***
Will

I'd picked a theater that was close to Paige's place, but it was still far enough away to warrant taking the bike. We lucked out with the traffic, but that meant we'd arrived too early. After buying popcorn and drinks, we waited in the small bar area in the inner courtyard.

I sat on one of the white plastic chairs, pulling Paige to me. She landed in my lap with a small "Oomph."

"There are plenty of chairs to go around, Detective," she said in a low voice.

"But this way I can touch you all I want."

She gave me a wicked smile in return. An important case had completely gone to hell. Usually, my coping mechanism was to throw myself into a new case, or in the rare instances one wasn't available, I'd dig up cold cases. I wasn't good company, because I was usually grouchy.

But Paige's voice had sounded so strained on the phone, and I wanted to be a good boyfriend. I knew how much she'd looked forward to tonight.

"Wanna tell me what was so shitty about the day?" she asked casually. I tensed, schooling my expression into a cool and relaxed mask, but before I could dismiss the question, she added, "I know you can't give any details, but just talking in general might help."

I hesitated, then admitted, "A case I've been working for over a year was basically discarded today. We know the guy is guilty, but the district attorney's office dismissed the case on a technicality. We can't charge the guy with jack shit."

"I'm sorry, Will."

"All that work, and... you know, it's not even the work that bothers me, just that he's going to walk free. That's why I became a cop. Our parents died in a hit-and-run. Guy was never caught."

"You can't catch every bad guy."

"I know." But somehow, it felt nice to hear it from her. "I just always worry about giving closure to those involved. Not having it eats at you."

Paige was silent for a few seconds, then kissed

my cheek, positioning herself even closer so that the side of her torso was pressing against my chest.

"I don't talk about these things, usually. But you've got a way of just making me want to... tell you everything."

"Tell me what you're comfortable with. And what I can do to distract you."

"Oh, you're distracting me enough with this dress."

She giggled. "And you haven't seen what's under it yet."

We watched the movie, though honestly, I was watching Paige more than the screen. Her laughter was contagious. I was suddenly very grateful I hadn't stayed back at the station, burying myself in cases. That was a way to escape, but this right here was making me *happy*.

After the movie, I barely kept my thoughts straight while I rode the bike home with Paige's hands tight around my waist. She wasn't making it easy for me. At every red light, her hands wandered.

"Paige," I warned, suspecting that my semi might turn into a full hard-on any second now.

"What?" she said huskily. "I'm taking advantage of the fact that you can't touch me for once. You're so bossy in bed. This is my revenge."

I wasn't sure how we'd made it behind closed doors, but the second we did, I moved in on her. I kissed her bare shoulder, unfastening the knot to her one strap. It came undone easily, and the dress fell to her waist. I kissed her spine, starting from the back of her neck, occasionally tasting her with my tongue too. She arched her back every time.

"There's a small zipper," she whispered. I found it, tugged it down, and then the dress fell to her feet, leaving her gorgeous ass right in front of me. She was wearing a tiny black thong. I touched the fabric, first the part with the elastic band, then the scrap between her cheeks. Paige trembled, opening her thighs. I touched between her legs, and she pressed her thighs together.

Spinning her around, I kissed her, walking her backward in the direction of the bedroom.

Her underwear came off in the corridor, along with my clothes. I kissed her hard, basking in her sweet mouth. I pinned her against the wall for better leverage, but I knew I had to get us to the bedroom. I stopped kissing her and just looked at her, caressing both her cheeks with my knuckles.

"What?"

I drummed my fingers over her lips, leaning in to steal a kiss. "You make me happy, Paige. Ridiculously happy. Being with you... I've never felt this way before for anyone. I just wanted you to know."

She smiled shyly. I lifted her off her feet, carrying her to bed. After I lowered her on it, she stood on her knees, leaning in to lick over my erection. Just the tip of her tongue on the crown electrified me. She looked up at me while her mouth worked me, and Christ, if I died now, I'd go a happy man. I held her hair in my fist so I could see her better, and I didn't hold back my grunts. I let her know just how much she pleased me, how good it was. Too good, because I felt a dangerous tightening in my balls and knew I had to hit pause.

"Paige, stop."

Instead, she moved her mouth faster. My eyes crossed. I wanted to pull back, but she didn't let go, moving her mouth until I went over the edge.

"Fuck, woman. You're beautiful like this, with your lips all swollen." I pushed her onto her back, settling between her legs, and nearly came when I realized how much pleasuring me had turned *her* on.

I stroked myself while working her clit, and when Paige cried out, I barely remembered to put on a condom. I lifted her legs from the mattress, putting them on my shoulders. Her panting was fueling me. I shoved a pillow under her, lifting her ass up a little, and then I loved her harder than I ever had. I wanted to get lost in this woman, and I didn't care if I never found my way back again.

Chapter Twenty
Paige

Like most people, I'd developed strategies to cope with shitty weeks. They included wine and some orgasms. Not necessarily in that order. But only three weeks after Greg had pawned off the water project on me, I was slowly reaching breaking point... mostly because four pitches I'd been sure were a done deal for my education center fell through, and I was facing the real possibility that my baby would be shelved. Greg had called me into the office on Saturday morning and all but slammed his fist on the desk, demanding I give *his* water project more attention. He had to send a progress report to Paris soon, and *I* was to prepare it.

Right now, I felt like screaming at the top of my lungs "TGIF." Well, more like "Thank God it's Saturday."

I needed a kickass plan to push this to the back of my mind, or I'd drown in endless angst the entire weekend. I needed an outing with the girls where we talked about everything and nothing and would just be silly in general. Euphoria filled me at the prospect, but I deflated like a balloon after a few phone calls. My sisters were taking the kids on a trip to Universal Studios. Faith had a date, and Luna was visiting her parents. I thrummed my fingers against the plastic case of my cell. I wanted to ask out the Connor girls. Since Lori's wedding almost two months ago, I'd been at three Friday dinners. The girls were fun to hang out with even when the guys were around. I could imagine that a night out with them would be a hoot. Would Will mind?

Surely a night out wouldn't cross a line. I shot Will a text, which included a lot of grinning emojis, an angel face, and a devil face.

Half an hour later, the party was ON. Lori, Val, and Hailey were in, and so was Maddie, Landon's wife. Apparently the guys had found my idea spectacular, because they were having their own outing.

Oh yeah, this day was shaping up to end much better than it had begun. I knew the problems would still be there on Monday, but I planned to thoroughly ignore them this weekend.

At eight o'clock sharp, I met the girls at a bar near Santa Monica beach. In true LA fashion, it was overcrowded and loud, but this just put me in a party mood.

The girls were already there, and I admired their outfits as I approached them. Val had an effortless bohemian chic thing going on: wide-sleeved blouse and black, wide pants. Lori wore jeans and a tank top, and Hailey was wearing the sexiest pair of red stilettos. The rest of the outfit didn't even matter. Those shoes were the essence of life, right there. Maddie had opted for a light beach dress, just like me.

I whistled when I reached the girls. "Are we hot, or what?"

Hailey rubbed her hands together. "This was a great idea."

"Looks pretty crowded," Val said, surveying the long line to the entrance.

Hailey wiggled her eyebrows at Val. "Use your magic powers, sister."

Five minutes later, not only were we inside, but we had a table. As we all slung our bags over our chairs, I made to take out my cell phone. Out of the corner of my eye, I saw that Maddie and Hailey had done the same.

Val cleared her throat, holding up a finger. "Hey! Girls' night out rule. No cell phones. It's a slippery slope. Starts with *Oh look, I have a notification* to reading urgent e-mails, and… well, you know where I'm going with this."

I grudgingly agreed, sliding the phone back in my purse. Hailey followed suit.

Maddie kept hers on the table. "I need it in case Grace calls. She's watching the baby."

"Stop worrying so much," Val said soothingly. "Have fun for a few hours."

We ordered fancy overpriced drinks, and I already felt the weight of the day lift off my shoulders.

"Shitty week?" Hailey asked sympathetically.

"Oh, yeah. But no talking about it tonight."

Val drummed her hands on the table. "I agree. Tonight is for fun."

I had an idea as I looked from one sister to the other. "And for getting some dirt on Will."

Val feigned offense. "Are you asking us to break sister code?"

We paused when the server brought our drinks, and clinked glasses.

Then I said, "I've known him for a while now. I've earned the right to some dirt." Wow. I couldn't believe that already two and a half months had passed since I'd met Will.

Hailey tapped her forefinger against her lips. "Yep, you totally have. I was bursting at the seams at the wedding already, so I've waited long enough."

Three cocktails later, I had enough dirt to fill a book: that one time Will had attempted to get a tongue piercing but the guy was a conman who ended up giving him an infection. The time Will was caught jumping the fence to the Hollywood sign. How he'd dated a string of bimbos over the years (I chose to slurp loudly from my cocktail at this point), and they hadn't liked any. But they liked me. Ha!

"Personally, I think his greatest achievement was when he saved Jace's ass and mine that night we sneaked out to go to a concert and you thought we'd run away," Hailey concluded. I was laughing so hard that my belly was aching, and so was Maddie. Lori threw a sheepish smile at Val, who looked... stunned.

"Wait, you and Jace were at a concert that

night?"

Hailey held up her hands, as if in surrender. "Whoops, forgot you didn't know about that."

Val opened her mouth, then closed it again, looking like a fish out of the water. "I think I'm too buzzed to process this."

Hailey shimmied in her seat. "Oh, come on. Someone had to shake things up."

I grinned. "You were the brat in the family. I happen to be the proud owner of that title in mine."

Hailey considered that. "Well, Jace and I competed for that spot, but between us, I think I won by a decent margin."

Everyone laughed then, Val included.

"So I'm forgiven?" Hailey asked Val.

"Just like that? Oh no, sis. You have to work for it."

Hailey jutted out her lower lip like a baby, just as the fourth round of cocktails arrived. Or was it the fifth? I was more buzzed than I'd thought.

"Well, I was waiting for the right moment to bring this up," Hailey said dramatically, "but it seems there is no time like the present. I, ladies, have gotten us tickets not only to the Oscars event, but also to one of the after-parties."

"Oh my God." We squealed so loudly that several other patrons turned to look at us.

Hailey batted her eyelashes at her sister. "Am I forgiven now?"

Val batted her eyelashes right back. "Depends, will anyone named Hemsworth be there?

Asking for a friend."

We clinked glasses, even though they were half-empty, and then Lori asked the question to which I dreaded the answer.

"Is this the fourth round of cocktails?"

Val wrinkled her nose. "Sis, we've reached the point where counting is counterproductive."

"But so is not feeling my toes," Lori countered.

Hailey snickered. "You always were a lightweight."

I, unfortunately, thought Lori had a point. I was feeling my toes... but I wouldn't be able to walk in a straight line.

I caught Val checking out a guy at another table. I scooted closer to her and whispered, "What are we talking here? Just ogling, or making a move to take someone home?"

Val smiled sheepishly. "Ogling."

"What are you girls talking about?" Hailey said. I motioned with my head toward Val's guy. Hailey followed my direction and whistled.

"He's hot. And so is his friend." She tilted her head. "Hey, Val, what are your top five qualities you look for in a guy?"

Val looked in the distance, giving the question serious consideration.

"So... he should be smart and charming," Val said, enumerating on her fingers. "Also, he should be tall. Taller than me so I can wear heels without looking like a giraffe next to him. Six-pack would be a nice bonus, but I'm more of a biceps type of girl. Strong arms that can just hold you, you know?" she finished dreamily.

"Strong arms are important." I nodded, thinking about Will and already missing him. I surreptitiously pulled my phone out of my bag, holding it under the table so the girls wouldn't see.

Shit, I saw my screen double. I squeezed my eyes shut, then opened them again. Now I saw it triple. I closed one eye, and I was back at seeing double. Right. No way could I text like this. I'd have to wait for the dirty talking until I saw Will in person. I slipped the phone back in my purse.

Hailey propped her head in her palm. "Smart comes first for me too. I'm attracted to intelligent men. But I'm also a six-pack type of girl. Washboard abs… yummm. But I'm willing to bend that rule. The only hard rule is that he must be good in bed. Sexy-time skills are important."

Val smacked her forehead. "How did I forget that? You're right. That's high on the list. Life is too short for crappy sex."

We ordered another round of cocktails and drank to that. Then we launched into the most serious debate of the evening: choosing the best shoe designer. Once we had enough alcohol on board, we felt like dancing, which meant we were a danger to anyone in a radius of two feet. We were drunk and full of energy, and we burned it off on the dance floor.

"When I'm drunk dancing, I don't know if

I'm rocking it just in my head or not," Val said. Yeah, probably the former, but why spoil our fun? Midway through the dancing spree, the guys Val and Hailey had eyed the entire evening approached and danced with the girls.

"Who here had the least to drink?" Val asked when we plopped back in our chairs, all sweaty and thirsty.

Maddie piped up. "I'm sober. No alcohol for me, remember?"

"Oh, yeah. I forgot. So... you'll make sure we're all going home, right?"

Maddie nodded once.

Hailey smiled at her older sister. "Val, I think the only time you actually let loose is during our girls' nights out."

Val grinned. We ordered just water from that point on, and sometime later, I thought I caught a glimpse of Will in the crowd. Huh? Was I imagining things because I was missing him? As he came closer, I had my answer. That was 100 percent my bragworthy boyfriend. Flanked by Landon, Jace, and Graham.

"How did the boys know where to find us?" Val asked in wonder.

I felt so proud. So proud. I'd managed to send that text message after all. I was just suffering from alcoholic amnesia and couldn't remember doing it. Then Maddie stomped all over my pride when she said, "I texted Landon earlier with the address."

The guys made it to our table, and because there were no extra chairs, each pulled his girl in his lap. Jace was the only one standing. Val looked from Will to Landon and Graham, and said, "You're all so cute." There was so much melancholy and affection in her tone that I had the strangest urge to hug her.

I leaned into Will, seeking as much body contact as possible... while remaining decent. Was it weird that I'd missed him?

"Hello, handsome," I whispered. Will whispered back hello, but his voice was so rough, and his hand slid so low on my back that I surmised that what he really wanted to do was to kiss me silly... preferably against a wall with my legs wrapped around him.

Jace was still standing, watching the guys with a shit-eating grin. The next second, our party was crashed by a gang of girls. They surrounded Jace, asking for autographs and pictures. He obliged them, but I thought his smile looked too practiced.

The bar manager did bring a chair for Jace eventually, but he was barely sitting because groups of fans popped up every few minutes.

"Well, this is annoying," he said after one such group had left, running a hand through his hair.

"Should we move the party somewhere else?" I suggested.

"Good idea. Somewhere where I'm not recognized."

Hailey patted his shoulder. "That would require a paper bag over your head."

"Or we could call it a night. It's late," Will suggested. To anyone else, it would seem like an innocent suggestion. But I was sitting *on* Will, so I had some *insider* information. Sleeping wasn't what he had in mind.

"We could do that," Val said. There was a general buzz of agreement, and everyone rose from the table. Jace headed out first, and the rest followed.

"Hey, have you noticed that Jace didn't flirt with even one fan?" Hailey whispered to Val. The girls were walking in front of Will and me.

Val nodded. "Yep. I'd take it as a sign that he's serious about that girl he's been seeing lately, but—"

"That's not it," Will interrupted. "Things didn't work out between them... at all. He just told us that over beers. He's been off all evening."

Hailey pinched the bridge of her nose. "Val, we need to stage an intervention."

"Shit. I'm tipsy. I need all my neurons for an intervention."

Hailey waved her hand. "Nah, just go on instinct."

Outside the bar, every couple ordered an Uber, and Hailey proclaimed she and Val were kidnapping Jace for a few more hours, going for drinks at his house. I could barely hold back my laughter at Jace's panicked expression when Val and Hailey each took him by the elbow and slid into a car with him.

"You think he knows he's about to be

ambushed?" I asked Will.

"Did you see the look on his face? Course he does."

We were the only ones left because our Uber hadn't yet arrived. Will wrapped his arms around my waist, keeping me close to him.

"You were the prettiest girl in there tonight."

"I think you're biased." I aligned my hips to his. "Your little friend is clouding your judgment."

Will blinked, and I immediately rectified my joke.

"I mean your very big and very hard friend."

Will slid his hands to my hips. God, I loved feeling those big, roughened hands on my hips. Or my back. Or my breasts. I didn't mind feeling them anywhere, really.

"Paige...."

I didn't understand the warning tone in his voice until the man immobilized my wrists with his hands. Whoops... my palms were roaming over the expanse of his chest. I tried to bat my eyelashes innocently.

"I have no clue how that happened. I'm blaming all those cocktails."

"Maybe I'm just irresistible."

"Pfft...." I feigned nonchalance, but I could feel myself failing. It was hard to keep up the pretense when all I wanted was to lift up his shirt and count those little squares on his washboard abs. I wiggled my hands out of his grip (to be noted: he could have stopped me, but he let go, so... he totally wanted to be mauled), and this time, I did slide my fingers under his shirt.

"Hmm… I wonder if I'd see a twelve-pack if I looked now. I'm already seeing double biceps."

"You'll look when we're alone." Will's voice was a delicious growl.

"Oh, once we're alone I'll do more than look. I'll trace them with my tongue, just to show my appreciation, of course."

Chapter Twenty-One
Paige

Will's gaze darkened. He kissed one of my palms, then the other, then placed my hands at the sides of his neck, as if he didn't want me to stop touching him. He just wanted me to keep the touching to safe areas. Cool. I could do that. I was buzzed and turned on, but I could pull it off.

"You look hotter than ever tonight, Detective." Was that my voice? Low and husky, wanton.

He feathered his lips against my cheek. The five o'clock shadow he had going on was grazing my skin in the most delicious way.

Thankfully, our Uber arrived, interrupting the moment. The heat was getting out of control.

The effects of the alcohol wore off on the journey, but I wasn't sorry. The slight buzz had been relaxing and fun, but I wanted my senses on alert for the sexy part of the evening. I scooted closer to Will.

"Do you think the driver knows we'll be up to no good once he drops us off?" I asked.

"Who said we will?"

Oh, right... he was playing hard to get, wasn't he? I pulled away, smiling saucily... or trying to. Will smirked back, which made me think my saucy smile looked more like a lunatic grin.

Well, that was just fine. I'd never managed to pull off saucy, but I had plenty of other talents. I got to work, tempting Will Connor like it was my job. I lifted the hem of my dress until I was showing plenty of leg. Then I accidentally on purpose rubbed my thigh against his. Will tensed. I grinned to myself. My plan was working.

When we climbed out of the car, Will kissed me before we even entered my building. *Ha! That was easy*. I was feeling very smug about it all when he suddenly lifted me off my feet.

"What are you doing?"

"Carrying you, or you'll rip off my clothes before we make it to your apartment."

Damn it. My hands had been under his T-shirt. Again. Oh, yeah. *Eyes on the prize, Paige. Eyes on the prize*. Being carried was nice, though. In fact, better than nice. I could touch him to my heart's desire, and there was nothing he could do to stop me. He was so manly, shouldering the doors open, not even breaking a sweat, as if carrying me was no big deal. He made me feel safe and protected. This big, muscly man was handling me with utmost gentleness, and it spoke to a primal part of me... a part I wasn't even aware of until now.

Will put me down once we got into the bedroom. God, that look in his gaze. It held heat and affection. No one had ever looked at me like that.

"You had fun tonight?" he asked.

"Oh, yeah. Lots of cocktails, and we danced. Val and Hailey even got two hotties as dancing partners."

"And you...?" He swallowed. "You danced alone all night?"

His tone was casual, but even so, I knew he'd be hurt if I'd danced with another man.

"Unless you count Lori and Maddie as dancing partners, then yes, I danced alone," I assured him.

He cupped my face, then kissed my lower lip. "I don't know if it's wrong to feel so possessive of you, Paige. But I can't feel otherwise. The thought of anyone else touching you...."

"You're the only one touching me, Will."

"That's right." He kissed down my neck, murmuring, "I love your dress." Before I could ask why, he whisked it away, providing the answer: it was easy to remove.

We tumbled into bed, clothes flying left and right until we were both naked.

"Ride me, Paige," Will said, sliding on protection. He was sitting with his back against the headboard, and he brought me on top of him in one swift move, positioning me with my back to his chest. He rubbed the tip of his erection across each of my ass cheeks, then gripped my hips, and I lowered myself on him slowly. Will's hands were on my waist, then skimmed further up so his palms pressed the side of my breasts.

His fingers teased the peaks. I was on top, but

he still had so much control, which I relished. I loved controlling every aspect of my life, but here, where it was just the two of us, I loved that he took over, that he showed me pleasure like I hadn't thought possible. I was moving faster now, bobbing up and down, loving this new angle.

My ass cheeks slapped against his thighs, and then Will took over completely, pounding hard inside me from below.

"Will, fuck. This angle... you're killing me."

He kissed my neck, my back, every part of me that he could reach. When he slid a hand between my thighs, pinching my clit, I gasped his name. I hadn't braced myself for the shot of pleasure.

My spine arched, and I bent forward, feeling the reverberations in every muscle. I heaved a breath, aware that my thighs were shaking. Will had stilled. He wasn't thrusting inside me anymore, just moving two fingers on my clit. My insides were clenching. I didn't know if he'd grown wider or I'd become tighter, but all of a sudden, the pleasure was too intense.

The muscles in my legs and belly tensed. I was going to come undone any second now.

"That's it, babe. I want to feel you come all over my cock."

I exploded around him. The orgasm engulfed every cell of my body. I felt on fire from the tips of my fingers to the ends of my hair. My eyes watered from the intensity of it. My body was pure sensation. I was wrapped in Will. He was holding me by the waist and raining kisses on my back. He held me like that until I was breathing normally again, then he switched positions, placing me on all fours.

I felt him behind me, and then he reached a hand between my legs, teasing my clit. I pressed my forehead against the mattress, breathing in deeply, already shivering in anticipation.

When the length of his erection rubbed between my cheeks, heat sparked up along my spine.

"Inside me. Now. Please."

I couldn't form full sentences, but Will obliged me. He slid inside me to the hilt, and then he moved faster than ever, slamming against me harder than ever. He gave me every ounce of pleasure I could take, while claiming his own. I was still tight from the first climax, and that feeling was otherworldly. Will rubbed against my inner walls, filling me up so thoroughly that I thought I'd tear up from the intense pleasure. I finished before him, and Will thrust into me right through it, until he climaxed too.

When he pulled out of me, he swore under his breath.

I tensed. "What's wrong?"

"The condom broke."

I sucked in a breath, turning around.

"Are you—" I'd been about to ask "Are you sure?" but I had the proof before my eyes. My stomach shrank to the size of a peanut. On shaky legs, I hurried to the bathroom. Will followed me. I wished he hadn't, because I needed a few seconds to pull myself together. I hopped straight into the shower. I'd begun to shake, and welcomed the warm spray of water.

Since my shower only fit one person, Will was standing right outside it, watching me. He'd cleaned up at the sink. What was he thinking? I wanted him to talk, but at the same time was afraid of what he'd say. I was still shaking, despite the warm spray.

"I'm sorry," Will said gently.

"It's not your fault. These things happen." I tried to work every ounce of bravado I could into my voice.

Will wrapped a towel around his lower body and stepped closer.

"Paige, you're shaking. You're nervous."

He could see that? How? I wasn't shaking that visibly, was I? I turned off the water, unsure of what to do, shifting my weight from one foot to the other. Will offered me a robe. Stepping out, I put it on. I knew we should talk, but right then I really wanted to feel Will's arms around me. I was too afraid to ask for a hug, though. As we left the bathroom, I caught a glimpse of myself in the mirror. I was seven shades paler, looking as if I'd lost blood. No wonder Will had guessed my terror. I went to the kitchen, though I wasn't sure why.

"Paige?" Will's voice was soft. "What do you need? I'll do it for you. You're still shaking. Tea?"

I nodded. "Tea would be good."

It was a good thing he'd taken over, because my fingers were too shaky to be of any good. A few minutes later, he handed me a steamy cup. We were still standing awkwardly in the kitchen.

"Now you're going to tell me why you're so terrified."

I clasped the cup tighter. "Because this can have consequences, and… I can't take the morning-after pill. I took it once a few years ago, and it messed me up hormonally. My ob-gyn advised me never to take it again. It's also why I'm not on any form of birth control. I have a hormonal sensitivity."

I was mentally building up arguments, waiting for him to push the idea of the pill. He didn't look angry, which was good.

"Okay, no pill then." The knot loosened a bit, but I was still on edge. "Paige, talk to me."

His expression lightened up, and the next words came out easier.

"I know the chances of… pregnancy are slim. I'm not even in the ovulation portion of my cycle. But we don't need this stress of uncertainty in our relationship now."

Will stepped right in front of me, taking my face in his hands. "It doesn't mean we can't handle it."

"And what if it happens?" I whispered.

"Then we'll have a little girl or boy. Personally, I'd keep my fingers crossed for a girl."

I blinked a few times, setting the mug on the counter. "You're not scared."

"Not one bit." He kissed my forehead and wrapped his strong arms around me, giving me that hug I needed so much. "I understand if you are, but I don't want any of that fear to have to do with me. Whatever happens, I'm here for you, Paige."

"Because you'd do the right thing."

He pulled back just enough to be able to make eye contact. "This isn't just about duty. I care about you."

Something amazing happened. A sweet warmth overpowered my fears. Then I was drowning in embarrassment. I fixed my gaze on Will's Adam's apple.

"I'm sorry I freaked out."

"Being scared is human, Paige. I'll be there for you through all of it."

I smiled. "Are you saying these things because there might be a mini-Will in here?"

"Maybe I've wanted to say them for a while but didn't find the right moment."

I felt flutters in my belly. "Is that code for you were afraid?"

Will pulled my bottom lip into his mouth, then kissed the bow above the upper lip.

"I did just say it's normal to be scared, so I'm gonna man up and admit that I was."

I felt so much lighter, even though I knew that if the unlikely happened, it would put a strain on our relationship.

"Are you going to finish your tea?" he asked.

"Well, I was thinking it might warm me up, but now I'm thinking there are better ways to warm up."

He tilted his head, offering a cute, lopsided grin. "Such as?"

"Body contact. Level of heat is disproportionate to number of clothes and proportionate to number of muscles. Know anyone interested?"

Will dropped his towel to the floor. I heated up before he even touched me, but then he scooped me up in his arms and I was *on fire*.

"You've read my mind," he informed me while carrying me to the bedroom. "I think we both have too much adrenaline to sleep."

"Pffft, maybe you do. I meant nothing more than a cuddle."

"And what makes you think I meant something else?" He did away with my robe before we climbed into bed.

"Hmpf." I'd tried to say actual words, but Will had licked one nipple, pulling it between his lips.

"What was that?" he moved to the other nipple. I didn't bother to reply. I was too busy squirming and enjoying his mouth. Will kissed up to my ear, and I became aware that every inch of my side was pressing against his body.

"Paige, are we good?" he asked softly.

I nodded, turning on one side too, watching him. "Yes."

He gave me a long, deep kiss and held me until I fell asleep.

Chapter Twenty-Two
Will

"Val, how much longer are you planning to torture us?" I demanded. We were at Friday dinner, and Val had brought samples from the office, asking our opinions, calling us her *testers*. The girls' group, which comprised Lori, Hailey, Maddie, and Paige, was ecstatic trying out everything, giving Val detailed reports on every fragrance.

"Until you give me your opinion," Val replied sweetly.

"Why do you need our input on women's fragrances?" Jace voiced my exact thoughts.

"Because I want to know if you'd like these on a woman. It's an important part of research."

Jace and I carefully avoided looking at each other.

I was always up for helping my sisters, but the most I could come up with was *I like it* or *I don't like it*. Val wasn't satisfied with that. She prodded us with questions like *"How about the undertone? The finishing notes? Do you feel the pepper at all? Would mint be better?"*

Milo had been the only one to escape this, and that was just because he was spending the night at a friend's house.

Graham and Landon were sharing my conundrum, but we all tried our best. We had our eyes on the prize. *Dinner*. Except the girls were having too much fun trying out the samples… so much fun, in fact, that it didn't look like we'd have dinner anytime soon.

"That guy I danced with the other night asked for my number, and we went out on Wednesday," Val told the girls.

She'd lowered her voice, but even so, bits of the conversation filtered through the living room. The girls were sitting at the dining room table, and the guys and I in the seating area on the other side of the room.

When the word *tongue* reached our ears, Landon cleared his throat loudly. "Val, how about continuing girl talk another time? We can hear you, you know."

Val glanced over her shoulder, smiling sheepishly. "Oops, didn't realize I was talking so loudly."

"Who is she talking about?" Jace inquired. "That guy from the girls' outing two weeks ago? He seemed like a schmuck."

I clapped a hand on his shoulder. "Brother, don't get her hackles to rise, or we might not get dinner."

Usually Jace wasn't one to jump the gun. That was my role. He took most things in stride, but he'd been on edge lately. He'd started dating a woman he was very much into, and discovered that she'd been more into his fame than into him. It didn't use to bother him, but my brother was changing. He was generous and trusted easily, which could be a bad combo, and I'd always worried for him.

Val finally showed us some mercy, and we moved on to dinner.

"Will, I've heard the case against the guy in charge of the car robberies was dismissed by the judge," Landon said after we'd all eaten and headed back to the sitting area.

I nodded. "Yeah. Fight's not over yet, but chances are high that the guy will walk away without a charge."

Val's eyes widened.

"Don't hold back. I can *feel* you wanting to say something," I urged.

She cleared her throat. "Maybe I'm just secretly observing."

I didn't manage to hide my smile. "Your secret observations are usually followed by comments."

She pressed her lips together, then turned to Hailey. "We didn't even get wind of this."

"Yeah," Hailey replied. "How did we not pick up on this? You're not displaying your usual broody forehead."

Val pointed to Paige, who was sitting next to me. "Is this your doing?"

Paige flashed my sisters a grin, then half turned to me. "I think it might be."

Her left hand was on the table, and I covered

it with mine. "I'm not going to confirm that. Might give certain people crazy ideas."

Paige wiggled her hand out of my grasp, pinching my thigh. Val was 100 percent on point. Paige was changing me. Or rather, I was willing to change for her.

Even when I wasn't with her, I found myself thinking about her, brainstorming about where to take her on dates. Pleasing Paige had become a goal. Right now, I was monitoring the Griffith Observatory reports for a meteor shower viewing. She'd talked a lot about constellations that night on my balcony, so I thought she'd like this.

When it was time to pop open a new bottle of wine, I offered to get it. Val was on my heels. We needed new glasses as well because we were moving from white wine to red wine.

I hadn't even realized that I'd whipped out my phone to check the Griffith Observatory homepage until I saw my sister peeking.

"Hey, stay out of my business," I admonished.

"But maybe you need pointers."

"Nope, I'm good."

"I always knew it."

"What?"

"That you've got a dreamy soul hidden deep inside there. Very deep."

"What made you think that? I was a punk growing up."

"No, you were trying to be a punk, big

difference. You were a sweetie underneath it all."

I stared at my sister as I grabbed the bottle and a few glasses, and she grabbed the rest. *Sweetie*, really? Out of all the ways she could have described me....

"Please explain," I said as we made our way back to the living room, though I wasn't sure I wanted to hear it.

"Well, you always pulled a lot of stunts, but you were so sweet with Lori and Jace and Hailey. Always volunteered to do activities with them. Even read them bedtime stories when Landon and I were working."

I tried to school my expression, because... damn, she was right. I hadn't done those things only out of a sense of duty, but because I'd genuinely enjoyed it. Spending all that time with my younger siblings had earned me snickers from friends at school, but I'd never cared.

"And what about you, lovely girl? More lemonade?" I asked Paige after Val and I had given everyone a glass.

"Yes, please."

She wasn't drinking wine tonight. It had been two weeks since the condom incident. She'd been so scared that night. I'd wanted to take away her fears any way I could. She'd seemed to relax after our conversation, but a part of me was still wondering if she'd been so terrified because she didn't see this going where I did. I'd been thinking about the possibility that Paige could be pregnant... a lot. I wouldn't admit it out loud, but a part of me was hoping the odds would work out. Was it crazy? Maybe. But so were my feelings for Paige. Intense and wild.

Chapter Twenty-Three
Paige

I was pushing my luck. I knew it, but I couldn't stop anyway. Greg had asked me to drop the education project, but I was still aggressively following every last lead. I just couldn't bring myself to give up. Not yet. I wanted to exhaust every possibility before shelving the project. Which was why I was working on a fine Saturday. Yesterday, I'd slept like the dead after Friday dinner and woken up energized. Will had some work to do as well, so I thought I'd put the time to good use. I was at my usual coffee shop in Venice.

At six o'clock, just as I shut my laptop, a shadow appeared on my table. I could make out the outline of a tall, muscly man. I swore to God, if another surfer annoyed me, I'd take drastic measures.

It was Will.

He was blocking the sun with his frame. Oh my, that frame. With the sun forming a halo around him, he looked even more handsome than usual. His skin seemed golden, and even his unruly hair appeared dark blond. He was wearing a black T-shirt that fit snugly over his broad chest. Yum... those pecs were just what the doctor ordered. He was carrying a backpack on one shoulder.

"Well, hello there, hunky detective. You didn't tell me you were coming." I'd texted him to let him know where I was, but he hadn't replied.

"Wanted to surprise you."

Will's gaze roamed over my body, and despite my knee-length skirt, I felt naked. He placed the backpack on the floor, then leaned in for a kiss.

Oh, la la. This wasn't just your run-of-the mill good evening kiss. Will tilted my head up, splaying his hand across the side of my face. His thumb pressed on my cheek; his other fingers reached my ear and hairline. His tongue entwined with mine, and the man kissed me until I felt as if my panties were on fire. My bra too. I was burning for him. Everything blurred except for Will Connor—the taste of his mouth, the feel of his skin against mine. I forgot where we were for a split second, but then I remembered with a jolt.

"Will, remember the rules about kissing in public?" I whispered.

He dragged his forefinger from the tip of my nose down to my lips. "Remember what I said about rules?" he countered. "Is this making you hot and bothered?"

"You know it does."

"I like hearing it." He brought his mouth to my ear. "Feeling it."

His hand moved to my thigh. I pushed it away half-heartedly because I loved his touch. But it was so scorching hot that I was at risk of forgetting all about decency. Will pulled back a notch, trapping me in his gaze. Yep, that hot look wasn't steering me on the path to Decentville. Sinnerland was looking more and more appealing. He kissed me again, hotter than before, as if I hadn't just scolded him. I detected a hint more possessiveness than usual.

"Every surfer boy here will know you're taken," Will explained after pulling his mouth away.

He sat on the chair next to mine. "Oh, I see. So you weren't just trying to kiss the panties off me. You had an ulterior motive."

"Saw the way a few bastards were looking at you when I walked up."

"And you're assuming the same surfers will be here next week?" I challenged. It *might* have been an underhanded tactic to get him to visit me next week too. *Might*.

"I don't know, but I'll be here."

Mission accomplished! He kissed that sensitive spot where my neck met my shoulder. At first he just feathered his lips... but then he brought his tongue out to play too, and I felt that little lick *all* over my body. Was he doing it on purpose? What was I saying—of course he was. He couldn't seem to help himself around me, and I couldn't deny it—I loved that.

"You're all I need, Paige."

I was so humbled that I was giving him what he needed. When I couldn't feel a hot exhale against my neck, I realized he was holding his breath, as if his own words had caught him by surprise. Then he went on, and I inched closer, because he was speaking in a low voice and I didn't want to miss one word.

"I think I've always avoided needing someone, but with you… nothing feels close enough." His warm breath landed on my skin again. "I'm not sure if I'm making sense, but I wanted you to know this."

"You are making sense," I assured him gently. I understood where he was coming from. I'd been afraid of losing Dad as a kid, but he *did* lose his parents. Needing someone had always seemed like a vulnerability.

I just couldn't get enough of his body heat, of the beauty of this moment. He'd shown me a vulnerable part of himself, and though I'd never been outspoken about voicing my feelings, I wanted to open up with Will.

"When I went shopping with Mom, she told me that I've always been afraid of love. But with you, I'm not afraid at all. Isn't that crazy?"

He pulled back a little, looking straight at me. I had never, *ever* seen Will smile like that. It was wide and warm, and he seemed immensely happy. I'd made that happen, huh? I'd made my hunky detective happy enough to warrant a smile so wide, I was a little afraid his cheeks would hurt.

"What?" I asked, even though I knew what. Maybe I wanted to hear him say it. But Will was out of words. He was too busy kissing the living daylights out of me. I was caught up in his magic and didn't give two hoots about the fact that we were in public. He wanted a sinfully scorching hot kiss? He'd have it. We only stopped when we were in danger of suffocating.

"Easy, Detective. I'm feeling so hot that I'm going to break into a sweat soon."

"Let's swim."

"I have a bikini, but you brought swim trunks?" I asked skeptically.

"Yes, I did. Also brought towels." He pointed to the backpack.

"Then let's go."

I left my laptop and bag with the barista, whom I'd befriended since I was here so often, and after we changed in the small cabins behind the bar, we headed to the beach, laying the towels on the sand before walking toward the water.

Will slipped into his vigilante mode, peering around the beach.

"I'm doing it again," he remarked when he caught me watching him.

"I don't mind. I got used to it."

He jerked his head back. "Really?"

I nodded. "It's part of who you are, Will. It just took me some time to accept it."

We ran toward the water, jumping in. It was cool, but not cold. I always preferred swimming at sunset anyway, after the sun had shone on the water all day, warming it up.

I swam breaststroke, and Will was by my side. I felt a slight twinge in my ovaries—like a cramp. My period hadn't come yet. I wasn't supposed to get it for another week, but the anticipation was killing me. I was reading into everything: was I too sleepy? Was I hungry too often? I swam faster. Whatever happened, I wasn't alone in this. I had to remember this. But despite Will's reassurances, I couldn't help worrying about the impact a pregnancy would have on us.

When I grew tired, I slowed my pace.

"Water's too deep here. Can we swim back to where I can touch the ocean floor?"

"I'm reaching it. I'll hold you."

He didn't need to tell me twice. I wrapped myself around him the next second. Legs around his middle, arms around his neck. I was making full boob contact with his chest. And below, we had a full cock contact situation. He had a hard-on, and the length of it was pressed against my belly.

"Hey, when did this happen?" I moved a few inches up and down, just to check I wasn't imagining things. Nope, I wasn't. Will was hard as all get out.

"When you were running in front of me in your tiny bikini." He skimmed his hands from my hips to my ass, palming each cheek and fondling it.

"Will...."

"My hands are under water. No one can see what I'm doing."

"You wouldn't dare—" Oh, and how he dared. Before I could even finish my sentence, he slipped one hand to the front. He moved the part of the bikini covering my center to one side and stroked my entrance. I shuddered in his arms.

He strummed his fingers on my sensitive flesh, and it was all I could do not to squirm. I pushed him away because the fiend showed no signs of stopping.

"Let's swim back," I said.

Will smirked. "You do that. I'm going to swim on my own for a while until my hard-on goes away."

Right. I'd feel guilty about him having blue balls, but it was his own fault entirely. Here I was, swimming innocently, and he had to go and get us both hot and bothered. He got what he deserved.

I shivered as I stepped out of the water, but the sun was still strong enough to warm me up. I peeked over my shoulder and caught Will watching me, so I made a big show of drying off, keeping my ass toward him and bending at the waist as I ran the towel down my legs.

After retrieving my bag and laptop from the barista, I sat down on the towel just as Will was coming out of the water. Lust coiled through me. He wasn't just yummy. He was... I had no words. Hotter than sin? The very definition of sexy? No words seemed to do him justice. He advanced slowly toward me, spraying water in all directions when he ran a hand through his hair. His dark tresses were sticking out in spikes, and drops of water were trickling down his chest. His gaze was on me, intense and molten. His eyes were hooded.

I tossed him a towel, and he dried himself off.

Then he propped a knee on the towel, between my ankles. Leaning forward, he moved over me until we were almost face-to-face.

"I know what you were doing earlier," he said in a raspy voice.

I planted a small kiss right in the hollow of his neck. "I was torturing you. No need to be coy about it. I'm owning up to it." A deep groan reverberated in his chest. It was a deliciously masculine sound. "It didn't help with the blue balls situation, did it?" He skimmed a hand up my arm, bringing it to the back of my neck. He lowered his head to whisper in my ear.

"You knew exactly what you were doing to me."

"Oh, yeah. Tit for tat."

"You'll pay for that. I won't let you come tonight."

I licked my lips. Holy hell, I had not been banking on that.

"What? I didn't hear you correctly. I think you meant, I will make you come repeatedly."

He took my earlobe between his teeth, tugged a little. "You heard me right. I'll eat you out, fill you with my cock, but I won't let you come." He moved, sitting right next to me, watching me as if he hadn't just turned me on *and* terrified me at the same time.

"You're that cruel?"

"Wait and see."

I debated going toe to toe with him on this, but I decided to keep my cards close to my chest: *I* could be just as cruel.

We had dinner on the beach and afterward we watched the water and the sun, and I couldn't remember ever feeling happier.

"Oh, I forgot, do you have time for a dinner sometime next week? At my parents' house?"

"Sure."

"It's going to be a crazy affair. I bet my brother will also make time to come."

"I already met your family."

Every single member of my family had dropped by the inn on the nights when it was my turn to supervise the handyman, under one pretense or another.

"Well, yes, but now they're all together. More intimidating."

"I'm a cop. I can't be intimidated."

"Won't stop them from trying."

"I'll handle it. Just don't schedule it on Wednesday. Actually, I wanted to ask you to keep it free."

"Why?"

"You'll see."

I lifted my head, watching him closely. "Tell me."

"No."

I poked his chest. He grinned. I poked below his navel. His gaze fell on my lips. When I moved my hand even lower, he gripped it. I had another free hand though, and I used it smartly. I went in for the kill, tickling his armpit. He was so surprised that he let my other hand go too. *Big mistake, Detective.* I tickled his other armpit too, straddling him. My attack only lasted a few seconds. He caught my hands, holding them suspended in the air. I became aware of our position. My groin was above his navel, and my nipples were practically in his face. As if knowing how close they were to Will's mouth, the girls perked up.

"Fine, you dangerous woman. I'm taking you to the Griffith Observatory."

"Oh?"

"You know your constellations, so I thought you'd like to see a meteor shower. I've been researching their page for something like that. And they announced it for Wednesday."

Wow. My muscles relaxed. In fact, my entire body felt lighter as I looked into those gorgeous eyes. He took advantage of my lack of attention, and in a few seconds, he pinned me beneath him. He was holding my hands captive, and I couldn't move my legs either.

"Happy now? You made me ruin the surprise."

"Just because I know about it doesn't mean it's ruined. I wasn't expecting you to be so swoonworthy, William Connor."

My heart was thumping wildly as he looked down at me with affection. I was so lost in him that I didn't even realize he planned to tickle me until his hands went to my armpits. I shrieked and kicked my legs, laughing like a maniac. Will knew how to do payback like no one else. I deserved it, true, but goddamn, I was going to embarrass myself if he didn't stop.

"Stop, stop, stop." I wasn't sure he'd understood any word I said, because I was shrieking. He must have though, because he stopped. Or maybe he just decided to show me mercy.

I was heaving out breaths while he brought his mouth to my neck. He was holding my hands above my head.

"Let's go over the things you're not allowed to do," he whispered against my skin. "You're not allowed to tickle me into telling you my plans for dates."

"So you're planning more?"

"Hell yes, I'm planning more."

I rolled my hips until my belly was flat against his hard-on.

"What are you doing?" he growled.

"Showing my appreciation for your effort. You're restraining my hands, and this is the only way I thought of doing it." I batted my eyelashes innocently. "You were saying?"

"You're not allowed to put your boobs anywhere near my mouth when we're in public and I can't taste them."

"Is there anything I *am* allowed to do, Detective?" Why was my voice so husky?

"Yes. You're allowed to go home with me and enjoy everything I'm going to do to you tonight."

I smiled, because it was clear he wasn't going

to make good on his earlier threats.

Chapter Twenty-Four
Paige

The next morning, I woke up at the crack of dawn for no good reason. The sun had just come up, but I couldn't figure for the life of me why I was up. That was until I looked to my left and noticed Will was propping his head on one hand, smiling lazily.

"Good morning." How could he sound so sexy in the morning? And look so damn gorgeous? It wasn't fair.

"Morning. How long have you been awake?"

"Half an hour. You're cute when you sleep." He slid closer, cupping my face. "You have a dimple here." He pressed his thumb above the left corner of my mouth. "And you were dreaming about me."

"Wait… what?" I had been dreaming about him, and it had been an embarrassingly sexy dream, but how could he know?

He circled the peak of my breast. My nipples were hard. Ah, yeah. Dead giveaway. I liked to sleep in the morning, but since I was awake, why waste a perfect opportunity for morning sex? I scooted closer to Will. He watched me with a lazy smile, skimming his hand lower to my belly, and then between my legs. I groaned when he slid a finger inside me.

"You woke up wet. What were you dreaming about, Paige?"

"Why don't I show you?"

His gaze darkened.

After the sexy action and showering, I changed into my clothes from yesterday, forgoing the panties. We were at his apartment, so I didn't have a change of clothes.

Will was slicing bread when I entered the living room. And he was only wearing boxers. Yummm.... He frowned when he saw me.

"Why did you dress up?"

"I need to work for a few hours."

"You can do that from here. You don't need clothes."

"I know it sounds weird, but I concentrate better if I'm wearing office clothes. You, on the other hand, should stay naked. I could use the view today."

He laughed. "The view?"

"What else would you call all that arm porn you have going on? You get a bonus if you drop your boxers too."

"Only if you take off your bra."

I considered this. On the one hand, the constraint of a bra was part of the "work mood." On the other hand, how the hell could I say no? It was a small price to pay to see Will walking around commando.

I awkwardly removed my bra and threw it on

the couch. When Will's gaze dropped to my chest area, I could see the fault in this plan. My nipples were showing—and they were awake... again—and Will was semihard as he dropped his boxers. This had temptation written all over it. But we were stronger than that, Will and I. Right? Right?

I'd almost convinced myself when he set the bread and knife on the counter and advanced to me.

He gave me a good morning kiss, then also kissed the girls through my pristine white blouse.

"Will," I groaned. "Maybe this isn't a good idea. How am I going to get any work done?"

He straightened up, bringing a hand to my face, skimming his thumb over my lips. I couldn't help myself and opened my mouth, suckling on it.

"If you keep doing this, you won't." He pulled back his hand, and I rolled my shoulders.

"I won't, I promise."

"Then we won't have a problem."

"Are you sure you want me to work from here? I won't be doing much besides writing e-mails and reports and making phone calls."

"And I'll make you breakfast and lunch, and give you massages when you're too stiff. I'll do my best not to distract you. No promises, though."

"What's in it for you?"

He smiled wickedly. "I didn't say where I'll be giving you massages."

We made sandwiches together, and after breakfast I started on my phone calls right away. I'd given myself a two-week deadline. If I didn't manage to bring more donors on board, I had to call the ones who had agreed to help and tell them the project wasn't happening. That prospect was worrying, because I knew once I did that, the likelihood of them collaborating with me in the future was slim. No one wanted to feel they'd wasted their time.

Ashley texted me during the day, which was surprising, because she never worked on weekends.

Ashley: I don't know what to do about Greg. He's being even more of an asshole than usual.

I felt for her. His misogynistic streak was evolving into downright emotionally abusive behavior. Ashely and I were considering how to best approach human resources about it.

By the time the afternoon rolled around, I was ready to face-plant on Will's couch. I'd gotten two vague promises, but even if they followed through, the money they were willing to donate was peanuts. At five o'clock in the afternoon, I curled on the couch and hid my face in the pillow.

"Babe?"

"It's not going to work out, Will. It just won't, and it's killing me. Those people are counting on me. I didn't make them any promises, but you should have seen the way they were looking at me when I talked to them about the possibility."

I felt his hand at the back of my neck, applying pressure just where I needed it.

"You're so good at that," I whispered into the pillow. "So damn good."

He sat next to me and I scooted a little to make space for him.

"I'm grumpy," I informed him. I'd been grumpy after the third phone call, and now on a scale from annoyed to fucking pissed off I was Godzilla. I was more emotional than usual, and didn't know if it was because of PMS, or a potential pregnancy.

"I gathered that. I've got a solution on the way."

I peeked at him with interest. "You mean there's an orgasm in the making?"

He smirked. "Early dinner and wine."

"Ooooh, that's even better."

"Now you're just stabbing my pride. Dinner and wine are better than orgasms?"

I saw my mistake and sought to rectify it immediately. Otherwise, this hottie might start again with his dangerous ideas, like *not* giving me orgasms.

"No, no. Not what I meant at all. But a grumpy Paige with a full stomach is better than a grumpy Paige with an empty stomach."

"I see. Are you done with your workday?"

"Yep."

He gave my ass a little smack. "Then lose these clothes."

"What?"

"Take a shirt from my dresser. And don't wear any panties. I want to see your sexy ass."

"Those are very... specific instructions. And by the way, I haven't been wearing panties the entire day."

Will stopped in the act of groping my ass. "And you didn't tell me."

"Well, no. Why tempt you?"

He bit my shoulder lightly, fondling my ass again. "Go change."

"Yes, boss."

I rose from the couch as Will's phone rang. I didn't move further as he went to answer it.

"Hi, Elliot!" He frowned, and nodded, dragging his hands down his face. "Well, we knew there was a good chance it would play out this way. Thanks for the call."

He was gripping his phone so tightly when he disconnected the call that I thought he might break it.

"I'm sorry, Will."

He nodded tightly, then pressed his palms against his eyes. I walked up to him and wrapped my arms around his bare middle—he was still wearing only shorts. He returned my hug, resting his chin on top of my head.

"Go change. Dinner will be here soon."

Now we were both grumpy. But as I searched through the stack of T-shirts in his bedroom, instead of drowning in my own problems, I was brainstorming ways to comfort him. Step number one: I would wear the shortest T-shirt he owned. It wasn't an easy task, considering he was as big as a mountain, but eventually I did find a T-shirt that looked like it had shrunk from washing. My ass cheeks were visible. Oh yeah, that would give him something to look at. I pulled my hair into a bun before remembering he liked to run his hand through it during our sexy times, so I let it fall around my shoulders.

Our dinner had already been delivered when I returned to the living room, and Will was setting it on plates.

"Smells delicious."

He looked at me over his shoulder, then slowly turned around, taking in my outfit. His gaze was on my bare legs. I twirled once, showing off my ass.

"You like this?"

He didn't respond. Well, at least not with words. The look in his eyes was... feral. I sashayed toward him until we were only inches apart. Will was standing with his hands at his sides, as if not touching me cost him all his willpower, but then he lost the battle. One hand went to my waist and the other slid down to my ass, pressing me against him.

"You're so fucking sexy, Paige."

"Back at you, hunky detective." I looked over his arms at the avocado nuggets he'd ordered. "Food's getting cold."

Will lowered his mouth on mine, tracing my bottom lip with the tip of his tongue.

"Maybe I'll just eat you instead, Paige."

Oh, my. I clenched my thighs, nibbling on his lower lip.

"Stay here tonight." It wasn't a question, but neither was it a request. I'd planned to go home because I needed fresh clothes, but when Will added, "I need you," it didn't even cross my mind to say no.

"Of course, I'll stay. I'll warm up your bed and make someone very, very happy." I ground my hips against his to drive my point home.

My big, strong man needed me. I rained kisses on his chest, from one side right to the other. Will fumbled with his fingers through my hair, and I sensed he had more to say.

"What would you say to working from here on my days off?" His shifts were at odd hours, so some days he didn't have to go in.

"You mean like making my home base here?"

"Yes. Or I could hang out with you at whatever beach you want to work from. I just don't like that we go days without seeing each other."

"I can do that. Except when I have meetings."

"I'm looking forward to it."

"You're going to take care of me every day like you did today?"

"I am."

"And you're also going to entertain me with the muscle view?"

He laughed. "Yes."

"And will you finally do a better job at tempting me than you did today?"

Will threw his head back, laughing. "You did not just say that."

I put on my most impish smile. "I most definitely did. You didn't even bother to check if I had panties today. You're losing your touch, Will

Connor."

Famous last words.

The man moved so fast, I was barely aware of what was happening until he'd pinned me against the wall. Oh, yeah. My legs were wide apart, and he slid one hand between them.

"What are you doing?" I whispered.

"Checking if you're wearing panties."

Bastard. He knew very well I wasn't, but he made a big show of *checking*.

He strummed his fingers on my folds, then circled my clit until I whimpered.

"You're still not sure?"

"Got to be thorough." He pressed his thumb on my clit, and a bolt of energy coursed through me. My entire upper body shot forward, and Will skimmed his hand over my thigh to cup my bare ass cheek.

"I like my shirt on you. I like having you here, in my house, sharing my clothes, and smelling your girly stuff in my bathroom."

I'd grown roots, I realized. My life was intertwined with Will's, and I liked it. I felt as if the roots made us stronger. We were both having a rough time at work, but here we were, laughing together, teasing each other. I knew this was just as big a step for Will as it was for me. I tried to push all my worries about the condom scare to the back of my mind, but didn't quite manage it.

"Do you want to talk about the case? No details, just… to clear your mind?"

"We did our best. The whole department worked on it, but at this point, there is nothing to do except let go."

"And you're okay with that?"

He gave me a rueful smile. "Oddly, yes. I think your sexy little ass is distracting me."

"Just my ass?" I batted my eyelashes, scooting closer.

"Your sassy mouth too."

"Hey, so question, if I bring some clothes here, can I still wear your shirts too? They're very comfy."

"Only if you don't wear panties."

I pretended to think about it. "Well, I suppose that's a fair request, since I'll be wearing your things *and* you've agreed to parade that muscly gorgeousness for me too."

Will set his empty plate on the coffee table and focused on me.

"Why are you looking at me like that?"

"I'm waiting for you to finish eating."

Hmmm… he didn't say more, but that glint in his eyes made it easy for me to fill in the gaps. I ate so fast, you'd think there was something chasing me. Then I pointed to the chocolate mousse.

"Moving on to dessert?"

"You bet we are."

***
Will

Paige set her empty plate on the table, but when she made to grab the ones with the mousse, I cuffed her ankles, pulling her where I wanted her, how I wanted her, which was spread out wide before me. I settled between her legs and pushed the T-shirt up and laid a trail of kisses on her bare skin, starting from her pubic bone, up in a straight line to her navel, then between her breasts, teasing each of her nipples with a single stroke of my tongue. I pulled the T-shirt over her head before moving my mouth down the same path. When my lips were above her pubic bone again, I brought one of the dessert plates closer to the edge of the table. I dug one finger in the white mousse and spread it on that patch just above her clit. Paige sucked in her breath as I licked it clean, careful not to touch her sensitive spot. Not yet. Then I moved up to her breasts, smearing mousse on the undersides, licking slowly. Then on top, licking even slower. Her nipples were so erect; they were just beautiful. But I still didn't lavish them with attention.

"I just discovered my new favorite way of eating dessert."

"Will, you're killing me." Her voice was breathy and husky.

I finally remembered my master plan when I realized Paige was grinding against me.

"I didn't say you could do that."

"You were too busy to say anything, so I

thought I'd show some initiative."

"You're not allowed to grind against me."

She reached for my boxers. I stopped her.

"Or touch my cock."

She licked her lips. *Fuck me.*

I continued to smear the mousse on her, this time from her pubic bone to her clit.

"Your pussy is so soft, so pink."

I licked in between words, and her thighs quivered. Suddenly, I didn't want to tease her anymore. I grabbed a condom, and after rolling it on, I slid inside her. *Damn.* I'd worked her up too good; she was so tight I wouldn't last long. I moved slowly, pressing my pubic bone against her clit on every thrust. She came apart beautifully, and I drank her all in. Her toes curled, and she dug her heels deep in the couch. Her legs were shaking as she rolled her hips into me.

"Will. Will. Oh God. I can't... Will."

I lasted two more seconds after she came, then exploded so violently that the air was knocked out of my lungs.

I rested on top of her, breathing deeply.

"I'm out of commission," Paige whispered. "I can't move."

"Can't talk" was all I managed.

I went for her mouth, giving her a deep, slow kiss. Her heated response and the way she pressed her breasts against me consumed me. But that was a running theme with Paige.

Today, the proverbial final nail had been

slammed in the case we'd worked on for a year, but I wasn't taking it as hard as I usually did, and it was because of Paige. I knew with a certainty I couldn't explain that she was my match. It was a powerful feeling—and frightening too. I hoped she felt just a strongly. I wanted to earn this woman's love.

Chapter Twenty-Five
Will

"This is going to be a lot of fun, I promise," Paige said when we arrived at her parents' house for dinner. It was the tenth time she'd said it. I took it as a sign that my girl was actually nervous. I interlaced my fingers with hers and kissed the back of her hand.

"I know it'll be fun," I reassured her.

Her family welcomed us as a group. Her sisters were practically jumping up and down, and Mrs. Lamonica straight-up hugged me. Her father and brother smiled pleasantly, but they practically crushed my hand shaking it, which I recognized as the general guy code for *if you mess with her, we'll come after you*. I gave Graham the exact same handshake when he joined us for Friday night dinner the first time. A handshake was worth more than a thousand warnings.

They'd set up a grill station in the backyard, and her dad was tending to steak, tuna, and salmon.

"Honey, you can't eat steak," Mrs. Lamonica admonished her husband once we were sitting at the table and everyone was helping themselves to food. "Have some fish. You know what the doctor said."

"Yeah, yeah. Steak will kill you. Butter will

give you a heart attack. What's the point of living?" Mr. Lamonica shook his head, but helped himself to salmon instead. Mrs. Lamonica was fussing around everyone, Paige most, I noticed. She was also loading my plate with three portions of everything.

"Sorry, she's just excited you're here," Paige muttered under her breath when her mom went to the kitchen for a fourth serving of mashed potatoes.

"Don't sell hot air to Will," her dad said. "Your mother is always like that."

"I don't mind," I said. Mom used to do the same. She'd fuss around us at the table, making sure everyone had plenty (read: too much) of everything. I smiled at the memory. I could get used to this.

After everyone was full, we relaxed at the pool, and I had a front-row seat to experiencing Paige in "brat mode." She'd definitely earned the nickname. She caused more trouble than even the kids. Her brother was at the edge of the pool, just dipping his feet, but Paige threw so much water at him, the guy was soaked.

She crooked her fingers at me a few times, but even though I had swim trunks on, I didn't trust myself anywhere near her when she was wearing that tiny bikini. I was fighting a hard-on just watching her. She was happy and relaxed, showing her nieces how to do a perfect breaststroke. Paige had gotten her period last week, and I won't lie, it had impacted me more than I'd expected.

Her mom was sitting on the sunbed lounger next to me. We were on the wide side of the pool, adjacent to everyone else.

"You're close to your family, Will?" she asked, just like that. Her voice was casual, but I was a damn good detective. I picked up the gist of the question.

"Yes, ma'am."

"That's lovely to hear." We both looked at the pool as Paige turned her focus on her father, splashing him.

"She's always been daddy's girl," Mrs. Lamonica added with affection. "She missed him so much when he was away. It was even harder than these days, where you have all this technology for video calls."

"That must have been hard, having your husband away so often."

"I got used to the distance, but not the danger." She smiled sadly, pointing to the hair at her temples. "My hair turned white here in a single night. We'd heard some bad news from his deployment unit. That his unit hadn't made it back after an attack. I tried to keep it together in front of the kids. They were young. Paige was eleven. She found me hiding in my bedroom, crying. Gave me a hug and said, 'Momma, we'll take care of you if something happens to Daddy. Don't cry.' I'm ashamed to say that there were many mornings when I could barely get out of bed. Paige would make breakfast for the other kids, make sure they had lunch packed for school. I think she learned from me to hide when crying. She's a tough girl, my Paige."

"She is," I agreed. I'd sensed that in her the

first time I'd seen her. She was a dreamer and a force to be reckoned with when needed, fighting for the project she believed in, determined to give it her best. She was an amazing woman, and it was a privilege to be by her side.

I knew that she wasn't entirely comfortable with my job. Yes, she'd said she'd gotten used to it, but I also knew her well enough to catch on to the telltale signs: getting used to something wasn't the same as liking something. I remembered how she'd reacted when she'd seen the scratch on my neck after our first night together, and wondered if that underlying fear would keep her from loving me. Was there something I could do to make this easier for her?

Paige interrupted our talk by splashing water on us, completely soaking me. When I glared at her, she shrugged. "Sorry, had to save you from Mom before she scared you away."

"And soaking me was the only way you could save me?"

She nodded with conviction. "Absolutely."

Mrs. Lamonica laughed. I jumped in the water and Paige half chuckled, half shrieked when I pulled her flush against me. We were alone in the pool, but everyone was on the edge, watching us.

"You're a naughty woman," I whispered.

"Everyone's watching. Nothing you can do about it," she said smugly.

"Not right now. But we'll be alone in a couple of hours."

I was still holding her flush against me, and positioned my growing erection between her thighs. Her breath hitched. I inched closer. She bit her lower lip.

"What are you going to do, Detective? Withhold orgasms again?" Her voice was very low, but very sultry, and my cock stirred at her words. I cupped her cheek, making sure it looked like a loving but innocent touch, and leaned until I was close to her ear.

"I'm changing tactics."

When I pulled back, I noticed with satisfaction that her pupils had dilated with lust. Fuck, I wanted to kiss her, pin her against the edge of the pool and spread her wide. A few hours. I just had to go through a few more hours, and then this incredible woman would be all mine.

"You two, get a room," Miranda called. Paige merely grinned at her sister. Remembering what her mother had said about Paige made my affection for her deepen. I wanted to make sure nothing ever brought her to tears unless they were of happiness. I hoped she'd share with me the vulnerable moments when she had them, that she'd trust me completely. How else could I take care of her?

Paige looked at me with those big, round eyes, smiling. "You'll have to resume your sexy threats later. I think Miranda can pick up the gist of this… conversation. There is no fooling her."

Now that I was near her, I only wanted to touch her more. I craved her. But if I didn't want to lose the points I'd gained with her family, keeping my hands to myself was the smart thing to do.

I swam for a while, and then Mrs. Lamonica treated us to a second round of dessert. Paige and I left just after the sun set.

"So, what did you think? I saw Mom cornering you. I hope that went okay," she asked once we were back at my place, lying on the lounger on the balcony.

"Paige, I loved getting to know your family. Don't fret so much."

"Uh-huh. I'll be patiently waiting for the delayed reaction."

"I was thinking about something. How would you feel about taking time off for a week and going on a vacation? You've worked hard, you deserve some time off. And I want to have you all to myself for a week."

She nestled into me, wiggling her toes. "I'd love that. Greg needs me for the next two weeks. We have a deadline. But after that, I'm sure I can take a week off."

"Have you ever been to a redwood forest?"

"I've been once when I was little, but I'd love to see one again."

"I'll arrange everything," I assured her. Then, just to tease her, added in a serious voice, "They have some of the best camping spots."

She deflated instantly. Not laughing at her reaction took up a lot of effort.

"We're going to sleep in a… tent?"

"Yeah. We can make a bonfire every night."

"But there are insects and… more insects."

Her voice sounded almost panicked now, and I started laughing in earnest.

"Ah! You were making fun of me." She elbowed my ribs.

"I have a nice cabin there." She tried to elbow me again, but I blocked her and shifted on top of her.

"Little Miss Princess, aren't we?"

She grinned. "Only caught on to that today? You're a lousy detective."

"Nah, today I just got the confirmation."

"So you're not going to subject me to tents and insects."

"Cabin's state of the art."

"What kind of heating?"

"Gas. Why?"

"Damn. I was hoping to see you chop wood. Shirtless, of course."

"There will be plenty of opportunities to see me shirtless, don't you worry."

She touched my chest with one finger, licking her lips. "But chopping wood would be different. I'd be hearing all those manly grunts. A girl can dream, mmm…."

"You drive me crazy when you make those sounds."

She drew out the mmmmm, then added, "What do you want to do now?"

"Devour you," I said seriously.

"Finally. I thought you'd haul me up against the door the second we came inside. Was afraid you'd changed your mind."

I kissed that mouth, bringing one hand under her dress, pressing my fingers into the soft skin on her thigh. I started unbuckling my belt, then undid the top button and lowered the zipper.

When Paige realized what I was doing, goose bumps broke out on her arms. I bunched her dress up and freed my cock, rubbing the length against her panties, over her clit. She lifted her knees and the angle changed. I felt the exact moment when she soaked her panties through, and I almost exploded, knowing that I could give her so much pleasure.

I had a surprise in store for her during our vacation.

Chapter Twenty-Six
Paige

Between the flight and the drive in the rental car, the journey to the redwood forest took a little over four hours. To settle my nerves when flying, I had a little too much wine, and kept fondling Will in my tipsy state. But the man was constantly touching me too, as if he couldn't be near me and *not* touch me, so I thought we were even.

"Wow," I exclaimed when the cabin came into view. I'd imagined a small wooden house. This was a villa. The exterior had elegant fake stone paneling, and the windows were immense.

"This is beautiful, Will."

"Jace and I bought it together about eight years ago to flip it. After I did all the work on it, I liked it too much, so we both decided to keep it. We rent it when neither of us needs it, which is most of the time."

I fell in love with the place the second I stepped inside. The walls alternated between crisp white and faux stone, and there was even a fireplace. I walked to one of the large windows, smiling at the sight of the redwood trees in the distance.

"This view is just stunning."

I felt Will come up behind me and hook an arm around my waist. "I'm glad you like it. We can come here anytime we want."

I loved the way he used the word we, as if it was the most natural thing.

"Why don't I give you a tour, and then I'll make us some dinner and we can watch the sunset in the sunroom?"

"Sounds great."

The house boasted three bedrooms and two bathrooms, one of which resembled a spa, complete with a huge tub with bubble function. Oh yeah, I planned to do sexy things to my sexy man in there.

I ended up taking a quick shower while Will went to the kitchen, then put on a long-sleeved wool dress that reached to my knees. I chose to forgo panties, but did put on stockings and garters. I was feeling feisty tonight. This place was inspiring me.

A delicious smell greeted me when I descended the steps to the lower level, and I followed it to the kitchen. He was dicing chicken, and there was an assortment of vegetables for salad spread out on the counter. We'd shopped for groceries on the way here. I was happy. God, I was. From the tips of my toes to the ends of my hair. I didn't think I'd ever felt so happy.

While he cooked the chicken, I made the salad. While I was dicing the herbs as tiny as possible, I heard Will snap a pic.

"What are you doing?"

"You look cute." He turned the phone so I

could see. I was fresh-faced and my hair was up in a ponytail.

"You can see my freckles."

"I love your freckles. You shouldn't cover them up." He kissed under one eye, then the other.

"I won't wear any makeup while we're here," I promised.

"That's my girl." He kissed me deeply, tangling our tongues, luring a moan out of me. I was so lost in his kiss that I barely noticed he was pushing the dress up my thighs until he let out a groan that sounded so primal, I instantly became wet.

"What's this?"

"Garters."

His breath came out in a hot rush. His pupils dilated.

"You were wearing these on the plane?"

"Nope. Put them on after my shower. You want to know what I'm *not* wearing? Panties."

His gaze dropped to my pelvis, then snapped back up. I tilted my head playfully. "Do you think you'll have problems concentrating on your dinner?"

Will skimmed one big hand from my shoulder to my breast, flicking my nipples through my bra. A bolt of heat shot straight between my legs.

"Nah, I have excellent self-control, Paige."

Game on, Detective.

Once the food was ready, we carried everything into the sunroom. It was decorated in natural shades of brown.

"It was smart to keep this. It's truly beautiful," I told him over dinner.

"I know. Plus, we get tourists all year round."

"So you flipped all the properties you rent?"

"Yes. A lot are in the LA area."

"I can't believe you worked in construction when you were in high-school. Most teens I know wouldn't bother."

"It was good money, and after my parents died we needed it. And keeping busy helped me cope. Then before my senior year, Landon bought a house, wanted to flip it. I offered to work on it, and did it all on my own. When he sold it, he wanted me to keep the profit. It was enough to buy two other small properties. From then on, it snowballed. I continued doing it during college. After keeping this one, I decided that vacation rentals were a smart investment, so I picked up places to flip that were in areas with year-round tourism."

"Wow." I crunched some numbers in my mind from the days my grandma was running the inn. "So you could just live off the rent."

He smiled. "Technically, yes. The decision to join the force wasn't motivated by money."

"And you have someone handling the daily operations in each location?"

"Exactly."

"That's very smart."

"Thanks."

I nodded, indulging in those last few bites of

chicken. Will was watching me with happy eyes.

"You know what day today is?" he asked once we'd moved to the couch in the living room, in front of the fireplace

"Ummm... Saturday?"

He chuckled. "It's three months since we started seeing each other."

It had been three months already? That's right, Lori's wedding had been at the end of July, and now we had the end of October.

"I have a present for you."

"Will...," I murmured.

He rose from the couch, searched his jacket, which was on the armrest, and got out a small jewelry box. He opened it, revealing a gorgeous bracelet: a platinum band with jade stones embedded in it.

"This is so beautiful," I whispered as he clasped it around my wrist.

"It's a family heirloom."

He was watching me with an adoring gaze. I glanced at the bracelet again, seeing it in a whole new light.

"I think I'm in love," I said happily.

"Just with the bracelet, or with me too?" His voice was full of emotion.

I snapped my head up, looking him directly in the eyes. "Both. You've made me fall for you, Will Connor."

He leaned in, giving me a deep, sensual kiss.

"I'm not good with words," he whispered when he skimmed his mouth to my cheek. "It's been years since I said those words out loud. My parents were still with us."

"Oh, Will. You're showing me. That's all I need."

I'd learned enough about him to know that Will had always been about expressing his feelings through actions.

We lay on the couch, entwined, and Will kissed me slowly, his arms wrapped around me tightly, as if he didn't plan to let go.

"Can we light a fire?" I asked a while later, pointing to the fireplace.

"Sure. I'll take care of it."

"Oooh, can I come with you outside while you cut the wood?"

He smirked. "The logs are already cut, Paige."

I jutted out my lower lip. "Can we pretend they aren't? So I can watch you sweat and make all sorts of manly sounds?"

Will dragged his gaze up and down my body before settling on my lips. He stepped closer, until I had to tilt my head back to look up at him. He stroked my chin, then drew his knuckles down my throat.

"You'll hear me plenty when I'm buried deep inside you."

Chapter Twenty-Seven
Paige

I must have fallen asleep, because the next time I blinked my eyes open, it was morning and I was in the bedroom. I barely blinked twice before I realized Will was snapping a picture of me.

I managed to only pull the cover up to my nose because Will was sitting on it, at the edge of the bed.

"Hell no. You aren't taking pics of me in the morning."

Will grinned lazily. "I already did. Also one where you were asleep and were holding both pillows under your head."

"I demand you delete them."

He leaned in and bit gently on the back of my hand. "Make me."

Shucks, I couldn't keep up with him seconds after waking up, but I did think I could pull off a distract-and-snatch move.

The first part of the plan played out without a hitch. I lowered the cover and showed him a nipple. Like the boob man he claimed to be, his attention immediately shifted there. The second part of the plan failed miserably. Will realized I was going to launch myself for his phone the second I moved. He threw it on the armchair opposite the bed, then attacked me. He somehow managed to pin me against the mattress.

"I misjudged your skills, Detective." Why was I breathless? Oh, yeah. Because he was shirtless, and his chest was almost touching mine.

"You need a lesson, Paige."

I swallowed. "Oh?"

"Yeah. You should know what happens when you provoke me in the morning."

"And what is that?"

By way of answering, he yanked the cover away completely and nudged my thighs apart. He moved on the bed until he positioned his mouth between my legs and nuzzled my clit with his nose, dipping his tongue inside me.

Holly hell! On pure instinct, I wanted to roll my hips into him, but Will stopped me. Instead, he slid his palms under my ass, lifting it up in the air for better access. And then his mouth was everywhere. On my clit. Pulling my folds between his lips. Biting my ass cheeks, then nipping at my clit before plunging his tongue inside. I shattered completely, calling out his name, pulling at the sheets.

"What a way to start my morning," I murmured as Will kissed up my body. "Why can't every day start like this?"

"I have a simple solution for that. Sleep every night at my house, and you'll have me every morning."

I expected to find him grinning, but I realized he meant it. "You really want me at your house every night?" I asked, holding my breath.

His face was level with my neck now, and he kissed along my collarbone. "I love having you with me, Paige. I miss you on the nights we're not together."

"I miss you too," I admitted. "I'd love to say yes, but... are you sure?"

Will pulled back to look at me. "Why would I be asking if I weren't sure?"

"Heat of the moment?" I suggested.

"You're the one who had an orgasm, sweetheart. My mind is all clear."

"Well then, Will Connor. Get ready to share your bed with me every night."

We enjoyed our breakfast while basking in the sun. We were sitting side by side at the wooden table.

"Where did you go just now?" Will asked.

I blinked, shaking my head. "Got lost in my own head. What you said about flipping the properties got me thinking... what if I turned Grandma's inn into an education center instead of selling it? I'd have to buy out the rest of my family because they need the money. That'll be a little tricky, because I have some savings, but not enough. I'll make an appointment at the bank when we get back, see about a loan. That'll show my boss that I have skin in the game."

Will pulled me closer. "I have a proposition. Don't take a loan. I'd love to be your partner on this."

I whipped my head in his direction. "Will, are you serious?"

"Hell yes."

"But... you haven't even seen the business plan. I mean, this wouldn't be a business. It would be a nonprofit."

"I don't need a plan. I trust your knowledge and your instincts. I trust you." My heart, which had already been beating wildly, was now in danger of jumping out of my chest.

"I'll show you a plan anyway. And then if you change your mind, I will understand."

He pulled me in his lap. "I won't change my mind."

"It would be a loan."

"No, it would not. I want to do this with you, as a team. If we can work together to make each other's dreams come true, well, I can't imagine anything better, honestly."

I was overwhelmed by this big, hunky man who wanted to intertwine his life with mine on so many levels. And I was ready to jump in with both feet.

"Are we hiking today?" I asked.

"Sure. We can go up to a viewing point and have lunch there."

He kissed the back of my hand, then turned it palm up and skimmed his lips from the center of my palm to my wrist, where he drew a small circle with his tongue. I bit my lower lip.

"You like this?" he asked wickedly.

"You keep this up, and there will be no hiking."

He moved his mouth further up my forearm. Holy hell. Why was this such a turn-on? It was the way he moved his tongue... just barely touching my skin with the tip, teasing me more than anything else.

We made it out of the house two hours later. The couch had seen some sexy action again, and so had the shower.

"I've gotten used to you parading around without a shirt," I complained, pointing to Will's white T-shirt. It was molded to his chest, so plenty of muscle was showing, but it wasn't quite the same.

Will was half hiker, half detective, looking on guard every time we passed a group. He gave me a sheepish grin when I looked at him pointedly.

"I told you it doesn't bother me. You don't have to change who you are for me. I just don't think you're truly relaxing, but that's okay too. I know a few ways to make you relax."

"Is that so?" he nudged my shoulder playfully.

"Oh yeah. You looked *very* relaxed this morning."

He gave my ass a little smack.

"Hey, what was that for?"

"Reminding me about this morning." He pushed a strand of hair behind my ear, adding,

"We're three hours away from the cabin. Don't tempt me."

"How about last night? Can I remind you about that?"

He pulled back, eyes flaring. His passion for me consumed me. He kissed my forehead, then took my hand, leading me further up the trail.

***

At the end of the week, after a day full of hiking, Will announced he'd made reservations in town. So even though every muscle hurt and I had imagined an evening where I'd soak in the tub— possibly with Will—I dressed up, ready for a night out with my man. Maybe I'd get my bathtub extravaganza anyway later on. I was wearing a knee-length sweater dress with long sleeves and not a very deep V-neckline. But Will stilled when he saw me.

"What? This isn't sexy."

"For me it is. Or maybe because I know what's underneath." He gave me a quick kiss, but still stroked my tongue, and I shimmied afterward as I worked a red scarf around my neck. Ufff… why couldn't we just skip dinner?

I realized why when we reached the restaurant. Will had reserved one of the smaller rooms just for us. We were surrounded by candlelight, soft music, and a mix of delicious smells.

"Will…." I didn't know what to say, but he must have heard the emotion in my voice, because he wrapped his arms around me from behind, tugging at my earlobe.

"It's our anniversary week, babe."

The food was delicious, the company even better. How life could be this good, I didn't know. I'd always liked my life, but this... this was different. It was like I hadn't known a part of me was missing until Will had come into my life.

After dinner we headed out to the parking lot behind the restaurant. When we reached the car, I realized I'd forgotten my scarf inside.

"I'll get it," Will said. "Go inside the car so you warm up."

He gave me the key, and he went back inside while I unlocked the car. I only had a light jacket on, but my parka was in the trunk, so I retrieved it to keep warm until the car's heating system kicked into gear.

I'd barely opened the trunk when I sensed something. Someone was behind me. My first thought was *Will*, but then I realized he couldn't be back so fast. I stiffened even before I heard the voice.

"Give me all your money and I won't harm you." It was a man's voice. I broke out into clammy, cold sweat. I didn't have a pepper spray on me, or money. But I didn't think that would go over too well. "Hand it over."

"I don't have any money."

"Don't be stupid."

"Look into my purse. I don't have a wallet. Just my smartphone."

With trembling hands, I opened the bag. A

hand snatched into it, grabbing my phone.

"In the car, then. There has to be money."

Could I cry for help? I figured I'd take a blow to the back of my head before that. Fighting back would only infuriate him.

"Let me look in the front. Maybe there's money there," I said quietly. And then I felt something sharp pinching my back.

"I have a knife. Don't do anything stupid."

Fear and adrenaline spiked my blood, the first overpowering the second. On shaky legs, I moved to the front of the car, my attacker right behind me.

I searched the front, but Will didn't keep money there.

"No money," I said.

"I'll have that pretty bracelet."

Hell no. Blood was rushing in my ears, adrenaline overpowering fear for a split second. Straightening up, I elbowed the attacker. He yelped, and I heard the sound of metal on the ground. I swirled around.

"You bitch."

I kicked and pummeled my fists into every bit of flesh I could find, but the man was tall and strong, and the only advantage I'd had was the moment of surprise. Now he was recovering from it and didn't like one bit that I wasn't as meek and scared as I'd appeared.

"Paige!"

Will's voice sounded through the parking lot. The thief whirled around, grabbed his knife, and braced for Will.

"He has a knife," I shouted, but then Will was on the attacker. I barely saw him move. One punch to the jaw, another to the chest, and the attacker doubled over.

My eyes were on the blade, which was still in the attacker's hand. He was swinging it blindly. My stomach constricted when he jabbed his hand straight toward Will's abdomen. Will caught his wrist in midair, then twisted the guy's arm and immobilized him.

"Paige, are you okay?" Will asked. He was shaking.

"Yes, you?"

He nodded. The next few minutes were a blur. Will only released the guy when the local authorities arrived and took over.

***
Will

It was another half hour before we made it back to the cabin because we had to give statements. I was running on adrenaline as we stepped inside. Paige was calm and composed, but I was still shaking.

"Will, are you hurt?" she whispered.

I shook my head. "No. Not at all. You're okay? Not hurt, or scared?"

"No."

I was clenching and unclenching my fists, and

she was looking at me as if she wasn't sure how to calm me down or why I was so silent. We went upstairs, and she prepared a hot bath for us. I didn't need a bath. I just needed her.

"The tub's full," she announced, coming into the bedroom. I was unbuttoning my shirt, and damn it, my fingers weren't steady. She came to my aid.

"Why are you shaking, Will?" she whispered.

I took in a deep breath, then brought my hands to her wrists, resting my thumb on the bracelet.

"Because seeing you there, I…. You have no idea how much I love you. How much I want to protect you from anything that might hurt you."

I claimed her mouth. I'd never kissed her like this: driven by a raw, primal need. I wanted her to feel everything I was feeling. My love for her, the fear of showing myself in such a vulnerable moment.

We didn't make it to the bathtub. Our clothes were out of the way even before we reached the bed.

She started trailing her mouth on my chest, heading downward, but in a zigzag rather than a straight line, teasing me. When she was low enough, she licked my erection from the tip all the way to the base and back. Then she took me in her mouth. I shut my eyes, turning my head slightly downward and to the side, fighting for control. She twirled her tongue, clasping her lips tight. When I blinked my eyes open, I looked straight at her. She didn't take her mouth off me until I was completely undone, grunting out her name.

Then I laid Paige on her back and went on to kiss every inch of her body, alternating between chaste and openmouthed kisses. On the insides of her thighs, on her belly and breasts. On her neck, then back to her thighs again. She was squirming and urging me, and I went on until I wasn't aware of my surroundings anymore, just her. My thumb was pressing on her clit, and I pulled each of her folds between my lips. Then my tongue was moving inside her, unrelenting, spurring her need for me instead of satisfying it.

"Will, fuck me. Pleaaaase." She tugged at my hair, and I kissed my way up her belly, smiling wolfishly.

In a flash, I had protection on, and then I eased her thighs wide open and slid inside her slowly. She felt tighter, and then tighter still. I leaned over her, capturing her mouth, pressing her thighs even wider apart, keeping her at the angle I wanted her, her breasts pressed against my chest.

I'd never felt the need to utterly possess her like this on a primal and emotional level. She came apart spectacularly, rocking her hips in a desperate rhythm until I couldn't hold back any longer. Then I kissed her, long and deep, and I knew I'd never, ever get enough of her.

"Thank you for loving me so fiercely, Will," she whispered between kisses.

Chapter Twenty-Eight
Paige

The worst thing about a great vacation? You don't want it to come to an end. I was still melancholic as I went into the office on Monday morning. It was time to return to the real world, where I still had some fighting to do on behalf of the education center. And now I had a plan too. I hadn't been able to help myself and showed Will the plan while we were still at the cabin. I hadn't wanted him to just glance over it, and at my insistence, he crunched the numbers himself. In the end he still wanted to go through with it. It made me immensely happy. Guess who it hadn't made happy? Greg.

"Let me get this straight. You want to go through with this even though I told you the project is dead?" Greg asked.

"It's not dead if I can provide enough funds," I replied calmly.

"It's dead if I say so." His voice was lethal, and for the first time, it occurred to me that there was more to this.

"Why do you want me to abandon it so badly?" I inquired.

"We have other projects to focus on. Paris is

pushing for the water project to happen, and I won't have you cost me a promotion."

I blinked, as if that could make me understand him better. "You were pawning that off on me so *you* could get promoted?"

"You're my employee. You don't question me."

Pulling myself to my full height, I crossed my arms. "I do question you when you're overworking me just so you can get ahead. That project was your *direct* responsibility."

"Jesus Christ, I knew you'd be trouble. That's why I don't like hiring women. One day I can rely on you, the next one you're PMSing and spouting shit. You're here to do what I tell you. You're not here to think."

"This is employee harassment, Greg. HR will have a few things to say about this."

He gave me a look full of contempt, as if he didn't think I'd follow through.

"I have a phone conference that will last the entire afternoon. Forget about the education center and get to work."

I left his office fuming. *Fuming.* But I wasn't giving up. So the next day, I went into his office at 8:00 a.m. sharp.

"I thought I made myself clear yesterday," he said when I brought up the subject.

"I have enough funding for this—"

"By using your personal assets. And then what?" Greg slammed a hand on his desk. "Jesus

Christ, can you just put your emotions aside? I need you for other projects. This is the problem with you women. Emotions get in the way, and one can't count on you anymore."

I clenched my fists and gritted my teeth. I'd always known Greg had a misogynistic streak, but this was... unacceptable.

"You're way out of line, Greg."

"So are you, disregarding my instructions. You answer to me."

"You are my boss, yes, but this doesn't mean I have to put up with insults. I have already contacted HR and filed a complaint."

"You did what?"

"You thought you could just insult me and I would accept it?"

He pointed to the door. I breathed in through my nose, releasing the air through clenched teeth as I left his office, taking refuge into mine. I was a little stunned and a lot angry as I sat behind my desk. I couldn't believe the nerve of him. The misogynistic bastard. I hadn't slacked off in my other tasks in the slightest, and now he wanted me to give up the project even though it was feasible? Well, I refused to. Not when I was *this* close to seeing it through. But what if he fired me? I'd been with Three Emeralds for so long that I didn't know what the alternative entailed.

Greg hadn't had time to circle back to the topic, but as I headed to Will's apartment later that day, I felt deflated. I hadn't come up with a way to come to an agreement with Greg. I wasn't even sure I wanted to anymore because I had another idea... a dangerous one.

Stepping inside Will's apartment, I smiled when I smelled grilled steak. I hadn't yet moved in with Will officially, but I hadn't gone home since we'd returned from our vacation.

And could I say that living with this man was just the best thing ever? I mean, here I was, having a crappy day, and now my mood improved just at the sight of him cooking bare chested, wearing only jeans.

After kissing me deep and good, he scrutinized me, and I felt as if I was under a microscope.

"What's wrong, baby?"

I told him quickly about Greg's reaction. My insides clenched tight when I laid out my *dangerous* idea.

"So, I thought... I could quit and dedicate myself to opening up the education center. I've always been in charge of funding only, but I could oversee operations as well."

I only realized after I'd said it out loud that this might sound as if I was taking advantage of him, or expecting things of him.

"I have savings, so I can live off them for a while. Then after I set it up and it runs smoothly, I'll look for a new job."

Will put his hands on my shoulders, his thumbs brushing the base of my neck.

"Paige, whatever you decide to do, I'm with you. I'm proud that you're willing to go to these lengths. And if you don't want to ever work again, that's fine by me too. As you recently discovered, I'm loaded," he said on a grin. "I can take good care of both of us."

"No, no. I don't want to be kept," I assured him. I was doing an inner victory dance, because my gorgeous man had just made my evening.

And he currently seemed more interested in feeling me up than finishing dinner. Somehow, he'd backed me against the counter and was trailing kisses up and down my neck, twirling his tongue over my sweet spot until I was aching for him.

"Will... dinner," I whispered weakly, and felt his lips form a smile against my skin.

"Dinner can wait."

***

Will

The next evening I headed to Paige's office building, even though she wasn't there. That was all right, because I wanted to talk to that Greg asshole. Paige was going to hand in her resignation in a few days, but I didn't want her to have to put up with any crap from him in the meantime.

While I waited for him to come out, my thoughts returned to the foundation. Paige was already setting everything into motion. So far, my only contribution had been capital, but I wanted to be actively involved and build something together with her. My shifts were not leaving me much time for anything else, but I was determined to find a way around it. Over the years I'd had colleagues move into less demanding career paths. I hadn't understood it then, but I was beginning to now. But what I did for a living had been part of my life for so long that even imagining myself doing something else was strange.

Greg sauntered out at six o'clock on the dot, as Paige said he usually did.

"Gregory Pemberton?" I asked.

He stopped. "Yes. Who are you?"

"Detective Will Connor. I'm Paige's boyfriend."

He cocked a brow. "So? She's not here. If you want to get a hold of her—"

"I'm here to see you. About the way you're treating her."

Greg bristled. "The way I what? I can't believe this. She's gone blabbing to everyone?"

"I will make this easy for you. If you mistreat her in any way, you'll have a bigger problem on your hands than your HR department."

"You can't talk to me like that. Or d-do anything."

"Try me."

I was taller than this schmuck, and in far better shape. His tiny piggy eyes widened, and he took a step back. I hadn't expected him to cower so fast, but I guessed he was a coward through and through.

"That's what I thought."

Chapter Twenty-Nine
Paige

I had always thought that I'd be terrified if I ever quit my job. Instead, I felt not only relieved, but downright excited.

I could quit effective immediately, so I did just that. On the day I went to collect my belongings, Will surprised me by saying he was coming with me.

"Why?"

"I want to be nearby in case Greg is there."

"He's not my boss anymore. I can hurl any insults I want at him."

"Babe. You're my woman," he said, as if this explained it all. I just smiled to myself, feeling weirdly proud, and already visualizing a standoff. Unfortunately, Greg wasn't there at all. But Ashley was, and I won't lie, our goodbye was a little teary. She accompanied us to the garage of the building when we carried my boxes to the car.

"You know, Greg hasn't been such a dick these last few days," she said.

"I had a word with him," Will explained.

I stared at him. "You talked to Greg?"

He gave me a half smile. "I might have had a conversation with him a few days ago. He might have shit his pants."

I just laughed, feeling oddly elated as we drove away. This was my first day of freedom. It was the first time I wasn't tied to a job in ten years, and it felt damn good.

Mom had been surprisingly negative about the whole thing.

"You sure this is the right thing to do, Paige? You'd be relying a lot on Will, with the funding, and living with him and everything. What if you don't find a job right away afterward?"

I'd soothed my mother's worries as best as I could and dedicated the next two weeks to sending grant proposals while overseeing the renovations on the inn. Since it would be an education center now, I needed to make some major changes as well as sell the old furniture and buy new things.

I was standing on a chair, securing a projector to the ceiling in what would be one of the classrooms, when my phone rang from the adjacent room. I'd already missed a call while I was installing this thing, but I didn't want a repeat. I climbed down, scurrying to the other room.

Val was calling.

"Hello, Val."

"Hi, Paige. Don't panic. Will just called me. They're taking him to the hospital. He said he tried to call you too, but you didn't answer."

"Oh my God. What happened?"

"He and his partner were in a chase. Some

glass panel broke and they got injured. I don't have a lot of details, just that they're going to do some surgery." Val's voice shook. "Can you meet me there? I'll text you the address."

"Yes. Yes. I'm... on my way."

I couldn't breathe. I felt as though I was running in a fog as I crossed the city in the back of a cab. I was in no condition to drive. We drove straight into a traffic nightmare on La Ciniega Boulevard, and it took almost *three* hours to reach the hospital. My phone's battery died midway through the ordeal, so I wasn't getting any updates from Val. What if I lost him? What if he.... No, I wouldn't let myself even think it. I knew I wasn't being rational. If he'd been in serious danger, he wouldn't have called Val. The hospital or the police would have contacted next of kin. My emotions were taking over though, and I couldn't fight them. I even cried a little.

When we finally, finally pulled in front of the damned hospital, I knocked over three people on my way to the floor where Val was waiting. I wiped my face clean, but knew my eyes were swollen, so there would be no hiding.

Val took one look at my face, then pulled me in a hug. "Oh, Paige. Come here. Calm down, please. You didn't get my texts?"

"Phone battery died."

"Surgery didn't last long. Come on, let's go see him."

I felt like my bones might liquefy, that's how relieved I was. Val led me to Will's room, and I wasn't surprised at all to see that Jace and Hailey were with him. I knew that Landon and Lori were in Hawaii with their spouses and little ones, or I was sure they'd be rallying around him as well.

His right arm was bandaged from his shoulder to the tips of his fingers, but other than that, he looked like himself.

"Paige," Will said brightly.

Jace shook his head. "I worked a good fifteen minutes to cheer him up, and nothing. You're here, and look at him. I'm losing my touch."

"Yeah, me too," Hailey said.

Val clapped her hands once. "Okay, both of you out before you give him a headache."

Jace and Hailey exchanged a glance, but it was Hailey who spoke next. "She still thinks she can boss us around."

The three of them left, but not before Val affectionately ruffled his hair as if Will was a kid. He grinned at his sister, then held his good arm out for me. I climbed right in next to him on the bed, and to my embarrassment, started crying again—this time out of pure relief.

Will looked stricken. "Paige, I'm okay. A glass panel crashed onto us, but I only had shards in my right arm. They managed to take them all out."

"I was so scared," I admitted, scrambling to pull myself together. "I didn't know what had happened, if you were okay. I didn't know for *three* hours. It was hell."

I was sitting right next to him, and then I lay

down, hiding in the crook of his good arm until my sobs subsided.

Will held me to him, whispering soothingly, and I felt more than a little ashamed that *he* was the one hospitalized, yet *I* was crying.

"I'm done now, I promise," I said, sitting up on an elbow so I could look at him. "Are you comfortable? Do you need another pillow? Something to drink?"

"I'm fine, Paige. I'm going to have to take a leave of absence from work. A few weeks at least."

"Are you telling me that you'll be mine to pamper twenty-four hours a day?" I was glad for a chance to lighten things up.

"That's right."

"I'll make you soup and stuff."

"No, thanks."

I glared at him. "You're in a hospital bed. How can you be mean even now? Besides, when you're sick, soup is good for you."

He was getting groggy, but he still managed to wink. "Other things are good for me too. Things at which you're *very* talented."

I gave him a kiss, which was meant to be soft and quick, but then Will's good hand went to the back of my head and he deepened the kiss before pulling me under him. Typical Will. He took over no matter what.

He fell asleep a short while later, courtesy of the pain meds. When I left his room, I was surprised to find that Val, Jace, and Hailey were still there.

"He's asleep," I told them.

"We wanted to talk to you," Val said. "About his care for the next weeks—"

"I've got it covered," I assured them. "I've been living with him anyway."

Jace grinned big, nudging Hailey. "Told you."

Hailey took a phone out of her bag. "I'm going to call Landon. He was already talking about hiring a nurse. I'll convince him not to come back from the vacation, though knowing him, he's probably on a plane already."

Jace pondered this. "Don't call Landon, call Lori. Have her make those puppy eyes at Landon and ask that they don't come back from Hawaii. The puppy eyes work."

Everyone stared at Jace. He shrugged. "What? They work on me."

Val gave him a thumbs-up. Hailey whistled cheerfully. "Finally you admit it, brother. And your strategy just might work. I'm going to call Lori."

Hailey stepped a few feet away, phone at her ear.

"But look, if you do want help at some point, call me at any time, okay? I'm actually getting better at working remotely, so I can stop by," Val said.

"Val, you're worse than Landon sometimes." Jace patted my shoulder. "Paige here said she can handle it. Stop micromanaging everything."

Val gave him the stink eye. "Okay, I'll try. But just so you know, Will can get grouchy when he's sick. Like, very grouchy."

Her mother hen tendencies were adorable. She projected an inner warmth and quiet strength that made me feel at ease, even though I suspected she was just good at not letting her turmoil show. She was so different from Hailey, who was boisterous and currently talking to Lori on the phone. I could see why she was good at managing PR crises.

"I'll let you know, Val," I assured her. Jace groaned. He seemed blasé, but he kept massaging the back of his neck, as if he'd spent the past hours in a state of constant tension.

"Please don't. That'll just fuel her micromanaging tendencies. If my brother does try to impersonate the Grinch, let *me* know, future sister-in-law."

"I'll keep that in mind." I grinned. I really liked Jace.

Chapter Thirty
Paige

Will was discharged two days later, and he was an excellent patient… in the beginning.

There were moments when he looked at me as if fearing I might burst into tears at any moment, and I regretted crying in front of him at the hospital. After a few days, grumpy Will made his appearance. Not being able to use his arm wasn't helping with the grumpiness in the slightest. I tried cheering him up by using my trusty techniques of seduction, but they only seemed to work half the time. I thought that maybe Will needed some space, and I was being overbearing. It turned out I had some mother hen instincts myself, as my repeated attempts to poison him with my soup showed.

But I couldn't exactly give him space because I had to be at the inn daily, and Will came with me, even though I didn't let him do any work. I'd set him up in the one bedroom that hadn't been converted into a classroom yet, and had also brought a lounger outside in the yard so he could lie in the sun, but Will had a mind of his own. He rarely stayed put.

"Will, you're still recovering," I said one morning.

"I need to occupy my time."

"You can entertain me. Start by removing some of those clothes. You don't really need the shirt, do you?"

"Paige—"

I made the mistake of looking Will directly in the eyes, and the fire in his dark gaze almost melted my resolve.

"Will, we have instructions from your doctor, and we are going to follow them."

"Remember my view on rules?"

I cleared my throat. "These are not rules. They're instructions. So sit outside on the lounger and do nothing. Except playing eye candy. If you're so inclined, you can kick off your jeans too until the workers arrive."

Will tilted his head, taking one step forward, and I almost felt my dress melting from the sheer heat and masculinity pouring off him. But I was saved by the bell... or in that case the electrician.

As days passed, though, Will's mood didn't improve, and I started wondering if the recovery was the only thing causing him distress.

"I've just booked someone to repaint my apartment so I can get my deposit back in full. My lease is up in one week," I said one afternoon, after we'd returned to his apartment.

I had my back to Will, facing a mirror, and I saw his reflection. He was frowning. I felt the first stab of fear that afternoon, after which I started reading into every little thing, overanalyzing every reaction. Was he having second thoughts? Now that my lease was up and I was officially unemployed, maybe he wasn't finding this whole thing appealing. Maybe he realized just how tied together we were and it wasn't sitting well with him. I tried to neutralize those thoughts the second they popped up, but I wasn't always successful.

I thought about talking about my concerns with him, but honestly, I was embarrassed. If they were unfounded, it would just be awkward. If they weren't unfounded... well, I wasn't sure I was equipped to handle the outcome, not with all the other changes occurring in my life at the moment. I was going to wait for Will to get better, and then I'd see if things changed.

One afternoon, Jace called.

"What's up, almost sister-in-law?"

"Jace, don't call me that." But I grinned at his words nonetheless. "So, you and Val were right. Will isn't... himself."

"Well, that took longer than expected. I was betting with Landon that this might be the first time Will isn't grouchy."

"I thought Will was your betting partner," I countered.

"I'm adaptable. So, listen. You remember my cousin Blake Bennett? He was at Lori's wedding."

"Hmmm, vaguely."

"He co-owns some bars and restaurants with his sister Alice in San Francisco, and now they've franchised their business here too. He's in town to oversee the opening of the first bar and wants to do a test run with the family on Saturday. Are you and Will up to it?"

"Oh, I think that's a great idea. And he's not on pain medication anymore so he can drink as well. I'll ask him. What time should we be there?"

"Afternoon. I don't know the exact hour yet, but I'll text you."

"Perfect."

I briefly considered asking Jace to ask Will if two weeks of convalescence was the only thing bothering him, but then decided not to. I wasn't *that* close to Jace.

***

Will

"Blake, you've certainly done well for yourself," I said. We were in Blake and Alice's first franchised bar. "I think I like it even more than the ones you have in San Francisco."

"Location's great," Blake agreed. "If things work out here, we're going to green light the opening of two more."

The bar was on the rooftop of a five-story building, overlooking the beach. Paige and I had arrived early, along with Jace.

The three of us were perched on stools in front of the bar, and Blake was behind it. The rest of the family would be filtering in soon.

"Impressive," Paige said. "You also own

restaurants, right? Do you plan to franchise those as well?"

Blake nodded. "Yes, we do. Eventually. We actually wanted to start by franchising the restaurants, but quality control is more hassle, and profit margins are higher for bars, so we'll stick to them for now. What can I get you to drink?"

Jace was studying the menu. "I'm usually not a cocktail kind of guy, but these look good."

Paige propped an elbow on the bar and parked her chin in her palm. "Aren't you supposed to stay away from sugary things during the season? Val wouldn't give you dessert yesterday at dinner."

"You've been around my sisters for too long," Jace grumbled. "One drink won't throw away my diet. But I'd better have it before the rest of the gang arrives. I can't fight off everyone at the same time."

Paige grinned. "I can still tell on you."

Jace turned to me. "Will you have my back at some point?"

By way of answering, I drew my chair closer to Paige's and kissed her bare shoulder. "Brother, I'm protecting my own interests. I'm with Paige on this one."

She gave me a warm smile, looking at me with those soulful eyes. I'd felt a change in her over the past few days, a reticence that hadn't been there before, and I couldn't help thinking that she might be sensing my own turmoil. Ever since my accident, the idea that I might not be what Paige needed in her life wouldn't leave me. Seeing her so hurt at the hospital gutted me. I'd watched her walk away from a job she loved to dedicate herself to a project that was dear to her, all with little hesitation, even though it was a big change. She'd been threatened with a knife that night at the restaurant, and she hadn't even shed a tear. Paige was a strong, tough woman, and yet she'd been inconsolable at the hospital. I'd put her through that, and the thought did not sit well with me. I wasn't sure what to do about it either.

"Blake, where is the ladies' room?" Paige asked. My cousin gave her instructions, and she hopped off the chair, swinging those sinful hips as she crossed the bar.

As Blake prepared Jace's drink, I noticed my brother was scrutinizing me.

"What crawled up your ass?" he asked.

I pointed at my arm, which was still bandaged. He didn't buy it.

"No, it's something else too. You haven't tried to make even one lousy bet with me since you arrived, and you've almost been mute."

"Just give him an hour," Blake interjected. "We'll get some cocktails into him. That'll loosen his tongue."

"So just because I don't fight you for air time, it means something is wrong?" I would be annoyed if he wasn't spot-on. In my family, nonverbal communication was more telling than actual words.

"Are things between you and Paige okay?" Jace went straight in for the kill. I wasn't sure what to answer, but Jace picked up on my hesitation.

"They're not," he said. A statement, not a question.

Blake shoved a cocktail in front of Jace.

"Things have been off," I said reluctantly. "I'm not sure this is the right thing—"

Blake cleared his throat. Jace turned in his seat and straightened as if he'd been electrocuted. I turned a second later. Shit. Paige had returned from the bathroom. And by the red color in her cheeks, she'd overheard at least part of the conversation.

"I'm going in the back to sort through some supplies that were delivered this morning," Blake said smoothly.

"I'll give you a hand," my brother added. They went out quietly. Paige hadn't moved. I walked over to her, despite the fact that she was shaking her head.

"Paige, I'm not sure what you heard."

"Everything you told Jace." Her voice was steely. "And I have to say, I always thought you'd have the guts to tell me to my face if something was wrong."

I swallowed, searching for the right words. "Paige, there's nothing wrong, per se... I just...."

I reached out a hand, but she stepped back, crossing her arms over her chest. I pointed to the bandaged arm, trying to find the right words. The trouble was, I didn't know what the right words were. I wanted Paige in my life more than I wanted anything else, but I felt guilty for having put her through a lot of worry. "At the hospital, you were so worried. That pain I saw on your face… to know I caused it pains me. I'm afraid you'll come to resent me for it."

She dropped her hands by her sides. "I was scared. So what? It's human. You said so yourself."

Her walls were up. I saw it in the defensive stance, in the slight change in her pupils. I'd seen it countless times when people were brought in for questioning and they were putting on a poker face, hoping we wouldn't see past it.

"Yes, it is human. You feel everything deeply, Paige. You love hard, you fight hard. And I'm afraid you'll resent me, that you'll come to think I'm not right for you," I repeated, then shut my mouth.

I was making things worse. Absolutely worse. Paige crossed her arms again, averting her gaze. When I made to touch her shoulder, she pulled back yet again.

"I think all that pain medicine has affected your ability to think clearly. If you ever get your head out of your ass and decide to make sense again, come talk to me. I'll be staying at the inn." She rearranged the strap of her bag on her shoulder. "Tell everyone else I had an emergency and I couldn't stay."

"Paige!"

She whirled on her heels, rushing out the front door of the bar. I recovered from my stunned stupor a few seconds later. What had I just done? Was I an idiot?

Judging by the fact that I was barely restraining myself from going after her, throwing her over my good shoulder, and bringing her back, the answer was a resounding yes. But I also wanted her to have no regrets. Right now every instinct told me to go after Paige, wrap my arms around her, and apologize for the fool I'd been, for hurting her. Somehow I managed to returned to the counter, fighting my own instincts. Going after her right now was the worst thing I could do. I wasn't thinking clearly, and I'd upset her.

"Well, that was the most stupid thing I've ever heard," Jace said.

I turned around. Blake and Jace and had just returned.

"You overheard us?"

Jace knocked against the wall separating the front area from the back. It sounded hollow.

"Thin walls, cousin," Blake explained.

"And you weren't exactly whispering," Jace added. "So… what was that all about? I'll tell you right off the bat, I'm siding with Paige."

I rubbed my hands up and down my face, sitting on a barstool. Jace joined me, and Blake poured bourbon in a glass, threw in some ice, then slid the drink to me.

"It's five o' clock in the afternoon," I pointed out. "Early for hard liquor."

"Said no one ever. Besides, you just let that woman walk out of here. Clearly you need this," Blake countered.

Jace nodded. "Keep them coming. Maybe he'll get smarter once he's drunk. Or we'll be able to knock some sense into him."

Blake had taken out the good stuff. Two glasses later, I was already feeling every muscle in my body relax, and I wasn't drunk.

"Cousin, I heard everything you've said, and it still doesn't make sense," Blake concluded after I explained my reasoning.

Jace jerked his thumb in Blake's direction. "I agree. Sounds to me like you jumped the gun."

"You two are driving me insane."

Jace shook his head. "No, you drove yourself insane all on your own. We're just pointing out the crazy."

Blake's phone buzzed, and he excused himself, walking in the back to answer it.

I spun the empty glass, eyeing the bottle.

"You can't control everything in life, Will," Jace said quietly. "I know you'd like to, we all would, but most of the time you just have to trust that things will work out."

It was easy to rebuff my brother when he was being loud and obnoxious, but I knew he was speaking from a place of concern right now. When Jace dished advice, I paid attention.

"In soccer, we train and prepare, but when we go out on the field, all we can do is play the game. Paige is one hell of a woman. She's smart, and she's crazy about you. Don't let her go."

Blake returned and made to pour me another drink, but I shook my head, moving the glass out of his reach.

"On a scale from one to ten, how sharp are your groveling skills?" Blake inquired. "Because I'm the Bennett expert at it, and I don't mind sharing my knowledge to help out a brother, or a cousin. I'm happily married, but I stuffed up royally before I got where I am."

"I don't need—"

"Minus fifteen. He's clueless," Jace filled him in. "Actually, so am I, so shoot. I'll be taking mental notes for later. I'm sure I'll be needing them at some point."

I squinted at my brother. "I thought you were happy with your bachelor status."

"Some habits just get old," Jace said with a half smile and a wink. "Wait until Lori, Val, and Hailey arrive. They'll hand you your ass. And I'll be cheering them on."

Chapter Thirty-One
Will

I resisted precisely twenty-four hours, and then I headed to the inn. I was still vacillating between *Fuck, that was stupid,* and *The point is worth considering.* But I wanted to talk things out with Paige. I felt her absence like a physical punch in my gut. Not listening to her soft breath at night and her slight snores in the morning was killing me.

The inn was quiet when I arrived, which meant all workers had left for the day. I gritted my teeth when I saw the front door open. What was the point of a state-of-the-art alarm system if she left the door open?

I went inside and found her in the kitchen, which was being remodeled to fit the new purpose of the inn. The fridge door was open, and Paige was rummaging in one of the lower drawers, her ass sticking up proudly into the air.

"Paige—"

She yelped, straightening up and spinning around in one move, nearly backing into the fridge.

"Oh my God. You scared me. What are you doing here?"

She rearranged her shirt, pulling at the hem.

Her body language tipped me off that something was awry. Her movements oscillated between too quick and too slow, like she couldn't control her reactions. I swept my gaze across the counter and found the culprit: a bottle of wine. It was open, but she couldn't have had more than one glass.

"Are you... drunk?"

"No, just a little... out of sorts. Luna is coming here tonight, so I brought out a bottle of wine. I only had one glass, and I haven't eaten all day. I'm fine, just... balance issues." She'd also pulled at her T-shirt too much, and now her breasts were practically spilling out and she wasn't even noticing, but I didn't see how that could earn me points, so I kept the observation to myself. "What are you doing here?"

"I thought we could talk."

She licked her lips, sighing, then looked at the floor. She was so damn cute that I just wanted to back her against the fridge and kiss her, sink inside her.

"I don't know, Will. Maybe you're right."

"What?" I croaked out, my voice raw.

"Well, if you think I'm some emotional whacko... if you can't even trust that I know who I want, that I know what's best for me, then maybe you're... not right for me."

"I don't think you're an emotional—"

"And if you want to pull out of the project, I understand. I just ask you for a little time so I can find another source of funding," she went on, as if I hadn't said anything at all. Panic was unfurling inside me now.

"Paige, of course I don't want to pull out of the project. Look at me." I walked up close and took her face in my hands, but she tugged at my wrists. I let go.

"No, you're not allowed to do that eye thingy." She emphasized every word with a wiggle of her forefinger.

"What eye thingy?" I asked, bewildered.

"That thing where you look at me until you make me all hot and bothered and I can't help squirming."

I saw my chance and leaned in, but Paige placed a firm hand on my chest, pushing me away.

"Oh yeah, really? You think you can kiss me if I don't even want you to do the eye thingy? No kissing."

"Okay." I held my hands up in surrender.

She was talking very fast as she shifted her weight from one leg to the other.

"I think you should lie down, Paige. Come on, I'll help you to the couch."

She shook her head. "No. You don't get to come here and be all nice and caring."

"So you want me to be a jerk and uncaring? I can't do that. I love you."

She swallowed and looked at her hands, twiddling her thumbs. "Then you should trust my judgement. You should trust my feelings."

"Paige—"

She was right in front of me, but it felt as if she was far away.

"Please leave. Luna will be here soon, and I can't vouch that she won't throw whatever she finds at your head."

I didn't want to leave. I wanted to hold her in my arms and talk to her until neither of us sputtered nonsense and we focused on the important part: that we loved each other. I'd had my proverbial come-to-Jesus moment sometime since I walked in tonight. Paige knew who she was and what she wanted. But I understood that she needed to process everything, talk things out with her best friend.

"I'll go. But I'm walking you to the couch first. It's nonnegotiable."

She huffed, wiggling her forefinger at me again. "Fine. But no touching me."

"And no kissing, no eye thingy. Got it."

I just walked a few steps behind her, and once she was safely on the couch, I left. I had my work cut out for me. Luckily, I had Blake's instructions.

I fashioned a plan as I left the inn. My first stop would be at the house of Paige's parents. That wasn't in Blake's instructions, but I was adapting it. As a family person myself, I knew how important it was to talk to her parents. I knew they'd be at her house because Paige had commented last week that they had movie night every Sunday. On the way there, I tried to play out in my mind her parents' reactions, as well as what I'd tell them.

When I arrived, I rang the bell and waited with my hands behind my back. Several seconds later, I heard feet shuffling through the door. A second later, a voice called through the house. "Harvey, it's Will." After a pause, she added, "Yes, yes, Will."

I kept my fingers crossed that her dad wouldn't open the door pointing a gun at me.

When the door finally swung over, I took in Greta and Harvey Lamonica. Her mom had a hand over her chest, looking at me apprehensively. Her dad didn't have a gun, but looked as if he'd do anything to point one at me.

"What are you doing here?" Harvey asked.

"Will, come on in. Tell us what this is about."

Her parents reminded me of my parents. My dad had always been something of a hothead, like me, and Mom had been calm and patient, balancing everything out. "I am assuming Paige has talked to you," I said as I stepped inside.

"Damn right she has," Harvey growled.

"Harvey," Greta hissed. "Hear the boy out. Why do you think he's here? It means he loves our daughter."

I stared at her. She could tell that… just like that? Women's intuition had always been a mystery to me.

"Is that right?" Harvey asked.

"Yes, sir. And I know I handled things wrong."

"And he's here because he wants to make

them right." Greta clapped her hands, then put them over her chest. "Oh, this is romantic."

Harvey glared at me, then at his wife. She elbowed him, not too gently. "Oh, don't pretend like you never screwed up. And I don't remember you showing up at my parents' house. Momma would've told me."

That shut Harvey up.

Greta patted his arm. "Let's go in the backyard and you can tell us what's on your mind."

Greta was smiling at me. Harvey at least looked like he wasn't planning to shoot me anymore.

We sat outside at the wooden table, and I explained my reasoning to both of them, and that I wanted to right things.

Mrs. Lamonica was smiling and then went on to give so much groveling advice that she'd make Blake proud.

"You know what? I'm going to bring us all some of our homemade cherry liqueur," she said eventually.

When she'd disappeared inside the house, Harvey said, "You still have something on your chest."

Well, yes, and it was weighing on me. "I know Paige is strong, but I don't want her to have to be strong. Or to worry. Does that make sense?"

I didn't want her to have to be strong for our children, or to have to pretend.

Harvey smiled at me for the very first time today. "You're talking to someone who used to be in the Army. Of course it makes sense. Let me ask you something. Why did you join the force?"

"Because I wanted to make a difference."

"And do you feel that your current position is the only way you can make a difference?"

I knew what Harvey was getting at because I'd given it a lot of thought as well lately.

"No, sir. There was a time I used to think that, but not anymore. There are alternative pathways in the LAPD where I could bring things forward without risk."

I'd always thought I'd needed the action… and well, in the very beginning I had. It had been a way to work out that residual anger I still held over the unsolved case of my parents. But lately, I'd moved on to other types of cases, which hadn't required as much action. And since Paige had entered my life, I'd learned there were more dimensions to making a difference than my narrow definition. A few months ago, I wouldn't even have thought about the change, but now I wanted it. The conversation with Mr. Lamonica had just solidified it.

"I will talk to my superiors as soon as possible." I was excited to explore all options, especially those that would leave me more time to focus on the foundation.

"Well, son, just make sure my daughter knows you're not making this decision only for her sake, or she'll hand you your ass, just like her mother did with me when I told her I'd retire early. She gets the stubborn from Greta."

"Are you badmouthing me?" Mrs. Lamonica inquired, appearing out of nowhere.

"No, dear," said Harvey on a slight wince.

I smiled, taking the glass she handed me. They were both happy and relaxed, but there was just one more thing I wanted to ask them before I left. One very important thing.

***

Paige

I was so proud of how I'd handled things. So proud. I'd stood my ground. I hadn't let those sinful eyes or lips sway me, or that sweet way in which he wanted to look after me. I'd wanted to say more, but I'd swallowed my words before I made a fool of myself. It pissed me off that he'd just jumped to conclusions because I'd had a mini-meltdown at the hospital.

It reminded me of Greg, who'd labeled me as an emotional nutjob because I was fighting for the educational center.

Truthfully, it had been because of Will that I'd become comfortable with expressing my emotions, whether they were happy or not.

My chest had ached since I'd seen Will, and it didn't seem to be fading. I wished I'd been sober when he'd arrived. I still wasn't sure why I was so unsteady... then I remembered that I'd only had a smoothie this morning, because I hadn't had time for a sandwich. So my last meal had been yesterday evening. That would explain it.

I had my phone on me, so I shot Luna a text, asking her to bring some food too. I wasn't in the mood for a girls' night in, but she'd insisted. I wasn't a quitter, damn it. What I wanted was to shake some sense into Will, make him understand that while I appreciated his concern, I needed him to trust me. If he didn't… how could things work out between us?

Over the next week, we threw ourselves into working on the education center. There was a lot to be done, and since I'd divided tasks once I'd quit my job, we barely saw each other.

On the first day, I found chocolate mousse in the fridge. Huh? I hadn't ordered it. Then I realized Will must have ordered it for me. Something tugged at my heartstrings as I ate it.

I shot him a quick message.

Paige: I found the chocolate mousse. Thank you.

Then a second one.

Paige: I hope it was for me. I ate it all.

Will answered a few minutes later.

Will: It was for you. Best energy shot, remember? Thought you'd need it.

This man. Did he really remember every detail about me?

On day two, I found a flyer from the Griffith Observatory on my bed. There were two tickets and a card next to it.

No meteor shower this time, but they do have a special viewing next week. I'd love to take you.

You don't have to answer right away.

(Take your time until the answer is yes.)

I smiled from ear to ear. I was still frustrated with him, but that frustration receded a bit every day. I couldn't lie, the little thoughtful gifts helped. On the third day, I realized this was probably his exact intent. He had an agenda. Yeah… I was slow to catch up, but hey, I had a lot on my mind. Also, realizing he had an agenda absolutely did not stop me from enjoying the gifts. The current one was a DVD of a movie I'd told him I want to see.

I hadn't texted him yesterday, but couldn't help myself today.

Paige: Just found your DVD. Wondering with whom I should watch it…

Will: With me, of course.

I imagined the growly sound he would have made if he'd said this in person and laughed. When was he even doing these things? I hadn't stopped to think about that, but surprising me required a lot of planning and some stealth maneuvers.

Oh, this lovely and infuriating man. Why had he upset me? I'd calmed down enough to see things from his perspective, though, and I could sort of understand it, considering everything I'd told him about growing up as the kid of an Army man.

On day four, I searched in vain for my gift. Instead, I received an impromptu visit from Luna, who informed me Will was treating us to a dinner out.

I'd actually thought it meant Will was joining us, but I was quick to hide my disappointment when it became clear that he'd just treated me and Luna.

"Tell the truth, did Will charm you?"

Luna made a sign as if to indicate her lips were sealed. "All I know is, he said this is a hectic week and you could need a distraction. So... ta-da, here is your distraction. He's quite thoughtful, isn't he?"

Hmmm, Luna had avoided my question, but by the way she was singing Will's praises—instead of considering which shoes would do more damage if she threw them at him, as she'd done during our dinner at the inn—I had my answer.

The next morning, I woke up to the sound of a door closing. I was in the only room of the inn that still had bedroom furniture. I patted the floor in search of my smartphone. I groaned. It was eight thirty. The workers would arrive in a few minutes, and I felt as if my bones weighed a thousand pounds. Luna and I had talked until the early hours of the morning. I'd had about four hours of sleep. But wait... who'd closed the door? I tried to remember if I'd set the alarm last night. Probably not. Will would have a thing or ten to say about that. Before I could panic, I noticed the tray of food on the empty half of the bed. All of my breakfast favorites were there. Fresh orange juice, cheese omelet, and blueberry pancakes.

How...?

I startled when I heard voices outside and scrambled to my feet, looking out the window. The workers were there. And a few seconds later, so was Will, coming out of the house. As if feeling my gaze on him, he looked up, straight at me, and gave me a devastating smile. I'd never eaten and gone through my morning routine so fast in my life.

When I made it downstairs, Will was already in action, ordering the workers around. Those jeans clung to his ass like their sole purpose was to tempt me. And that shirt, huh? It showed off his muscles— all of them. Even what the fabric covered was still visible—the shape at least.

"Good morning," I said.

The workers greeted me, and Will turned around slowly, watching me with a bemused expression. It was the first time we were seeing each other in days.

"I thought you'd sleep longer."

"I woke up when you closed the door. Thank you for breakfast."

"Welcome."

"You'll be here the whole day?"

Will flashed me a smile full of mischief. "And tomorrow, and the day after that. I still have two weeks free."

"I sense you're going to take advantage of this."

"You're sensing right."

My heart was hammering like mad. What did this mean? Was he just looking out for me? Fulfilling his part of the deal? If we were going to be partners in the education center and not in any other way, well... this would be excruciating, honestly. He still hadn't come closer to me. He'd also made no attempt to kiss me, or otherwise seduce me with that eye thingy. But he'd sent me all those cute and thoughtful gifts. So where did we stand?

Chapter Thirty-Two
Paige

I was required to stay indoors for most of the day, overseeing the floor replacement as well as calling the most promising candidates from the pool of educator applicants. But even so, I was aware every time Will was in the same room. Since that happened more often than was necessary, I'd concluded he was purposely forgetting tools or "needing" a glass of water.

But then again, I was peeking out the window as often as I had the chance, so who was I to judge?

In the afternoon, after I'd made a shortlist of candidates, I went out in search of Will. I thought we could decide together which ones to interview in person. I found him in the back of the yard, next to a freshly painted section of the fence. He was guzzling down water. His eyes were closed, so I took a second to shamelessly and unapologetically let my gaze roam over him, taking in the way his throat moved with the shape of water, the way his chest expanded with every breath.

Damn, how could he look even sexier after a full day of work? Wait... he had worked? He was only supposed to supervise. He was still recovering.

But he had a few drops of green paint on his jeans, and there were no workers on this area of the fence. I stalked toward him, careful to stop at a *safe* distance.

"Will, what's this?"

He blinked his eyes open, giving me a lazy smile. "Your freshly painted fence."

"You were supposed to just supervise."

He took a step closer, blowing my safety net to smithereens. Being this close to him and not knowing where we stood was torture.

"I have a tendency to misbehave, Paige. You should know that by now."

There was no escaping that dark, all-consuming gaze, but I tried my best. I focused my attention on the stack of papers in my arms.

"I've sorted out the best applicants and selected my favorites. Want to go through them to give me your opinion?"

"That's your domain, boss," Will said.

"*Now* I'm the boss? How about when I say you're only supposed to supervise?" I made the mistake of looking up.

"I didn't say you're the boss of *me*, Paige."

He'd leaned into me a bit. I hadn't seen it, but I'd felt it, and now all I could think about was feeling his hands on my skin, his lips on mine. Did he still want that? He had to, right? Or he wouldn't be here.

But then he took a step back, motioning to the house. "I still have some things to finish out here. I can look over them later."

I nodded, my chest tight. Was that a brushoff?

What else did he have to do? The workers were gone. Resigned, I returned to the house, holding the résumés against my chest. I wasn't sure what was happening.

I stayed in my temporary bedroom, sitting cross-legged on the bed, plugging in my headphones. I listened to music as loudly as I could, drowning out thoughts of Will as I went through the résumés. I was determined not to look outside again. I had no idea how long Will wanted to stay, but I had to leave in three hours anyway to meet Mom for dinner.

Later, as I reduced the volume, intending to get ready for the outing, I realized I had three missed calls from Mom, and called her right back.

"Hey, Mom. Did you decide where you want to eat?"

"Honey, didn't you see the message I sent you last night?"

"No, sorry. It got buried in a million other messages. Why?"

"I'm sorry, I have to cancel. Something came up with one of my friends, and I can't make it in time."

Mom was leaving me high and dry? This wasn't like her, especially since I'd told her what had happened with Will.

"Okay. No problem. Take care of your friend."

"I'll do that, and we'll reschedule soon, okay?"
"Sure."

She was also not offering to stop by later... or

asking me anything in her usual nosy way. I was getting more suspicious by the second.

I glanced at the empty breakfast tray I'd been too lazy to carry to the kitchen, and a small detail caught my attention. Will had brought me blueberry pancakes, even though I'd never specifically told him they were my favorites. This morning I'd thought that was a coincidence, but now….

I climbed down from the bed and headed downstairs. It was almost sunset, and it was just me and Will, unless he'd left too.

When I didn't see him anywhere in the front, I went to the backyard where I'd left him hours ago, and then I was… stunned.

There were twinkle lights in the tree and a blanket on the ground underneath, as well as a picnic basket. Will was in the process of laying something on the grass. When I squinted, I realized they were candles.

It happened in a fraction of a second. My heart went from feeling tiny but heavy to feeling impossibly big and full. I made a sound somewhere between a giggle and a yelp. Like the fool I was, I gave myself away instead of enjoying these stolen moments. But I just couldn't contain my joy. Really, that was all it was.

Will straightened up and held his good arm up in surrender.

"Caught in the act."

I practically flew to him. It felt that way, at

least. Like I was so light that my feet weren't even touching the ground, merely skipping over the surface.

I stopped right in front of him, smiling. "I see what you're doing. You're groveling."

He groaned, lowering his head. "You didn't even realize I was groveling until now? Blake will never let me live this down."

"Nah, I caught on to it a few days ago. I'll save your honor when it comes to Blake. After all, I saved you from Pippa too. It's becoming a running theme. But what's your cousin got to do with this?"

"He's got this theory about the science behind groveling.... Never mind. Gave me some pointers."

"Did that include talking to my mom?"

He snapped his head up, looking directly at me. "No, that was my idea."

"Why did you do it?"

"Who knows you better? I had to know if I had a real chance here."

"You know you did. I told you when you came by that night I was half drunk."

"You also asked me not to kiss or touch you."

"That was a defense mechanism," I countered. "So... why did you talk to her?"

Will came a little closer. There were now maybe three inches separating us, and I desperately needed to feel his warm skin on mine, but I wanted to hear what he had to say first.

"I wanted to make sure they were on my side. Didn't want to risk anyone else wanting to throw things at me, like Luna."

"So, technically, you wanted me ambushed."

"Not sure if it's an ambush or an intervention. My sisters could clear that up."

"You just wanted pointers, didn't you? Blueberry pancakes?"

"Made an impression, I see. Since I'm making confessions, I spoke to your dad too."

"Wait... on the phone or in person?"

"In person."

"That was brave, Detective. You risked him shooting at you. My dad is very chill. Until he isn't."

"He was *not* chill at first. But I won him over. Both of them."

"What did you tell them?"

The humor faded from his eyes. "The truth: that loving their girl is an honor for me. I wanted them to be convinced that I was going to make their daughter happy. That I'd only acted out of a deep fear that maybe I wasn't able to make her as happy as she deserved, but that I was a complete fool not to trust that she could handle absolutely anything. And I was an even bigger fool for ever thinking I could let her walk out of my life. I can't. I won't."

The deep emotion in his voice wrapped around my heart.

"Will—" I said the word softly. Maybe too low for him to hear, because he continued right away.

"And one more thing. I spoke to my superiors, and I will be moving to another unit, one that involves no risk."

"William Connor, you'll do no such thing."

"Listen to me, it's what I want. For me, for us. The hours will also be more reasonable, and I'll be able to involve myself in the foundation too."

"Will... are you sure this is what you want?"

"Yes. One hundred percent. I mean it." He smiled. "You know, it was easier winning over your family than mine," he said with a half smile.

"Don't tell me they sided with me."

"Every single one of them. Traitors."

"Even Jace?"

"Especially Jace. Cornered me right after you left. My sisters gave me an earful... my brain is still ringing. Not even my bandaged arm softened them. They were ruthless."

"Maybe they thought you deserved it." I was feeling very smug, but I was also very grateful to the Connors.

"They sure did. I can't promise not to upset you again—"

"By all means, upset away. Your way of winning me back is quite charming. But since I have a heart, I'm going to tell you that you don't have to keep doing it. I'm yours. It's hard to stay mad at someone who puts my happiness above his."

Will hooked his good arm around my waist before I even finished my sentence. I laced my hands around his neck the next moment, pulling him to me. Our lips met fiercely, our tongues tangling with mad lust and deep love. Our chests were crushed against each other's, and still, I wanted to be closer to him.

He skimmed his lips over to my ear.

"I love you, Paige."

I laughed, though it sounded a little like a sob because my emotions were running high.

"I love you too."

I was shaking, and he was shaking, and when he looked at me, his gaze was smoldering, which meant my clothes were seconds away from being yanked away. My lady parts tingled in anticipation. Did I want to distract him? Or not?

"What's in the picnic basket?" I whispered.

"All your favorites. But right now, I need you, Paige." He feathered his mouth on the side of my neck. "I want you naked."

"I'd call you out on it if you didn't."

Will lowered his hands down my back, cupping my ass and pulling my hips against him. He was rock-hard.

"Do you feel that? It's all for you." His voice was gruff, and I rocked against him gently. "Let's go inside, or we're getting that citation for indecent exposure."

"Here I am, seducing you, and you're still thinking about a citation? I ought to become a better temptress."

We'd barely reached the bedroom when Will started undressing me, but he took his time, as if he was on a mission to rediscover every inch of my body. He stood behind me, kissing the back of my neck, circling his fingers on the peaks of my breasts.

We were both naked, and his erection pressed along my left ass cheek, spurring my need for him. I was hungry for him. When it came to Will, I was insatiable.

"Will, please," I muttered, feeling like I might come out of my skin. My nipples were tight and tender. With every swirl of his tongue on my skin, more heat rushed between my legs. He flipped me around, lowering me on the bed. He was still standing, and his erection was level with my face.

I wrapped my hand around the base of him, taking him in my mouth. Will groaned, wrapping one hand in my hair, bending at the waist, nudging my thighs apart with his other hand and touching between them.

"You're so wet for me."

I couldn't bear it. His touch was setting me on fire. He was circling my clit with his thumb, and when he slid two fingers inside me, I looked up at him. He curved his fingers in a come-here motion, and my insides spasmed around them. I came the next second, rocking against his hand, clamping tight around him.

"You're so beautiful when you surrender to your pleasure, Paige." He moved me to the center of the bed, climbing over me. "I want to fuck you hard and love you gently." His mouth was everywhere, as if he was so greedy for me that he wasn't sure where to kiss first.

"Yes. Yes, please."

He knelt between my legs, focusing his

molten gaze on me.

Clasping his hands around my ankles, he lifted my feet off the mattress.

"Lift your legs and put your hands under your knees." I did as he instructed, opening up for him. He put on protection and slid inside me until his pubic bone was pressing on me, and he claimed my mouth, his tongue teasing mine in a seductive dance. I thought I might splinter from pleasure, from being so full of this man.

"So deep," he grunted, caressing my cheek with his knuckles. "I want this every day for the rest of our lives. The certainty of your love. Do you trust me with your happiness, Paige?"

"Yes."

How could I not? The way he looked at me, God… as if he'd do whatever it took to make me happy, as if he'd be at my side no matter what.

"This is home for me. You are," he whispered.

He moved faster then, and on every thrust, I felt our connection grow stronger, deeper.

Afterward, we had our picnic, but not under the tree. Will brought the basket in the bedroom because we hadn't had nearly enough of each other. Currently I was eating apricot jam with a side of hunky detective. I'd smeared it around his navel and was taking my sweet time cleaning him up.

Ah, life was so good. *So* good.

"Paige, come up here. If you're not stopping, I'm going to—"

"I'm sorry, but you're in no position to make threats."

I tapped one finger just under his navel to drive my point home. In a fraction of a second, the balance of power changed. The man had impressive speed. I barely blinked twice and then I was under him. He was holding my hands hostage at my sides, his body pressing me down.

I cleared my throat. "All right. Point made."

"What am I going to do with you, hmm? Pushing my buttons all the time."

I wiggled under him. "My proudest moment is still the one where I kind of pushed you to line up for the garter."

"When I saw you up there, I knew I couldn't let anyone else touch you. So I got the garter."

"Ummm... correction. You elbowed your way to the garter."

"I certainly didn't." He bit my shoulder lightly.

I gasped, but I wasn't going to go down without a fight. "I definitely saw someone being elbowed out. And a guy practically bounced off you."

"I just went the extra mile. To get my girl."

Chapter Thirty-Three

Will
One month later

"Will, I'm afraid this confirms my initial diagnosis," the doctor said. He was looking over the charts and notes from my physical therapist. A month ago, the doctor made the unpleasant discovery that a nerve in my hand had been damaged in the accident. It was a small enough issue that it didn't interfere with regular daily activities, but a trip to the shooting range and a physical therapist confirmed that I wouldn't be able to properly fire a gun again—which meant I couldn't keep my badge.

"I was sure it would. The therapy didn't help much."

Paige was sitting by my side in the doctor's sterile office. He prescribed more physical therapy, but made it clear that a 100 percent recovery wasn't possible.

When Page and I exited the clinic, we strolled through the small green space surrounding it.

We came across a bench, and I sat on it, pulling Paige straight into my lap. She let out a small sound of surprise before lacing one arm around my neck. She rested the other on my chest. Correction. *Felt up* my chest.

"What are you doing?" I inquired.

"You're pulling me in your lap to feel up my ass. I'm taking advantage and touching your chest. I'd say it's a fair deal." She grinned. I knew what she was doing: cheering me up. It was working.

"I'm going to talk to everyone at the station today and confirm that I'm leaving."

My superiors had explained my options, but if I had to face such a big change, I wanted to do it on my own terms.

"Hmmm… I'm only detecting a small frown." She traced a line on my forehead. "This requires neither an ambush nor an intervention."

"What?"

"Your sisters asked me to report." She spoke nonchalantly, even as she squirmed in my lap. "But there's nothing to report. Tell the truth. Are you okay, or is this blasé reaction because I'm distracting you with all this squirming?"

"A mix of both." I gave in to her game. "Mostly, I'm just looking forward to having you to myself all day long, every day."

She stopped fidgeting. "William Connor, just because we're going to be partners does *not* mean you can just do *this* whenever you want." I'd slipped one of my hands under her skirt, touching her midthigh.

"Yeah it does. It absolutely fucking does."

When we first discovered the problem with that nerve, I'd known I wouldn't continue on the

LAPD. Not being able to carry a gun limited my options considerably. I hadn't taken it as hard as I'd expected, probably because I'd already decided on a change in careers, and because I'd already been looking forward to building something with Paige. Now I could dedicate more of my time to this.

We were going to grow the foundation, and I also planned to work on expanding the rental network. She was going to be my partner in all things. It made perfect sense. Our skills complemented each other's.

We'd discussed what the additional centers could be about. Between the two of us, we had plenty of ideas, and seeing Paige light up at all the prospects had been one of the proudest moments in my life. It humbled me to know I could make her so happy.

Giving up my badge was still something I had to get used to, but instead of mourning the end of my career on the force, I was excited for what our future together would bring. I was smiling, and then I took her by surprise, kissing her bottom lip, then biting it lightly. Paige giggled, and I let go just as she burst out in a full belly laugh, then covered her mouth.

"You don't care much about a citation for indecent behavior, huh?" she whispered.

"Not particularly, no. I love you, Paige."

"I love you too. And I promise this will all work out."

"I'm sure it will. I have a great feeling about

what we're going to build together."

My happiness had been deeply entwined with my cases since I'd joined the force, but Paige had severed that tie. In fact, my happiness was now deeply entwined with the sassy brunette who might or might not be purposely squirming in my lap.

***

"I can't believe this doesn't even require an ambush," Hailey said wistfully at the next Friday dinner. Next to her, Val sighed.

"Yeah, I'd been bracing for a full-on intervention when Lori arrived."

The three of us were on Val's porch, waiting for dinner to be ready. Jace and Paige had offered to prepare dinner. I was keeping my fingers crossed, and the food-ordering app on hand. I should have known that the only reason Val would give up the reins of her kitchen was because she thought an intervention was required. Also because we were having another dinner on Wednesday to celebrate Christmas.

"Sorry, girls, no ambush needed," I teased them, though I secretly enjoyed that they were doting on me.

"So… we know you made a business proposal to Paige, but are you planning to make any other kind of proposal?" Val asked, her tone casual. She feigned studying her fingernails, but she was stealing glances at me.

"Are you trying to fish out of me if I'm planning to ask her to marry me?"

Val nodded. "Yes, I am. Actually, I'm sure you do. The question is when. And how? Do you need tips?"

"You could have been more subtle about it," Hailey critiqued.

"Or… you could have asked me when Hailey wasn't around," I supplied. Annoying my little sister was one of the simple pleasures in life. Why deny myself?

Hailey made a choking sound, and in that moment, she looked more like her younger, bratty self than the polished PR-pro.

"You too? How long am I going to have to pay for past mistakes? I work with celebrities now. I've learned to keep secrets."

Val and I carefully avoided looking at each other.

I schooled my tone to appear apologetic. "Hailey, I love you, but you've busted more surprise parties and gifts than I can count. Whatever secret-keeping abilities you've developed, I'm sure they come in handy at work, but when it comes to family stuff…."

Hailey groaned. "Damn it. I can't even bribe you with anything. Any celebrity you'd like to meet?"

I cocked a brow. Then she held up a finger, as if struck by a sudden idea. "What if I promise *not* to hire a stripper for Paige's bachelorette party if you tell me now? Keep quiet at your own risk."

"You're not bringing her a stripper," I said through gritted teeth.

"That's not for you to decide, is it? Oh, brother, when are you going to learn that you can't outmatch me?" She wore a shit-eating grin now. I turned to Val, looking for support, but our oldest sister was too busy being impressed by Hailey's blackmailing skills.

"Hats off to you," Val said.

"I'm going to call your bluff," I said as we entered the house. She smirked at my confidence, but I had means of stopping any ill-advised plans. *Game on, little sis. Game on.*

"Where are Pippa and Eric?" Val asked once we were inside.

Our cousin Pippa and her husband, Eric, were also here. Her stepdaughter Julie was studying at UCLA, and they had come to take her home for Christmas.

"I'm here," Pippa called, coming in from the direction of the kitchen. "Eric and I wanted to give Jace and Paige a hand."

Well, now I was more confident about our dinner.

"How is Julie?" Val asked.

"Happy. Enjoying college, and dating... which is why she isn't here tonight. Had a goodbye date before Christmas break, much to Eric's chagrin." Pippa smiled saucily.

"Not used to Julie being all grown up?" I

asked.

"Not at all. But at least Mia and Elena still have a few years of childhood left. He's a great husband and father, but stresses too much over the girls. In a perfect world, he'd like to veto anyone who asks Julie out."

Julie was Eric's daughter from his first marriage. He'd had her when he was very young, hence the large age difference between Julie and her younger sisters.

"Hey, if any boyfriend needs vetoing or being scared away, our brothers can be of excellent use. Right, Will?" Val asked.

I grinned. "Absolutely. At your service, cousin. I can be extra smooth, or extra scary. Depends on what the situation requires."

"Oh, I'll keep that in mind. I'm always in favor of smooth, though I think my dear husband might prefer scary."

"I can always team up with Jace. He can play the smooth part, and I can do my part if scary is required," I offered.

"That sounds very promising. And speaking of Jace... is it my impression or is he...." She narrowed her eyes, as if searching for the right word.

"Afraid of you?" I filled in the blanks.

"Yes, yes he is," Val declared.

Pippa put her hands together, tapping her fingers against each other. "Well, well, my last matchmaking attempt was too successful, huh?"

"Sort of. They hit it off, but since she wasn't

from here, nothing came of it," Val said.

"You want some insider knowledge?" Hailey asked.

I shook my head. "This is exactly what I mean about secrets, little sis."

Hailey ignored me. Pippa whistled appreciatively. "And Jace won't hand you your asses?"

"We'll take our chances. We can go toe to toe with him," Hailey said on a laugh.

"I will bow out of this conversation," I informed them. "Or I'd have to report to my brother that you're... conspiring."

"It's for his own good," Val said with a wink.

Later that night, once we were in bed, I asked Paige, "So what was that about girl talk after dinner?" The girls had all huddled on the couch, and when I or any other guy tried to approach, they informed us it was *girl talk time*.

"Because *girl talk* are the magic words for getting manly ears out of the way." Paige was lying with her head on my chest, tracing a pattern on my stomach.

"Duly noted. What did you talk about?" I wouldn't put it past Hailey to already have dropped a hint.

"Brainstorming potential dating pools for Val to increase her chances of getting laid."

I blinked, then blinked again. They went from planning Jace's demise to this? How did they even work so fast?

"Right... I'm better off not knowing the outcome of the conversation."

She smiled sheepishly. "That came out wrong. The best way for her to meet a decent guy. Getting laid is part of the package."

"No further details required," I insisted.

"Okay. Just keep your eyes open for a smart and very sexy guy. Strong arms are important. Six-pack always a plus. Great skills in bed are also a requirement, but obviously, there's no way to check that beforehand."

"I can't believe we're having this conversation." I made a mental note never to ask about girl talk again.

"Why? You could help brainstorming. It's not so easy to meet people once you're settled into working life. Not everyone has my luck. And Val deserves to be happy."

"Of course she does." When we were growing up, she put her life on hold for us for a while, and then she'd thrown herself into building her cosmetics company.

"Tell the truth. Did you ever scare the shit out of a man she introduced to you?"

"No. Just asked what their intentions were and called them out on it if they seemed to just want to jerk around."

Paige chuckled. "Doesn't surprise me. Well,

what are all these muscles for, if not for flexing when you sense foul play? We'll make a great team. So many advantages to working together."

"And speaking of working together, I want you to keep the weekend after the official opening of the center free."

She lifted her head, narrowing her eyes in suspicion. "Okay. I didn't have anything planned, but why?"

"I want you all to myself." I shifted us on the bed and kissed her neck, just under her earlobe.

"That sounds promising." She was almost breathless.

"I want us to celebrate this beautiful life we have. And maybe not share you with the world for another week."

"That's an outrageous thought."

"I promise it'll be worth it." I traced her collarbone with the tip of my tongue. She arched her back, then rolled her hips into me. One lifetime with this woman wasn't going to be enough. But I was going to make every single minute count.

"Sold."

Epilogue
Paige

"Hey, you! No stealing food." I swatted his hand away from the ice cream. It was the third time I'd had to do it in the last five minutes. Tomorrow we were officially opening the education center, and we were knee-deep in preparations. "I will ban you from the kitchen if you keep doing that."

"No, you will not. You want me to distract you. You just don't know how to say it."

He had some nerve. Homemade ice cream required attention. Of course I didn't want him to distract me. Except... now that he'd said it out loud, it didn't seem like such a bad idea. I turned to face him, and as I often did since he'd handed over his badge, looked for signs that everything was all right. He'd assured me that he was ready for this new phase, and he'd thrown himself into our new life together with such passion that I didn't doubt it.

I dipped my forefinger in the small bowl of leftover ice cream and smeared it all over his cheek.

Will grinned, and then the game was on. He hooked an arm around my waist, keeping me in place while he smeared ice cream over my lips. Then he drew his tongue sensually over them, licking it off. We might have a lot to do for tomorrow, but we always had time for a sexcapade. Oh, yeah.

"I've been watching you dance around this kitchen for hours, moving those hips. I've fantasized about bending you over this counter and sinking inside you." His gaze was smoldering. The arm around my waist had moved lower, and his hand was splayed on my ass.

"So what held you back?"

He let out a low growl, and his palm pressed me into him so I could feel how hard he was. Sweet heavens, how long had he been so aroused? And I'd been wasting my time making ice cream?

"I'd better take care of this," I whispered, shimmying against him.

He touched my earlobe. "Yeah. Needs thorough attention."

"What if I'm not... *thorough*? Will I get some of your deliciously sexy threats?"

"Only if you insist."

"I do."

"Well, then... how can I not play along?"

He scooped me in his arms, and I flailed my legs in the air, grabbing his shirt for support. Will *distracted* me right until dinnertime, when Maddie and Landon dropped by unexpectedly with their daughter Willow.

Landon had offered his support in our joint venture, and while Will and I were grateful for it, we were doing just fine on our own.

"Won't keep Landon from insisting," Maddie had warned me the first time the subject had come up. And as the two of them helped themselves to some ice cream, Landon brought it up again. Maddie and I exchanged amused glances. We'd adopted the Connor betting habit, and I'd lost this round.

"What's that?" Will asked suspiciously when I offered Maddie a five-dollar bill.

I figured it was best to come clean right away. Looking between the brothers, I said, "We just made a bet on how long it would take Landon to bring up the subject of investing."

Both brothers glared at us. Then Landon turned to Will.

"Is it just me, or are our girls getting more and more daring?"

"Nope, not just you," Will agreed.

"Maddie won this round, obviously," I said.

Will tilted his head to one side. "This round? There are more?"

Ah, I'd shared too much. Maddie threw me a warning glance.

"Yep, but they involve girl talk, and I remember you clearly telling me you want to be kept out of it, so…."

Will grimaced. Landon held up a hand. "Say no more."

Truthfully, our other bet had been a more elaborate business. Maddie, Hailey, Lori, and I had made a bet on what kind of man would steal Val's heart, but there was no reason to share that with our men.

Maddie and Hailey were betting on some sort of Hollywood hunk. Hailey in particular was *very* excited at that prospect. Lori and I veered toward a businessman.

We chitchatted about everything under the sun, and when Will held Willow, I furtively snapped a few pictures. He was expertly holding Willow on one arm, and she sighed adorably, snuggling up to her uncle.

Later, after Landon, Maddie, and Willow had left, Will caught me looking at the pictures as we were doing one last check to ensure everything was in place for Monday.

"What's this? I thought you kept all images here." He tapped his temple.

"Some should be photographed. You look cute with her."

"Cute?"

I nodded with conviction. "Don't get your boxers in a twist. You're still all muscly and manly, but also… cute. I can't explain it."

Will flashed me a smile. Wait a second… that was an unusual smile, as if he was harboring a secret. Hmmm, what could it be? He came close enough that I only had to lean a few inches to kiss him, but I was no closer to guessing the secret.

"How do you think I'd look with one of our own? Or more? Personally, I think we'd do great with more. Of course, we could luck out and have twins. Two in one shot." He pushed a strand of hair behind my ear.

I was stunned that he'd envisioned our future in such detail. I tried to keep my composure, but his words touched me deeply, and my voice wobbled a little when I spoke next.

"You've been giving this some thought."

He dragged the tip of his nose across my cheek to my jawbone. "Since the condom scare."

"You've been keeping secrets from me."

"Just waiting for the right time."

"I think you're forgetting something."

"I am?"

"We're not married."

He pulled back a little, and his secretive smile morphed into a teasing grin. "Paige Lamonica, are you proposing to me?"

I felt my cheeks heat up, then my neck. I decided to take out my embarrassment on him, and poked one of those superb biceps. "I was hoping *you* would propose to *me*, but if you don't, I'll reconsider a few things."

His gaze was intense. In a fraction of a second, Will had an arm around my waist, keeping me against him.

He kissed me deep and hard, and when he pulled back, he said in a gruff voice, "You can't very well do that if I'm kidnapping you next weekend, can you?"

Everything around us seemed to still. I was only aware of my thundering heartbeats, and how impossibly warm Will's body felt against mine.

"You… are planning to propose?"

"Yes. Down on one knee, with a ring and a very romantic speech."

My heartbeat was out of control right now. Then I remembered a particular conversation and started laughing.

"Sorry, I just realized that's why Hailey was so curious about the trip. Kept asking if we had some fancy dinner reservations."

Will groaned. I kissed just under his jaw, then rested my nose in the crook of his neck, inhaling that delicious masculine scent.

"You really want to be tied to me?" I checked. "For the good and the bad?"

"Legally and forever," he confirmed. I shimmied against him.

"That sounds lovely."

He pulled back a little, bringing a hand to the back of my head. His mouth close, he feathered his lips over mine. "So you'll say yes?"

Warmth unfurled in my belly. I felt my pulse thrum in my ears as I placed my palms just under his broad, strong shoulders.

"Depends," I said coyly, fighting to maintain my seriousness as I lifted a brow. "Are you okay with a huge wedding?"

"Yes."

"I want all the bells and whistles. I'll also want a huge dress."

"It'll be my pleasure to take it off you during our wedding night."

He brought his other hand from my waist to my hip, as if he wanted to lift up my dress. I pushed his hand away. "I already know you're good at taking off my clothes, William Connor."

"Thought you need more convincing—an incentive to say yes." His eyes flashed. "Any more conditions?"

"Just one last thing. I want to officially be part of any ambushes and interventions your sisters plan."

"That's negotiable."

"I'll take it as a yes."

He cocked a brow.

"What? I have solid proof that my negotiation skills are sharp enough to win you over."

"Is that so?" He made another attempt to slide his hand under my dress. I pushed it away. *Again.*

"Uh-huh. Every time."

"That's not how I remember it, but I'll let it slide."

"Out of the goodness of your heart, or as another incentive to get me to say yes?"

"Both. Did I succeed?"

"I promise to love you, and torment you, and reward you with scorching-hot sex my entire life, William Connor. How is that for a yes?"

He grinned, leaning in for a kiss. "Makes me want to marry you right now, future Mrs. Connor."

Other Books by Layla Hagen

The Connor Family Series

Book 1: Anything For You (Landon & Maddie)

Book 2: Wild With You (Graham & Lori)

The Bennett Family Series

Book 1: Your Irresistible Love (Sebastian & Ava)

Sebastian Bennett is a determined man. It's the secret behind the business empire he built from scratch. Under his rule, Bennett Enterprises dominates the jewelry industry. Despite being ruthless in his work, family comes first for him, and he'd do anything for his parents and eight siblings— even if they drive him crazy sometimes. . . like when they keep nagging him to get married already.

Sebastian doesn't believe in love, until he brings in external marketing consultant Ava to oversee the next collection launch. She's beautiful, funny, and just as stubborn as he is. Not only is he obsessed with her delicious curves, but he also finds himself willing to do anything to make her smile. He's determined to have Ava, even if she's completely off limits.

Ava Lindt has one job to do at Bennett Enterprises: make the next collection launch unforgettable. Daydreaming about the hot CEO is definitely not on her to-do list. Neither is doing said CEO. The consultancy she works for has a strict policy—no fraternizing with clients. She won't risk her job. Besides, Ava knows better than to trust men with her heart.

But their sizzling chemistry spirals into a deep connection that takes both of them by surprise. Sebastian blows through her defenses one sweet kiss and sinful touch at a time. When Ava's time as a consultant in his company comes to an end, will Sebastian fight for the woman he loves or will he end up losing her?

AVAILABLE ON ALL RETAILERS.

Book 2: Your Captivating Love (Logan & Nadine)
Book 3: Your Forever Love (Pippa & Eric)
Book 4: Your Inescapable Love (Max & Emilia)
Book 5: Your Tempting Love (Christopher & Victoria)
Book 6: Your Alluring Love (Alice & Nate)
Book 7: Your Fierce Love (Blake & Clara)
Book 8: Your One True Love (Daniel & Caroline)
Book 9: Your Endless Love (Summer & Alex)

The Lost Series

Lost in Us (James & Serena)
Found in U (Jessica & Parker)
Caught in Us (Dani & Damon)

***

Standalone USA TODAY BESTSELLER
Withering Hope

Aimee's wedding is supposed to turn out perfect. Her dress, her fiancé and the location—the idyllic holiday ranch in Brazil—are perfect.

But all Aimee's plans come crashing down when the private jet that's taking her from the U.S. to the ranch—where her fiancé awaits her—defects mid-flight and the pilot is forced to perform an emergency landing in the heart of the Amazon rainforest.

With no way to reach civilization, being rescued is Aimee and Tristan's—the pilot—only hope. A slim one that slowly withers away, desperation taking its place. Because death wanders in the jungle under many forms: starvation, diseases. Beasts.

As Aimee and Tristan fight to find ways to survive, they grow closer. Together they discover that facing old, inner agonies carved by painful pasts takes just as much courage, if not even more, than facing the rainforest.

Despite her devotion to her fiancé, Aimee can't hide her feelings for Tristan—the man for whom she's slowly becoming everything. You can hide many things in the rainforest. But not lies. Or love.

Withering Hope is the story of a man who desperately needs forgiveness and the woman who brings him hope. It is a story in which hope births wings and blooms into a love that is as beautiful and intense as it is forbidden.

AVAILABLE ON ALL RETAILERS.

***

Wild With You
Copyright © 2018 Layla Hagen
Published by Layla Hagen

Published: Layla Hagen 2018
Cover: Uplifting Designs

***

Acknowledgements

Publishing a book takes a village! A big THANK YOU to everyone accompanying me on this journey. To my family, thank you for supporting me, believing in me, and being there for me every single day. I could not have done this without you.

<<<<>>>>

LAYLA HAGEN

MEANT FOR YOU

9 781635 765083